Praise for *L*

"Autumn is a multi-dimensional character, and she is given so much relatable baggage, even if pieces of it will touch readers in different ways. Her internal conflict, emotional struggles, reluctance to face her past, the tension with her family—her mother, in particular—and the absolute complexity of her feelings illustrate her depth and solidify an already exceptional arc. Maplewood is so thoroughly immersive in how it and its surrounding areas are described that it almost becomes a character itself, and the landscape is used metaphorically in some cases. There is a perfectly written forest pursuit scene, dripping with fear, and that journey through the forest becomes a symbolic representation of external factors hammering at internal strife, using the forest to convey abstract concepts through tangible elements. This is a great, thought-provoking, and touching story, and I look forward to seeing what Lizbeth J. gives us next."-

—Asher Syed, Five Stars from *Readers' Favorite*

"Author Lizbeth J splashes romance, drama, and suspense into this absorbing tale about finding love and inner strength while navigating the treacherous terrain of trauma. Beneath Autumn Leaves shows how cycles of abuse can manifest malignant toxicity in relationships through people who, at some point, were victims themselves. The author takes a nuanced approach to the sensitive topic of domestic abuse, using the narrative to showcase how hard it is for victims to disclose the truth, even to their friends and family. Autumn and Emmett play off each other brilliantly, and their palpable chemistry makes it easy to root for them. I also liked Autumn's circle of friends, especially the twins and their constant back-and-forth. All in all, *Beneath Autumn Leaves* is a captivating story that romance lovers are bound to love."

—Pikasho Deka, Five Stars from *Readers' Favorite*

"Lizbeth J doesn't just tell a gripping story. She doesn't just create believable characters. She takes us into Autumn's mind and heart. We experience the fear, the sense of betrayal, the hurt of a daughter desperate for her mother's approval, and the yearning for the sense of security that comes with being truly loved. Reading *Beneath Autumn Leaves* forces you to, for a while, be Autumn Evans. Lizbeth J takes us into the world of the deranged abuser, showing us precisely how his manipulation confuses his victim and destroys her sense of self-worth. She shows us how the victim becomes isolated and full of shame. If you have never experienced spousal abuse or been close to someone who has, this story might help you understand its profound effect. It might offer a glimpse into the workings of the minds of some abusers. Yet this is done with tact and discretion, in a manner that does not distract from the entertainment value of the story. This is a story with depth. It's a story that evokes a powerful emotive response. But it's also a story full of hope and reassurance of the healing power of love and genuine friendship. It's a fantastic read for anyone who loves great women's fiction, psychological thrillers, and stories that entertain us while shining a light in the darkest corners of our world."

—Lorraine Cobcroft, Five Stars from *Readers' Favorite*

beneath autumn leaves

a novel

LIZBETH J

Beneath Autumn Leaves
Published by Alegria Ink Publishing LLC.
Denver, CO

Copyright ©2024 Lizbeth J. All rights reserved.

This is a work of fiction. Names, characters, businesses, places, events, locales, and incidents are either the products of the author's imagination or used in a fictitious manner. Any resemblance to actual persons, living or dead, or actual events is purely coincidental.

No part of this book may be reproduced in any form or by any mechanical means, including information storage and retrieval systems without permission in writing from the publisher/author, except by a reviewer who may quote passages in a review.

All images, logos, quotes, and trademarks included in this book are subject to use according to trademark and copyright laws of the United States of America.

ISBN: 979-8-9896074-0-2
FICTION / Women

Cover Illustration by Janna Bruns, @mystic.mind on Instagram
Cover and interior design by Victoria Wolf, wolfdesignandmarketing.com, copyright owned by Lizbeth J.

All rights reserved by Lizbeth J. and Alegria Ink Publishing LLC.
Printed in the United States of America.

Alegria INK
PUBLISHING

For every survivor who has ever felt alone.

And every survivor who wishes to love again.

1

New Mexico *should've been my home. It should've been safe.*

Autumn tightened her grip on the steering wheel as she turned onto Century Street, feeling a knot in the pit of her stomach. The closer she got to her old home, the more tempted she was to turn her thunder grey Volvo around, gather her belongings from the storage unit she had rented in town, and disappear from the state—again.

When Autumn left Maplewood seven years ago, she had been hopeful for a fresh start, but what she found was quite the opposite. And now she was back—albeit for a short while—on the street she grew up on in a small town in Colorado, where members of the community were over involved in each other's lives, whether you wanted them to be or not.

She hesitated at a stop sign. "You need to be there for her, it's her special day," she lectured herself, slamming her hand against the steering wheel. "Darn it, Ortus, why did you have to find someone to fall in love with?"

When Autumn pulled into the driveway of her childhood home, she realized nothing had changed since she had last been here. A white picket fence still surrounded the large front yard, and the tree holding the swing their dad had made for them was still standing. She couldn't help but smile at the memory of it. The swing had been Autumn's safe space, where she dedicated hours to reading her veterinary books in secret. Her mother had never been as supportive of Autumn's career path as she was of Ortus's.

After killing the engine, Autumn grabbed her luggage and trudged toward her childhood home. The two-story ranch-style building was painted chestnut brown, and its ledges were chipping, but still white. Autumn let out a deep sigh. The house was full of more unpleasant memories than good ones.

She stood on the doorstep in silence, with her eyes closed, listening to the birds chirping around her and the sound of her own heartbeat.

Breathe, Autumn, breathe.

After a long minute, she reopened her eyes, took a step forward, and knocked.

The door swung wide open. "Autumn, you made it!" Ortus jumped toward her, wrapping her arms around her sister's neck, pulling her into a warm embrace. She was already wearing her white mermaid dress and had her natural brown curls hung loose under a crown of blue lotus flowers. She looked stunning, and it hit Autumn that her younger sister was getting married.

"Of course I did!" She pulled away from her sister but kept hold of her hands. "Did you think I would miss my own sister's wedding?"

"No, but..." Ortus looked at the ground. "We haven't spoken much over the years. I was beginning to think Mason wanted you all to himself." Ortus scanned behind Autumn, "Speaking of which, where is my brother-in-law?"

Autumn froze and her smile dropped. The sound of his name made the hairs on her arms rise. How would she begin to explain to her sister where it all went wrong? Ortus, noticing Autumn's discomfort, changed the subject.

"Dad is going to be happy to see you. You look stunning in that color, it brings out the blue in your eyes." Ortus winked.

Autumn relaxed, grateful. As children, they had always been close. They could read each other like books, although not even Ortus knew of the breakup.

"Of course you love this dress. You're the one who chose it," Autumn said.

Ortus shrugged. "Hey, someone must be the fashionable one around here. I can't have my maid of honor looking like a mess, but you obviously can't look better than me."

With a playful gesture, Autumn rolled her eyes, grabbing her bags from the doormat, and heading inside her parents' home. Due to the unchanged exterior, she had expected to see the same home she left, but as she entered the room, there were noticeable changes—the walls were now white, the floors were covered in golden-oak wood, and the stairs that connected to the living room were now light gray.

She tilted her head to the side. "Um, major remodeling happened while I was gone?"

"You know Mom and Dad, they like to change things up every few years," Ortus said as she closed the front door, brushing past Autumn to the staircase.

Autumn followed her sister but came to an abrupt stop halfway up the stairs. The old photo frames on the wall had stayed the same. There were photos of outings, proms, and various graduations, plus several of Ortus alone, including a professional portrait of her in her police uniform and another taken on the day of her graduation from the academy.

She studied the photo of her college graduation, where Autumn stood between both her parents displaying her Bachelor of Science in biology—the first of several certifications she went on to obtain. To her left, her mother was beaming proud. It was one of the few times Autumn saw her smile.

Her mother, Dr. Marie Evans, graduated top of her class in medical school, and she *never* let Autumn forget it. Autumn grew up under the pressure of living up to her mother's expectations, and when Autumn veered from the career path her mother had planned for her, needless to say, she wasn't thrilled.

"Autumn, are you coming?" Ortus called, snapping Autumn out of her thoughts.

"Oh, yeah. Sorry." She hurried up the last few steps, arriving at Ortus's childhood bedroom, where she placed her bags on the floor. "Your room looks like a teenage girl still lives in it," Autumn observed.

Their parents had left the room as it was before Ortus had moved out. The walls were the same light teal, posters of her sister's favorite singer, Maxwell, still decorated the walls, and the corkboard of their childhood photos remained intact.

Ortus placed her hands on her hips the same way their mother always did. "Don't judge, you scientists never can appreciate creativity. Plus, Maxwell remains my favorite musician." She paused, flashing a flirty smile. "And the man I would run away with."

"Does Jordan know this?"

Her sister nodded as she grabbed a makeup brush from her vanity. She added the finishing touches with her bronzer. "Are you going to wear the red lipstick I told you about?"

Autumn walked up behind her sister. "Nope."

Ortus pouted. "Aw, come on. You're already gorgeous but think how everyone will be in awe of you!"

"I'm not looking for attention," Autumn said.

Ortus turned to face her, holding out a navy-blue eyeliner. Autumn took it without prompting and swiped it over her sister's eyelids.

"Autumn, you should know you can't say no to a bride. It's the law."

"Is that what they taught you at the academy?"

Ortus hummed. "Yes. They also taught us that red lipstick looks *amazing* on people with blue eyes." As Autumn pulled away and slipped the cap back onto the eyeliner, Ortus fluttered her eyelashes up at her. "Please!"

With a groan, Autumn threw her head back. "Fine! Give it to me."

Ortus cheered and reached into a drawer to pull out a red tube, which she handed to Autumn. Autumn leaned close to the mirror and smeared it across her lips. She stood back a moment later to admire the addition to her look.

She didn't recognize herself. It was as if the woman standing before her, were a complete stranger. When she was with Mason, he had always told her the less makeup she wore the better, so she stuck to wearing nude colors to please the man she loved. Autumn had forgotten how confident red lipstick made her feel.

Her sister stood behind her. "Didn't you have blonde hair when you left Maplewood?"

"Yeah, I decided it wasn't my color anymore."

"Your natural brown has always been my favorite anyway."

Autumn was about to say, "Mine too," when Ortus gasped, her eyes focused out the window. Autumn frowned. "What?" she asked.

"The florists have tied white ribbons around the table arrangements. I asked for blue to match the flowers!" She threw her hands up either side of her head and turned back to Autumn. "No. No, I refuse to be stressed on my wedding day."

"That's a little unrealistic, don't you think?" Autumn lay back on the bed.

Ortus rolled her eyes. "Jordan gave me blue lotus flowers on our first date. This detail is important."

They heard footsteps climbing up the stairs. Autumn's heart jolted in her chest, and she jumped closer to the wall so she wouldn't be visible from the door. "Mom isn't here right now, is she?"

Ortus gave her sister an odd look. "No, she's outside helping the vendors set up."

"Autumn, is that you?" a voice called.

Autumn released a sigh of relief as her childhood best friends, Brooke and Bradley Knight, entered the room a moment later. They were fraternal twins, both of whom had light-hazel eyes. Brooke was wearing a sapphire-colored dress similar to Autumn's, with her long, straight hair pulled up into a neat bun; its color, however, singled her out as the edgier twin.

"Purple, huh?" Autumn said.

"Duh." Brooke smiled. "Thought I heard your voice. Good to see you. It's been a long time."

Autumn tried to conceal the wave of regret that simple sentence brought upon her. The last time Autumn had seen Brooke was at their college graduation, and it pained Autumn to know she distanced herself from her friends on purpose.

"Yeah," Autumn said, "it has. How are you both? I've missed you!"

"We're great! Neil and I are starting to prepare for our big day," Brooke said, pulling Autumn in for a hug. "You're coming to my wedding next year, right?"

Say no, Autumn.

"Yes," she nodded.

Idiot.

"Hello, Earth to Autumn!" Bradley said, waving his hands in front of her. "Do I get a hug too?"

Autumn chuckled and opened her arms for him. He closed the gap between them and lifted her off her feet in a gentle squeeze. Bradley was more social than Brooke, was obsessed with food, and was one of the sweetest people Autumn knew.

And yet while the old friends caught up, Autumn found it difficult to engage in their conversation as they spoke in turn about the adventures they'd embarked on over the past few years. Autumn felt out of her element, so for the most part nodded and pretended to listen, all the while wondering what possible place she had in the lives of her friends now.

"Are you all right?" Brooke asked.

Autumn wiped away the distant look she knew was on her face. "Yeah. I was thinking about our childhood. Our lives are all so ... different now."

"But you're here now." Brooke nudged her. "Remember when we would go to the local fair? We had so much fun."

Bradley crossed his arms. "It was fun until I started losing every game."

Autumn pressed her lips tight together to keep herself from laughing. "It was the one thing that would get you out of your house after ..." Her smile flickered and her face fell.

Brooke reached out a hand each to Autumn and Ortus. "After our parents died," she said, "Bradley and I had a hard time adjusting without them. Our aunt tried her best, but it was both of you who got us through it."

"We're not best friends." Bradley smiled at each of them. "We're family."

"Don't send a search party, I have arrived!"

The group broke from their reverie, and Brooke rolled her eyes at the six-foot man who had knocked himself out on the doorframe. "No one was going to. We know you love being late."

"You mean *fashionably* late." He winked.

Autumn giggled. "Hi, Josiah."

Josiah Jacinto was their college friend who had lived across the hall from them. Often, they had referred to him as their third roommate, as he spent a ridiculous amount of time in their rooms instead of his own. Regardless, they loved his energy and the drama that would follow him.

Josiah removed his glasses, cleaned the lenses with his sleeve, and put them back on. "Oh my, I thought my eyes were deceiving me. It *is* you, Autumn!" He ran toward her and pulled her into a lung-crushing hug.

She squeaked out of surprise, and for a moment she wasn't in the room anymore. Her throat constricted and she tried to remain focused on the voices around her as she fought through the numbness in her arms and patted him on the back.

"I missed you too, Josiah, but can you put me down?"

"You know you can call me J.J." he said, setting her back on her feet. "You're going to have to catch me up on what you've been up to. I have missed you."

Autumn gave him a warm smile before turning toward the window. She took a couple small and quiet breaths, hoping her friends wouldn't notice.

Ortus waved her arms in the air. "Okay, enough of this. Let's get this show on the road!"

"The spotlight should be on Ortus. Noted," Brooke teased.

"Ortus, your wedding doesn't start for another hour." Autumn turned around, pointed at the clock above the door. "I'll go make sure everything's ready. You stay here and *relax*."

Before Ortus could complain, Autumn slipped from the room and headed down the stairs. When she made it to the bottom, she stopped upon hearing voices.

"Everything seems ready."

It was her father. Not quite ready for a reunion, she contemplated slipping around the banister and escaping through the front door, but her mother's words found her next.

"Well, it seems the maid of honor is still missing." Her tone was contemptuous, a sneer hidden under it.

"I'm sure she won't be long, dear. Autumn would never miss such an important day for her sister. You know how close they are."

Marie scoffed. "She could have fooled me. The girl hasn't cared to visit in years. She's been slipping off the rails ever since she left this house. Where did I go wrong?"

Autumn stepped out of her hiding place and into the kitchen. "If you're going to talk about me, can you at least wait until I'm in the room?"

Marie raised her eyes, tucking a strand of her gray, shoulder-length hair behind her ear. Her mother's genetics hid her age, not a wrinkle in sight on her porcelain white skin. As their matching-colored eyes locked, Autumn noticed the shock in them and for a moment thought her mother would cry.

"Autumn. What a surprise." Marie walked toward her, giving her a brief hug. The awkward embrace caught Autumn off guard. It wasn't like her mother to, well ... hug. "I didn't think you would show up for your sister." She paused. "But I'm glad you took a break from whatever it is you do nowadays."

And ... there it is.

Autumn folded her arms across her chest. "I'm still a veterinarian, Mother."

"And I *still* don't understand why," Marie said. "We had a plan for you to follow in my footsteps."

Autumn rolled her eyes. "No, Mother, *we* didn't have a plan. *You* did. It was always *your* plan. After Maggie died, I felt so helpless. I wanted to know how I could've saved her. I never wanted to be a medical doctor."

"I have the dog to thank for all of this?" Marie threw her hands up in the air. "You couldn't even make a *relationship* work, Autumn, how do you expect to have a fulfilling career cleaning up animal feces?"

"That's not—" Autumn stopped, narrowing her eyes. "Wait. What do you mean I couldn't even make a relationship work?" Autumn hadn't told her parents, sister, or friends about the breakup.

Marie turned her back on her daughter and picked up a cloth to polish the already sparkling kitchen island. "When Mason told me about the breakup, I couldn't believe it. I was beginning to think you were getting your life—"

"You ... spoke to him?" Autumn stuttered, casting a furtive glance at her father, who seemed to be doing his best to keep himself out of the line of fire by blending into the curtains.

"Yes. This morning."

Autumn wiped her clammy hands on her dress, her heartbeat racing, causing a tightness in her chest. She looked back at her mother. "Is he here?" she managed to say in a faint voice. Her father's eyes fixed on her, observing her with intensity.

"Of course he is. Mason is such a good man, I can't believe you let him go." Marie continued oblivious, "I even asked your sister if she knew anything, and she was as shocked as I was!"

So, Ortus knows. Autumn's body loosened, realizing she didn't have to keep the breakup a secret anymore. Autumn was grateful Ortus hadn't pushed her for more information, compared to how her mother was now.

But Mason is here…

The painful memories of her time with Mason rushed to her. The way he wooed her when they first met to the horror of the end of their relationship. If Mason was here, she had to run.

Before she could act on her plan, Bill stepped forward, rubbing his temple in frustration. "Marie, now is not the time to make passive-aggressive comments. We haven't seen Autumn in almost seven years." He met Autumn's eyes, tears glistening in his own. "Come here, kiddo." He pulled her into his arms as her own tears formed.

Don't cry. You can't. So instead, she laughed and said, "I don't think I've ever seen you out of your uniform."

He chuckled next to her ear. "I clean up well."

Returning home and being in her dad's arms made her feel complete and somehow *safe*. The heartbreak and the obstacles all vanished so long as he was holding her. With her loved ones by her side, she hoped it would discourage Mason from making impetuous decisions.

Brooke strode into the kitchen. "Sorry to interrupt, but the bride is getting antsy."

Autumn sniffed, and in a gentle manner, pushed her dad away. "I need to go."

He kissed her forehead. "We'll talk later."

Brooke and Autumn walked to the French doors at the back of the home.

Autumn had expected the cold verbal greeting from her mother, but it was the warmth of her father's embrace that had caused tears to pool at her eyelashes. She blotted them away, careful not to ruin her makeup.

"So, you and Mason broke up?"

Feeling a lump in her throat, Autumn remained speechless, responding to Brooke with a simple nod. It was enough for Brooke to drop the conversation. She handed Autumn a small bouquet of lilies. "I'm going to make sure Neil has the camera ready for when Ortus walks down the aisle. Wait here."

Brooke walked up to Neil and held on to his arm as she laid her head on his shoulder. When they were younger, Brooke made it known she would never get married, and for a short time, Autumn almost believed her. But at the grand opening of her gallery, in walked Neil, a local photographer. They were each other's muse.

Their relationship inspired Autumn; it reminded her what true love was. It wasn't about power and control, it was about care and support. When Brooke and Neil disagreed, there was no violence. They worked together to come to a solution. They were good for each other, they cared about one another, and she had no doubt in her mind they would make each other happy once they tied the knot.

Autumn stood by the door, dazzled by how the yard had been decorated. The sun was beginning to set, casting a brilliant golden aura over the scene. Twinkling string lights wrapped around the trees, while elegant blue lotus flowers were at the end of each row of seats. Nearby, a pianist played a soothing melody. Her eyes landed on Jordan, who was tapping his foot at the altar, waiting for his bride. Autumn smiled at the thought of Ortus getting married to her best friend.

"This is so mesmerizing," she whispered to herself.

"It is, isn't it?"

Autumn felt a sudden chill on her neck. She observed Mason through the corner of her eye as he stepped in next to her. He was wearing a traditional tux, his dark hair slicked back into a manbun.

"How did you find me?" Autumn managed to say.

"I found a wedding invitation stowed away in one of your photo albums."

"Of course," she replied, voice small.

"You'd think if you were going to do something stupid like leave me ..." he sneered, "you'd be better at hiding. It's almost like you wanted me to find you."

She remained hushed, anxious not to provoke his temper.

He sighed and stood closer to her. Goosebumps erupted on her arms. She could smell the peach cologne she used to love so much. She was sure Mason wanted her to notice, wanted to get a reaction from her.

"Are you still mad at me? You know I never meant to hurt you. I love you," he whispered into her ear.

From a distance, she spotted the groomsmen and bridesmaids gathering nearby, while Mason remained unaware. She fought the rising panic inside her and built up the courage to turn and face him. There was a gleam in her eyes. "I wish I could say the same."

They stared at one another. Frustration and anger filled his face, forcing Autumn to turn her eyes away from him. Silence fell over the backyard as all the guests rose from their chairs. The pianist began to play, and all eyes turned to the French doors.

Autumn swapped her frown for a smile and clasped her flowers close to her. Even though she was turned away from Mason, she felt him glaring at her until it was her turn to stroll down the aisle.

Mason had broken her heart in inexplicable ways, and as she watched Jordan and Ortus exchange their vows, she wondered if one day she would ever feel the same love again.

2

The wedding ceremony was touching and there were tears—*lots* of tears. After taking photos of the wedding party, the old home transformed into the wedding reception. The aisle became the dance floor, surrounded by white rectangular tables with the lotus flowers as centerpieces. Bradley, Brooke, J.J., and Autumn sat drinking champagne as they watched the married couple dance to their song.

As Autumn observed her sister and new brother-in-law, she noticed how Ortus couldn't stop smiling. Tomorrow they would go off on their honeymoon, and Autumn would be far gone from the town that drove her away.

She watched Brooke and Bradley argue next to her, pretending to listen. She couldn't help but wonder what life would've been like if she had never left this town. Would she have been happy or … not? Autumn thought leaving for Los Angeles was the best decision, but the reality was leaving had also brought her pain. She would often find herself asking, *what if*? But the truth was, it didn't matter what could've been, because in the end, this is the reality she had chosen.

"… and that's why I'm the better twin," Bradley finished, taking a hearty swig from his beer bottle as if to end the discussion.

"Oh, please. Because your *side job*," Brooke emphasized with a pointed look, "is to style people who don't know how to dress themselves doesn't mean you're the better twin. I mean, if anything, I'm the true artist in the group. I make art, I inspire others to think outside of the ordinary—like how I inspired you to wear a cashmere suit."

I made it clear I didn't want to see him again. What does he want to prove?

She couldn't stop thinking about him. Ortus was her sister, so of course Autumn couldn't pass the opportunity to visit the people she loved. Mason knew the negative mark Maplewood had left on her. Autumn thought she convinced him she would never return. She had even been strategic toward the end of their relationship by dropping subtle digs about Maplewood and hiding any indication of her sister's wedding. Autumn was naïve to think she could stop by for one night.

"What do you think, Autumn?" J.J. asked.

Autumn crashed back to Earth. "I'm sorry, what?"

"You left our world for a second, didn't you? You all right?" Bradley asked, his forehead furrowed.

"Um ... yeah, a little sentimental over my sister getting married. Wedding feels, you know?"

Before Bradley could respond, his eyes flicked above Autumn's head. "Oh. Hey, Mason."

Autumn hadn't heard him approach them, and when she turned to face him, he had a huge smile on his face, as if he was about to say something he knew would hurt her.

"You always did have a thing for weddings, didn't you? Almost makes me wish we'd tried it sometime," he said.

Autumn's intuition had been right. She pivoted, turning away, not wanting to confront the sneer he insisted on wearing every time they spoke. Instead of playing his game, Autumn pushed her chair back, avoiding his shins, and walked away. She walked toward the front of the house, to the one place she knew she could feel safe.

Behind her, Brooke's deep growl was directed at Mason. "I don't know what happened between you two, but you leave her alone ..."

Their voices faded the farther Autumn walked, allowing the tears she was holding back to come streaming down her face. Autumn assumed she'd gotten rid of him by running to New Mexico and that he would have given up by now. But she should have trusted her gut. He would always find a way to her.

A tree wrapped in lights illuminated the front yard. She walked to the swing under it and looked at the wooden seat where a plaque read, "Property of Ortus, Autumn, Bradley, and Brooke."

Autumn smiled. *I can't believe this is still here.*

During her time in Maplewood, Autumn and her friends had always fought over who would be the first to sit on the swing every Sunday afternoon. As they got older, they realized they were too old to continue to fight, and instead agreed to take turns, giving priority to the person who'd had the worst day. It had become their safe space to voice their frustrations and share their deepest secrets.

Autumn sat on the swing, looking up at the night sky. She closed her eyes, took a deep breath, and listened to the sounds of the owls hooting. A small breeze blew against her hair, and she was in her safe space again. But that split second of bliss was replaced by a tingle up the back of her spine—someone was watching her. She opened her eyes and looked about her surroundings but saw no one.

Mason being here is starting to mess with my head. How was it possible after everything that happened, he still had control over her? She wanted to be happy, but what if happiness was an impossible reach? Would she always be haunted by her past?

Screeching tires and the agonizing cry of an animal tore Autumn from her thoughts. Acting on instinct, she sprang from the swing. On the road ahead, neighbors had already gathered around a golden retriever who lay on the ground, whimpering in pain. Without a thought, Autumn ran to her car and grabbed her veterinary bag.

"I'm a vet, get out of the way!" she yelled. The small crowd parted, allowing her to sink onto the tarmac beside the poor animal. "Hey there, you're going to be okay," she whispered.

The car that had run into the dog hadn't stopped. She couldn't understand how inhumane the person had been to leave behind a dying animal without taking responsibility; it was a cruel act. Blood was dripping from the dog's mouth in addition to the nasty cut on her front paw. Autumn grabbed a clean cloth from her bag and wrapped the dog's paw to staunch the bleeding.

"Looks like a minor fracture, but possible head injury," she murmured to herself, shouting to the crowd, "We need to get this poor girl to an animal hospital for an X-ray. Someone help me get the dog in my car!"

As the neighbors worked together to place the dog in her car, she rushed to start it, the wedding—and Mason—now at the back of her mind. She grabbed her phone and searched for the nearest clinic.

Dr. Pierce's veterinary clinic, five stars ... this will do.

"I have you girl, don't worry," Autumn spoke to the panting dog in her rear-view mirror. "What were you doing out there all alone? What fool would let their dog wander the street?"

As Autumn drove to the clinic, she was glad Mason had scared her off when he did. She felt the dog's pain as if it were her own. There had been a point in Autumn's life when she couldn't reach for help either. A point when she was hopeless too, with no one listening to her cries of pain. She wanted to help, she needed to save the dog.

I promise, I won't let you die.

When Autumn arrived at Dr. Pierce's veterinary clinic, she pulled up to the entrance, ignoring the several free parking spaces nearby. She rushed into the clinic.

"Help! I have an injured dog in my car that needs immediate attention," she called into the building.

The receptionist, whose name tag read "Jackie," followed Autumn and helped to carry the dog out of her car.

"Is this your dog?" he asked as he rushed the dog to one of the back rooms.

Autumn shook her head as she followed. "No. She was hit by a car in front of my house."

An older woman in a white coat barged into the room as Jackie set the retriever down on an examination table. She walked over to the sink counter and pulled on some gloves. "What do we have?" she asked.

Before Jackie could answer, Autumn interrupted, "There are no major fractures from what I can tell, besides one of her paws that might be broken. She's bleeding from her mouth, it might be due to a head trauma from the impact of the car."

"Jackie, get the X-ray room ready, and we can go from there."

"Right away, Dr. Pierce." He nodded, running from the room.

Dr. Pierce turned to face the dog and touched different parts of her body, waiting for any cries of agony. "There seems to be no immediate pain, but she is breathing heavy, which could be because of her low blood pressure." She removed her gloves, looking back at Autumn. "I'm assuming you're a veterinarian?"

Autumn nodded.

"We'll have to wait for the X-rays. Why don't you go sit in the waiting room?"

Autumn conceded and found a corner of the waiting room to settle in, leafing through a magazine without focus. An hour went by, and she noticed the waiting room was growing busier, packed with a variety of cats, dogs, and hamsters. Each owner entered the clinic claiming it was urgent. She studied the system they had in place and concluded that Dr. Pierce was alone helping patients today.

After another thirty minutes, Dr. Pierce approached her. "I know you're not Max's owner, but I figured I'd give you an update."

Autumn tilted her head to the side. "Max?"

Dr. Pierce smiled. "I've already called her owner." She raised her glasses. "We did some X-rays, and the paw seems to be the one visible fracture."

Autumn stood and crossed her arms. "And the head trauma?"

"Her scans were clean, but we do have her on IV fluids to elevate her blood pressure. We'll keep her on them for a bit, but she seems to be responding well to them."

Autumn let out a big sigh. "What a lucky girl."

"Lucky indeed, although we still need to do the surgery on her paw."

"Okay," Autumn nodded, "will that be done tonight?"

The doctor sighed. "We're understaffed. There are three veterinarians in this clinic, and one of them is on maternity leave. It might have to wait until we can get the second vet here."

"Wait." Autumn frowned. "No, that's not happening." She grabbed her bag from the seat beside her and fumbled through it, pulling out her work ID. "Let me help. I'm qualified."

Dr. Pierce remained silent for a moment. "This is unorthodox, but … okay. I don't want Max to be in pain." She turned to the reception desk. "Jackie, please show Dr.… ." She looked at Autumn.

"Evans. Autumn Evans."

"Please show Dr. Evans to the operating room and prep Max for surgery. I'll handle things in here."

Autumn hovered over Max, stroking her head as she awoke from sedation. It had been a challenging procedure, but with the help of Jackie, she was able to mend Max's paw.

"I told you I wouldn't let you die." She kissed Max on her forehead.

"You did a great job," Dr. Pierce said, entering the room.

Autumn smiled. "Thank you for letting me assist."

"I should be the one thanking you. You did such a great job with Max, and I can see you care for the animals you help."

"My dog, Maggie, was also a golden retriever, and I loved her so much. She got hit by a car and had a severe head trauma. They couldn't save her."

"I'm guessing that's why you became a veterinarian?"

Autumn nodded. "I felt so helpless. I never wanted to feel like that again."

Looking back on the memory, she also thought of how empowered she was when she became a veterinarian. Autumn knew she could overcome anything that came her way. The feeling of empowerment was torn from her during her time in Los Angeles.

"As I mentioned earlier, we have two doctors working at the moment, and if I'm being honest, we could always use an extra pair of hands," Dr. Pierce hinted.

Autumn's hand stopped stroking Max's head, and she looked at the older woman, who held her gaze.

"I'm offering you a job, Dr. Evans. You have a gift with animals, and I'm sure the dog you saved is going to be one of the reasons you will take this job," she said with certainty.

An awkward laugh escaped her, lifting her hand to tuck a strand of her hair behind her ear. "Thank you, Dr. Pierce, but I don't plan on staying in town for much longer. I returned for my sister's wedding."

"You could work for as long as you want to. We need the help, even if it's temporary. Think about it, okay?"

The woman's honey-brown eyes implored Autumn with such desperation, Autumn sighed and gave her a sad smile. "I will."

"Perfect. Now, if you'll excuse me, I have a waiting room of animals to tend to."

Dr. Pierce left the operating room, and Autumn took a moment to breathe in the air of a successful surgery. She scanned the room, admiring the soft-olive walls, how spacious it was, and how organized it had been laid out for her. This had been her first surgery in months. When she was in New Mexico, she worked as a receptionist; it had been the way she was able to lay low for so long. Taking a job as a veterinarian would have ended Mason's search much too soon. Conducting this surgery helped fuel her with the energy she needed to get back to what she was destined to do.

After transferring Max to a recovery cage, Autumn, tired and unwilling to change back into her bridesmaid's dress, walked back to the reception desk in her scrubs. As she walked, she couldn't help but be tempted by Dr. Pierce's offer. This clinic was much smaller than the clinic she'd worked at before, but there was something homey about it.

But she brushed the thought out of her mind, knowing that the sooner she left, the better it would be for everyone.

As she arrived in the waiting area, a man rushed through the front door and paused when he noticed Autumn. He tilted his head, giving her a confused look, and walked toward her. "Have you seen my dog, Max? She's a golden retriever and was brought here after some jerk ran her over."

Autumn placed her hands on her hips, "You're her owner? It was a complete miracle her injuries weren't more severe. She has a cast on one of her paws."

"I had my front door open, and I got distracted looking at—" His cheeks turned pink, and he scratched at the stubble on his jaw. "Eh, it doesn't matter, but I looked away for one second, and she took off."

Autumn couldn't help but notice he was an attractive man. She would do anything to have Maggie with her, so witnessing an irresponsible owner lose sight of their own pet for such trivial reasons was frustrating.

"Well, was the distraction worth it?" Autumn snarled. "Dogs have a lot of energy, so you need to be more careful and keep an eye out for them."

The man's eyes widened, and his cheeks turned an ever-deeper shade of red. He opened his mouth a few times without producing any words. She could see the conflict behind them, defensiveness mixed with guilt and fear.

Crap. Maybe I'm being too harsh.

"But she's doing well." Autumn rubbed her arm, giving him an empathetic look. "Her blood pressure was a bit low, and we gave her some fluids. I operated on her paw, and she should heal within the next two to three weeks. She'll need a lot of bed rest and regular check-ups at the clinic. I care about these animals, and I want them to be safe."

The man nodded. "You don't know how thankful I am," he said, meeting her eyes. "Max is always there for me on my dark days, always puts a smile on my face when I need it. Thank you for saving her."

Autumn grinned. "You're welcome." As she was about to walk away, the man's hand shot out in front of her, whipping back when she looked down at it, startled.

"I didn't catch your name, Dr...."

She looked over her shoulder at him. "Evans. My name is Autumn Evans."

"It's nice to meet you, Dr. Evans," he said with a shy smile. "I'm Emmett. Are you passing through town?"

"Something like that, I'm not planning on staying around for long. Although, Dr. Pierce did try to hire me."

He looked at her, stunned. "That's impressive. Dr. Pierce isn't one to hire anybody around here, which means you must be special."

They stood in silence for a moment until Autumn cleared her throat. "Promise me you'll be more careful with Max? I want to avoid having to stitch her up again."

He smirked. "I will, Dr. Evans, and that's a promise to you."

"Good, I'll hold you to it." She glanced at her watch. "I have to get back to my sister's wedding. It was nice meeting you," she said, skirting around him to get to the door.

"It was nice meeting you too. I'll see you around!"

And she had a feeling she would.

By the time she returned to the wedding, everyone had gone home. Autumn felt guilty for missing most of the party but was relieved to know Mason was no longer there.

"I'm sorry I left so sudden, Ortus. You should've seen her, though, the dog was on the verge of death," Autumn explained as she helped clean the backyard. Her sister had been understanding as she recapped how she'd saved Max's life.

"Was he cute?" Ortus asked as she placed her wedding gifts on a small wagon.

"The dog? I guess, but I was more focused on—"

"No, silly, the dog's owner. Was he cute?"

Autumn rolled her eyes. Ortus never missed an opportunity to play matchmaker. "He's the reason his dog ended up at the clinic. He was not cute," Autumn snapped.

Ortus pouted. "If you say so ..."

They pulled the wagon of presents to the front of the house, where Jordan was waiting. While Jordan loaded the car with gifts, Ortus turned to Autumn and held her hand.

"I know it was hard for you to be here. Thank you for coming to celebrate this day with me."

Autumn pulled her into a hug. "You're my little sister. I wouldn't miss it for the world."

"You'd tell me if something were bothering you, right?" Ortus whispered.

"I don't want to talk about Mason, I-"

Ortus released the embrace, "I'm not referring to Mason."

"What are you hinting at?"

"Some of our extended families were eyeing us, like when we were kids."

It dawned on Autumn why her sister was checking in. "Oh, now I feel *horrible* for leaving you alone to deal with them."

"We cannot control what they say." Ortus leaned against the car, "Are we always going to get weird looks when we're together?"

"Being bi-racial is like a foreign concept to our relatives, and it's disheartening." Autumn attempted to lighten the mood, "They act like we were born yesterday, we've been bi-racial for twenty plus years. Get a life."

Ortus giggled, turning to Autumn. "I'm glad you're here, I wish you'd stay in Maplewood," she pleaded.

Autumn stiffened, but Jordan interrupted the moment.

"Okay, we're all set."

Ortus and Autumn shared one last embrace.

"Enjoy your honeymoon," Autumn said.

"Oh, we will." Ortus winked. She spun around and slapped Jordan on the bottom as he stooped to get in the driver's seat.

Autumn chuckled and watched them drive away. She had made it through the day, and by this time tomorrow morning, she would be heading to another state, ready to start over … again. Her smile fell, and she headed back into the house.

Before getting to the stairs, she passed the kitchen. Her mother glared from where she sat, eating a piece of wedding cake. "I was beginning to think you'd left."

Autumn didn't even stop. "Don't worry, I'll be out of your hair soon enough."

"Where did you even go?" Marie looked her daughter up and down. "And what are you wearing?"

"Someone ran over your neighbor's dog. I took her to the clinic and did emergency surgery on her."

Marie shook her head. "Those could have been people."

Autumn scowled. She wanted to tell her mother how wrong she was, how selfish she was for saying such things. But instead, she said the complete opposite, "You're right."

"I always am, honey."

Without another word, Autumn headed to her bedroom. When she turned on the lamp by the door, she smiled. She was half-expecting to walk into a new home gym or office, but her walls were still pastel pink, and white fairy lights still hung throughout the room. At the large window, the curtains were open, revealing a bright crescent moon hanging over the front yard.

After she showered, she placed her dirty clothing in her luggage. She turned her lamp off and headed to her bed. The bright headlights of a car driving up the street cast moving shadows across her walls. As she approached the window to close the curtains, she noticed a car pull into the house across from her parents' home. A man got out of the vehicle. It was difficult to see through the dark, but when he picked up a large, golden dog from his backseat, Autumn knew this had to be Emmett.

He dropped Max off inside and ran back to lock up his car. Without warning, he glanced up, catching Autumn watching him. Her cheeks turned pink as he smiled waving at her. Mortified, she waved back and closed the curtains.

Emmett watched as Autumn closed her curtains. He'd been caught off guard by her coldness earlier, but he realized it was because she cared for the animals she treated, and she cared for Max as much as he did. There was something intriguing about Autumn Evans.

He walked back inside and locked up behind himself. Max lay on the grey couch, still drowsy from the anesthetic. Emmett sat next to her, placing his legs on the wooden coffee table in front of him.

"Don't you ever scare me like that again, Max," he said, scratching her forehead as she gave a gentle yawn before falling asleep on his lap.

Emmett's eyes wandered around, observing his sage colored living room. His mom had chosen the color a couple of days ago, claiming he lacked the creative eye required to design the interior of a home. When they'd finished, he'd tried to convince her to stay with him, but she declined.

"I love you, but it would be odd if your mother still lived with you," she explained. "You'll find someone soon, Emmett."

Emmett scoffed. "If she can't understand the love I have for my mother, she isn't the one."

His mother sighed. "You can't keep pushing everyone away. Lily would've wanted you to move on, be happy. You know that, right?"

Emmett's mother had good intentions. He knew she wanted to see him happy again. The problem was, he didn't know how to be himself anymore. Before losing the love of his life, he'd been excited to get married and have children. Now, he felt like he was at a stalemate, unable to determine what would fill the emptiness he felt in his chest.

He grabbed the photo album from under the coffee table and, as he turned each page, smiled at the photos of Lily and his old best friend Jayden. Their lives were different now and each of their paths had taken a different turn.

He paused at the next page, feeling as if he had been punched in the gut. It was a photo of an eight-year-old Emmett smiling on a boat after catching his first fish. His father stood next to him.

The vibrations of his phone in his pocket brought him back from his thoughts. He glanced at the caller ID, not recognizing the number.

"Hello, this is Emmett," he said in an exhaustive tone.

"Emmett, it's your father."

Emmett's lips pursed. With her head on his lap, Max blinked awake at the shift in tension. The sound of his father's breathing on the other end of the line filled the quiet.

"Son ... we need to talk."

Emmett's heart dropped to the pit of his stomach. An anger boiled in his blood. Twenty years. After twenty years he needed to talk?

"Don't ever call me again," he said before hanging up the phone and heading to bed.

3

Autumn finished packing her belongings the following afternoon. She hadn't told anyone she was leaving, so when there was a sudden knock on her bedroom door, she shoved her luggage under the bed.

"Come in!" she called out, running to sit by her window.

J.J. entered the room, with Brooke and Bradley following behind, dressed in matching red flannel shirts.

Must be a twin thing.

J.J. gave her a thoughtful look. "What happened to you last night?"

"You ran off, and we couldn't find you anywhere," Bradley added, brows knitted into a frown.

"Oh, the neighbor's dog was hit by a car, so I took her to the animal hospital," Autumn said.

She shook her head, but Bradley continued to observe her. "You and I both know that's not what J.J. meant," Bradley said. "What happened with Mason? Why did he upset you?"

Autumn suppressed an eyeroll. Leave it to Bradley to be observant when Autumn didn't want him to be. She knew he meant well and his focus on her was coming from a place of concern, but it was a concern she didn't wish to burden him with.

Much to Autumn's appreciation, Brooke answered first. "Bradley, Autumn doesn't need a reason. Mason is her ex-boyfriend now, and if she doesn't want to talk to him, she doesn't have to."

"Wait, they're broken up?"

The twins continued to argue, but Autumn stopped listening. It didn't matter where she escaped to, Mason always found a way back into her life.

When they were children, Autumn never kept anything from her friends. They knew everything about her, and she knew everything about them. After what happened with Mason, she had been close to calling them but hesitated. Being forced to push them away and omit the embarrassing truth of what her life had become was one of the most challenging things she'd experienced.

"She's gone again." J.J. nudged Autumn, bringing her out of her thoughts.

Brooke gave her a worried look. "Autumn, we want to know if you're okay. We're your friends, you can tell us anything."

Autumn shook her head. "I'm fine, don't worry about me."

Brooke looked at Autumn for a moment, mouth pulled to the side in a way that told Autumn she was suspicious. "California … changed you, didn't it?"

The question was soft, not accusatory, as if she knew something bad had happened.

A sick feeling enveloped Autumn. "You could say that," she expressed in a faint voice.

Brooke sighed in defeat. "Fine. I won't keep pushing, but can you hurry up and get ready for tonight?"

Autumn cocked her head. "Where are we going?"

"The annual Battle of the Bands is being hosted in the downtown park. We went every year as teenagers, remember? I thought it would be nice for the four of us to go, seeing as you're in town."

Autumn looked down. "I'm not in the mood to go out to a concert, Brooke."

"Oh, c'mon Autumn. Let's go. It'll be like old times!" Bradley pleaded. Without warning, he slumped onto the window seat beside her. She flinched, shifting closer to the wall.

The twins gave her matching puppy eyes, and J.J. rolled his eyes at their tactic. It had been seven years since Autumn last saw her friends, all they were asking of her was to spend time with her. Why was she stopping herself from rebuilding relationships with those she cared about?

She reflected back to the wedding, to how Brooke had berated Mason without a word from Autumn. She had spent years pushing her friends away, but they had stood up for her without question.

"Fine, but one of you is paying for my ticket," she said.

Brooke winked. "I've got you."

Bradley clapped and sprang to his feet. "Awesome. Now, you get ready while I sort this one out," he said to Autumn as he grabbed his sister's wrist and began pulling her toward the door.

Brooke scoffed and looked down at her outfit. "We're wearing the same thing!"

J.J. shook his head. "We'll see you at the park."

The door closed behind them, and as they disappeared down the hallway, Bradley's muffled voice said, "We all know I pull it off better."

Autumn chuckled and rolled her eyes, though for a moment she sat there staring at her closed door. With a sigh, she pulled her suitcase from under the bed and flipped it open.

"Okay ... concert ..." she muttered to herself as she scanned the folds of fabric. It had been so long since she'd been to one. Mason had never been a fan of crowds. Now that they'd broken up, Autumn realized it might not have been the crowds he disliked, but the fact he would have to share Autumn's company.

After rifling through her luggage, Autumn settled on a burnt orange mini overall dress over a white long sleeve. She pulled her long, brown hair into a ponytail and applied some mascara, finishing the look with the red lipstick Ortus had made her wear at the wedding.

She admired herself in the mirror for a moment. Mason had never allowed her to dress like this. He preferred Autumn look like what he called "a respectable woman"—dresses, curled hair, and manicured nails. This small act of rebellion made Autumn smirk, and after pulling on a pair of black Doc Martens, which she found buried in her closet, she made her way out.

Autumn met Brooke, Bradley, and J.J. at the park entrance. The sun had almost set by now, and the bass of the music beyond the trees rumbled through the ground.

Brooke waved Autumn over. "Girl, you look awesome!"

"Couldn't have dressed you better myself," Bradley said, trailing off. "Well—"

"Shut up, Bradley," Brooke said, looping her arm through Autumn's and pulling her down the path that led to the stage.

Once they broke through the trees, lights of all colors filled Autumn's vision. Enticing food trucks glowed from the edges of the clearing, and farther up the field, audience members lounged on blankets while they enjoyed the music. Closer to the stage a crowd had gathered, swaying and jumping to the rhythm of the music.

"I love this song!" Brooke squealed and headed for the stage with a skip in her step as if she'd regressed ten years in a second.

Autumn giggled, following Bradley and J.J. They wove through the crowd until they found Brooke, and there they danced and laughed and sang until their stomachs groaned for sustenance and their throats complained for water.

While Autumn and Brooke sat on the grass near the trees, Bradley and J.J. went to grab them some food and drinks.

Brooke sighed and leaned back on her hands to watch the stage. "Glad you came?"

Autumn smiled. "I haven't had this much fun in a long time." And it was true.

Brooke glanced sideways at her. "You didn't get out much in LA?"

"Ah ..." Autumn stuttered, averting her eyes from her best friend's studying gaze. "I was busy with work ... *we* were busy. Mason and me. Well, more so him than me, but it's okay—"

"Didn't you have any ... friends you could hang out with?"

"We, er ... we kept to ourselves ..." Autumn said.

In truth, her life in Los Angeles had been monotonous. Her routine included waking up in the morning, going to work, and returning to Mason in the evening.

By the time they were both home from work, he was exhausted, and Autumn was fed up. Neither tried in the end, leaving Autumn to also blame herself. After spending years in isolation, she had forgotten what it was like to have fun, and what it was like to have friends.

"Brooke!"

Both women looked up to see Bradley a few feet away, waving his arms at them. "They're giving out free cotton candy!" he yelled and pointed.

"Cotton candy?" Brooke said, but Bradley had already turned and was running toward the stand, pushing through anyone who got in his way. Brooke shook her head and turned to Autumn. "I better go after him before he attacks the vendor. I'll be right back."

Autumn had forgotten how silly Brooke and Bradley could be together. The twins had been inseparable since the death of their parents. After such a tragedy, it made sense for them to find joy in the little things.

Autumn sighed, closing her eyes and listening to the sound of the guitars and drums, allowing herself a moment of bliss.

"I guess it's a party of one now," she whispered.

A hand landed on her shoulder. "Care if I join you?"

Autumn gasped, reached up, and slapped the hand from her before whipping around, fists raised.

"Whoa, there! That's one tough grip." Emmett shook the pain from his hand.

Autumn scowled. "You startled me. Didn't anyone ever teach you about personal space?"

The music had stopped playing and the emcee had taken the stage to wish everyone good night. Emmett studied Autumn, his demeanor still. She knew he was trying to understand why she had snapped at him; she'd seen that look before—on her dad, on Ortus, on Brooke and Bradley.

Autumn sighed. "I'm sorry." She crossed her arms. "It doesn't take much to startle me. It's one of the reasons why I don't like surprises."

"No, I'm sorry. I'll be more careful next time." He gave her an encouraging smile. "I'm guessing that's a yes to joining you?"

"That depends. How's Max doing?"

"She's a lot better. She's been getting as much rest as possible, per doctor's orders." He winked. "I don't want to risk her being in more pain than she is already."

Autumn settled back on the grass. "I suppose a little company never hurt anyone …"

Emmett took a seat beside her, leaving a comfortable gap between them. "I still don't know how to thank you for what you did for Max," he said, rubbing the back of his neck. "I feel guilty you had to leave Ortus's wedding."

She gave him a puzzled look. "You know my sister?"

"It's a small town. Everyone knows everybody around here. I was on my way but … you know the rest."

"I do." Autumn glanced at a group of women who were whispering to one another while casting furtive glances toward her and Emmett. "I guess some things never change, there's no such thing as privacy around here, huh?"

"Oh, don't get me wrong. Sure, it's a small town, but everyone is always here for each other. We're one big community," he reassured her.

But it never felt like a community to me.

Autumn's resentment toward her mother tainted how she felt about the town. Marie was praised by the people of Maplewood, so Autumn never bothered to get to know the people of the town for fear they would see her the same way—as a disappointment.

"What do you say?" Emmett asked.

Crap. "I'm sorry, what did you say?"

He looked at the ground, nudging a rock around with his knuckle. "I asked if I could walk you home."

"I'm supposed to let a total stranger walk me home? What if you kidnap me or something?"

Emmett placed a hand over his heart. "Promise I won't. Besides, the town would know it was me. I'm a sucker for brunettes."

Autumn looked away, feeling her cheeks flush. "I guess you can walk me home."

The park wasn't too far from Autumn's parents' home, or at least that's what it felt like when she talked to Emmett. They talked about their hobbies, favorite movies, and favorite books. To her shock, they had a lot in common. Walking with Emmett brought her a strange feeling of contentment, a feeling she hadn't been exposed to in a long time.

When they arrived, Autumn guided him to the swing so they could continue talking. She sat while Emmett pushed her.

Autumn shook her head in disbelief. "I can't believe you don't like thrillers. I used to love the buildup of suspense, the adrenaline you feel throughout a good film is amazing!"

"Used to?"

"Yeah, I haven't watched one in a long time." She planted her feet on the ground to stop swinging. "I guess I don't like being startled, anymore."

Emmett circled the swing so he could see her. "Hey, it's all right. I don't enjoy feeling scared either, but what type of person doesn't like comedies?" he challenged.

Autumn scoffed. "Films nowadays make comedy feel so forced. What's even more astonishing is hearing of someone who enjoys taking risks but doesn't enjoy a good thriller. You say you like skydiving?"

He shrugged. "Everyone's a critic."

Autumn chuckled and stood. "Well, thanks for walking with me. You didn't have to."

"Are you kidding? You saved Max, I owe you the world."

"You make me sound like a superhero. I love animals. I did my job."

"You're a superhero to me."

Silence fell. A smile snuck onto Autumn's lips, but through the dark, she could see Emmett's face heat much like how it had been when she berated him in the veterinary clinic.

He scratched his jaw. "Umm ... I mean to *us*, Max and me."

"Noted. Would you like a go on the swing?" Autumn stepped aside, extending her hand to the hanging bench.

Emmett sank onto it with hesitation, as if he feared the ropes would snap under his weight, but they held strong and Autumn stepped behind him, giving him a little push. He laughed, and they remained that way in silence for a moment, enjoying the calm of the night air. Silence had often made Autumn uncomfortable, but being in this moment with Emmett somehow felt natural.

"My dog, Maggie, was my best friend growing up. When I cried, she would run up to me and lick my tears away," she said.

Emmett chuckled. "Max does the same thing. I think they like the salt."

"Dogs are what got me started in my veterinary work, but all animals deserve the love we give them. They're looking for their partner in crime as much as we are. I love them."

Emmett planted his feet and twisted so he was looking at Autumn. "There's something I need to tell you—"

"I couldn't help but overhear …" A figure separated from the shadows of the neighbor's house. Emmett stood in alarm, but Autumn recognized his voice in an instant. Her hands began to tremble as Mason stepped into the light spilling from her parents' kitchen window.

"You know, Autumn's love for animals is almost as big as the love she has for me. Isn't that right, my love?"

Autumn stepped around Emmett, putting herself between the two men. "What are you doing here, Mason?"

"Your love?" Emmett said.

Autumn turned around at the hint of disappointment in his voice. When she met his eyes, Mason came up behind her, breathing down her neck, sending chills up her spine. She didn't know what to do or say, so she stood there, frozen.

Emmett appeared to grasp the situation and crossed his arms. "She seems to be more scared than in love with you."

"I don't think that's any of your business, now, is it?"

Autumn knew that tone. It seemed calm on the outside, but beneath it hid fury. Autumn broke from her paralysis and turned to face her ex.

"Mason, what are you still doing here?" she whispered.

"I was heading back tomorrow morning, but there was something I needed to take care of before I left. I also wanted to talk to you about something." The frown dropped from his face, replaced by a smile that could melt butter. "Autumn, my love, I want to bring you with me."

She stared at him in disbelief, but Emmett responded before she could.

"She can't go with you."

"And why not?" Mason said.

Emmett scowled. "Because she accepted a job in Maplewood."

Mason's jaw dropped, but he clamped it shut. "That's impossible. Autumn hates this town. She was mistreated by her own mother. She would never stay here."

Why aren't I saying anything? Why am I letting Emmett speak for me?

Autumn half turned to look at Emmett. His expression had changed to one of concerned confusion when he heard Mason's revelation about Dr. Marie Evans's narcissism.

She sighed and turned back to Mason. "That's where you're wrong. I am staying. You're right. I ran away from this town because of my mother, but maybe I didn't give it a fair chance. I'm staying."

"Autumn, you can't be serious—"

"Things change, Mason. You of all people should know that."

Mason rubbed his jaw. Autumn knew that look. It was the look he always wore when he didn't get what he wanted, but also the look that meant he wouldn't stop trying. There was a time when she'd found it charming, but after being with him for so many years, she knew it to be a part of his manipulation cycle.

He broke eye contact with her, pulled his phone from his pocket, and started tapping away on it. "I'm going to stay in town. You deserve better than this place. *You're* better than this place, Autumn." He met her eyes one more time before turning and walking away.

Autumn's shoulders loosened. He was walking away.

He never walks away.

Perhaps he has changed.

A sense of hopelessness and irritation washed over her. Once again, she was trying to see the best in Mason. She was stuck in a cycle that she couldn't seem to break out of.

"Are you okay?"

She scowled and rounded on Emmett. "I can't stay in this town. Why did you do that?"

"Because you're innocent and pure, sort of like a dove." He took a long pause before continuing. "Lil' dove, why are you so afraid of him?"

Autumn fidgeted with her hands, and it took her a moment to calm herself down. Emmett was suspicious, and she didn't want to give him an opportunity to question her further. Today had been a taste of what could happen if anybody tried to get between her and Mason, and she was certain things weren't over yet.

After a couple of breaths, Autumn said, "You should go, Emmett." She turned and made her way inside without a backward glance. She knew he was staring at her as she walked away. She was sure he was confused, but this was none of his business. They'd only met, after all.

When Autumn walked into the house, she noticed her parents had finished eating dinner. She tried to sneak upstairs but was called by her mother.

"Did Mason ever find you?" Marie called.

Autumn walked to the threshold of the kitchen. "Yep. I'm guessing that was your doing?"

"He came by asking where you were. Are you going to say yes to his proposal?"

She snorted. "Of course not."

Marie rolled her eyes as she placed the dishes in the dishwasher. "Don't be foolish. He's an established detective, and he seems to love you. Don't let him go."

Autumn rubbed her arm. "You don't know what you're talking about, Mom," she whispered.

"Foolish. I promise you you're going to regret not taking him back."

Autumn wasn't at all phased her mother had taken Mason's side. There hadn't been a moment where her mother had stopped to ask what had occurred to cause their breakup. Somehow, she had assumed that it was Autumn's fault.

Holding back tears, Autumn shook her head in disappointment and headed to her room, hoping to get a good night's rest. But as she lay in her bed, memories of her time in New Mexico returned.

She had moved there on a whim after an explosive breakup with Mason, had rented an apartment, cash in hand, and was employed as a dental receptionist. But she still felt too close to Los Angeles for comfort. Not a day went by that she didn't find herself making odd turns to make sure she wasn't being followed, didn't go out of her way to use an ATM as far from her apartment as possible, didn't loiter outside a police station, debating whether to out one of their own as an abuser.

Autumn knew she was safe staying in Maplewood. Mason wouldn't risk hurting her, knowing her loved ones were watching nearby, and yet it felt like she was letting him influence her decision to stay in this town. She considered buying a plane ticket, leaving her car behind, and heading far away from Maplewood. She could run away, and he wouldn't know where to find her this time.

But she was trapped.

How could she run away when there was something telling her to stay?

4

Autumn spent the night feeling paranoid, tossing and turning at the idea of someone watching her. Footsteps in the morning had caused her to spring out of bed, to discover it had been her parents getting up for the day. Although she was exhausted, she called Dr. Pierce and agreed to hear more about her offer. After getting dressed, she headed downstairs to eat a quick bowl of Cheerios.

"Cereal?" her mother said, taking a bite of her bacon.

Autumn rolled her eyes. "It's not like you made enough for the three of us."

"We're not used to having you around, and to be frank, I thought you had already left."

"I'm going to stay in town for a bit."

"You won't lie around and do nothing, right?"

"Autumn can stay here for as long as she wants," her father said without looking up, flipping through another page of his newspaper.

Marie narrowed her eyes at her husband, a second later shifting to Autumn. "No one lives in a house for free."

"Don't worry. I'll pay rent with the job I'll take at the veterinary clinic."

Great, now I've got no choice but to take it.

Not wanting to commit to anything else without thinking, Autumn wolfed down the rest of her cereal and placed her bowl in the sink. "I can't argue with you right now, I need to go," she said as she left.

The clinic wasn't too far from her, but driving allowed her to think. She was sick and tired of running away from the people who caused her pain, of making decisions on a whim based on fulfilling someone's expectations of her. It felt as if she were on a constant loop, running laps and arriving at no realistic solution.

Regardless of what Dr. Pierce said, she would stay in Maplewood for a couple of weeks. She hoped it would buy her time to plan her next move. But above all else, if she was close to her dear ones, she may feel safe for once.

Autumn pulled up to the clinic. For a moment, she lingered in the driver's seat, doors still locked, watching the pet owners who came and left. She looked to the trees that bordered the parking lot, to the shadows beneath them. After a long pause, she took a deep breath and headed inside the clinic.

"Nora made it through the surgery," a woman expressed on the phone as Autumn held the door open for her. "I can't imagine life without that cat. There are no words to explain how grateful I am to Dr. Pierce."

Autumn smiled upon hearing this. She longed to feel the warmth of a patient's gratitude again; it made everything worth it.

"Good morning, Autumn. Dr. Pierce is in her office," Jackie said as she walked through the door.

"Thank you, Jackie." She paused, grabbing a candy from the jar on the reception desk. "Good job the other day, by the way. I couldn't have done it without you."

He grinned. "No prob, doc. I'm studying to be a veterinarian, so it's helpful to see you in action."

Autumn smiled. "Well, as long as it's okay with Dr. Pierce, I'm always happy to let you sit in on a surgery."

"I'll hold you to that offer."

After a couple minutes of wandering, Autumn found a door decorated with a golden plaque which read, "Dr. Elizabeth Pierce, dvm, ms, dacvs." She lingered in the hall and took a deep breath. *Suck it up and get in there.*

After knocking twice, she walked into the office, and her mouth fell open.

"What the heck are you doing here?"

Emmett, who was wearing scrubs and smiling, leaned on Dr. Pierce's desk. "I thought you'd be a lot happier to see me."

"How am I supposed to react? You're in scrubs in my potential supervisor's office. I repeat, what are you doing here?"

"What's going on?"

Autumn spun to see Dr. Pierce standing by the door. Autumn's cheeks heated. "I'm sorry, Dr. Pierce, but this man—"

Dr. Pierce waved her hand, frowning past Autumn. "Emmett, get your bottom off my desk," she said, brushing past to sit in her chair. She looked up at Autumn from over her glasses. "Is my son causing you trouble, Ms. Evans?"

"Your … son?" Autumn looked between the two. How could she have been so naïve? As they both stood in front of her, she could see their similar facial features, their matching eyes and smiles.

Dr. Pierce nodded, patting her son on the arm. "This is my son, Dr. Emmett Miller. Veterinarians run in our bloodline."

Emmett cleared his throat. "We've met, Mom."

This revelation didn't appear to faze Dr. Pierce in the slightest. "Good! Because you two will be working together a lot, and it's important we all get along for the sake of the clinic." She waved her hand across the table. "Both of you have a seat."

Without hesitation, Autumn sat down. Behind Dr. Pierce, she noticed a cabinet on which sat photos of her and Emmett. There were no father figures in any of the pictures.

"As I mentioned when we met, I won't be able to stay here for long. I can help for a couple of weeks."

Emmett sat next to her. "You're skilled, so we appreciate any help you can give us."

Dr. Pierce nodded. "I agree. What would you say to a month?"

My, she is persistent.

"The doctor I said you'd be covering for let us know she is moving to Oregon. It will take time until I can find an official replacement. We need the help, or Emmett and I will be swamped every day." Dr. Pierce reached into a drawer and pulled out a manilla envelope. She slipped it across the desk to Autumn. "All the information on the position is in there."

Autumn picked it up and peeped inside, spotting a pile of documents. She sighed. "I'll need some time to look these over, but when can I start?"

Dr. Pierce smiled. "You can shadow me or Emmett today. I want to make sure you transition well into our team."

Autumn could feel Emmett's cheeky smile on her, but she avoided looking at him as she said, "Dr. Pierce, I would love for it to be the two of us. I think I should learn from the person who built this place."

Dr. Pierce grinned. "Wise woman."

Emmett coughed and leaned back. Autumn suppressed a smile of her own as he stood up. "I'll let you get to it," he said before leaving them alone in the office.

Dr. Pierce glanced at her. "Let's get started."

After a tour of the clinic, offices, and break room, and a few general appointments that Autumn watched from the corner of the room, Autumn headed to the local café, leaving her car in the clinic parking lot. Brooke and Bradley had called her, demanding she meet them there.

As she walked the streets of Maplewood, she watched the crowds, cautious of those around her. Walking alone stopped being enjoyable the moment her relationship with Mason ended. She quickened her pace at the thought of him.

When she arrived at the corner of Magnolia Street, she spotted the café's rustic red brick exterior. She looked over her shoulder and let out a sigh of relief. When she walked into the café, she noticed how busy it was, yet the atmosphere was quiet. Almost every seat was taken; it seemed many were using the place as a workspace by the laptops, notebooks, and folders scattered across the tables.

Heading past the people waiting in line, Autumn searched for her friends. She walked toward a small stage at the back of the room. A chalkboard next to it read, "El Café del Poeta presents: Open Mic Night every Tuesday and Thursday." At the windows beyond, her eyes met the twins' scowling faces. It was in that moment Autumn realized she hadn't followed up with them after the Battle of the Bands concert.

"Wait, so you ditched us for some guy?" Brooke said, unimpressed after a quick explanation from Autumn.

"You ran off to get cotton candy, so who left who?"

"Hey, don't blame the cotton candy!" Bradley interjected, taking a bite of his croissant.

Brooke relaxed, stirring her iced hazelnut latte. "You worried us, Autumn." Her eyes were soft, filled with concern and empathy, while Autumn was consumed with guilt. She'd gone without friends for so long, she'd forgotten even the basics.

"I thought you saw me leave, I'm sorry," she murmured.

For a moment, no one said anything. She couldn't tell if they were still upset or if they were being dramatic. Brooke broke the silence.

"Well, what's his name? Is he cute? Does he like puppies as much as you do?"

Dramatic—got it.

Before Autumn could respond, she saw Brooke's eyes glance above her head.

"I do enjoy puppies," a voice said.

You've got to be joking. Autumn turned in her chair to see Emmett standing behind her. "Are you following me or something?"

"It's a small town. This also happens to be the best café in town, the coffee they make here could raise a man from the dead," he said.

"Good to know what places I need to avoid," she said, turning back around.

She heard him take a deep breath, though she couldn't tell if it was out of frustration or sorrow. "Autumn, I want to apologize. I know I should've told you sooner, and I'm hoping you'll give me a chance to explain?"

A part of her still felt embarrassed for what had occurred earlier, but the other part—which had been rather smug—was beginning to feel guilty for turning him away. She looked over at Brooke, who was giving her a nod of approval.

Autumn rolled her eyes and turned to face him again. Their eyes met, and for a couple of seconds, they stared at one another in silence. As if they were the only two in the room.

"Fine. One chance to explain," Autumn said.

He smiled. "Great, I'll pick you up at eight."

Before Autumn could object, he was already gone. She turned to look back at her friends. "What the heck just happened?" she asked.

"Looks like you're going on a date with Emmett Miller." Brooke took a bite of her chocolate muffin, giving her a pointed look.

"First of all, it's not a date. Second, how do you know his name?"

Bradley and Brooke looked at one another with mischievous smiles. Growing impatient, Autumn crossed her arms. "Well?"

Bradley sighed. "Emmett is Brooke's ex-boyfriend."

Autumn looked down at her hands, shocked but also relieved. Her best friend had been in a relationship with the handsome man she was intrigued by, but at least now Autumn had to honor girl code. The date was off.

Laughter made Autumn look up.

"You believed me?" Bradley said through chuckles.

Her ears turn hot. "You were lying? Why would you say that?"

Brooke placed her coffee to the side. "Isn't it obvious? We wanted to see how you felt about him, and now we know."

"You're the worst. Do you even know the guy?"

"We do!" Bradley said. "His mom owns the local veterinary clinic. He followed in her footsteps and became a vet. Ortus was the first to befriend him, but that's a story she should tell you herself."

"He's mysterious, all right." Autumn's gaze was distant as she looked into her hot chocolate. "I work with him now."

"Wait, what?" Bradley dropped his croissant back onto his plate. "You're staying?"

"The night of the wedding, I saved Emmett's dog. She was hit by a car. His mother offered me a job and now ... here I am."

"As easy as that?" Bradley said.

Autumn shrugged. "I've been looking for a change. Even if I don't stay here for long, it'll give me some time to think."

Brooke sighed and shook her head. "If you don't take all this as a sign, there's something wrong with you."

Autumn smiled but didn't respond. Was this a sign, or was there something wrong with her?

After finishing her coffee and listening to the twin's gossip, Autumn headed back home. Although they liked to make fun of her, she'd be lying if she said she didn't enjoy her time with them.

Back at her parents' home, she was surprised to find them sitting in the living room, watching the classic film *Good Will Hunting*. Her father had his arms around her mother, and although Autumn didn't have a good relationship with Marie, she couldn't deny the love her parents had for one another.

Movie nights were her favorite when she was a kid. They would choose a film to watch together, and afterward go to the ice-cream shop and discuss how they felt about it. It had been their tradition.

Autumn studied her parents, wondering how her relationship with them had become so strained.

"Are you going to stand there, or are you going to come watch with us?" Marie asked.

"I can't." Autumn continued to the bottom of the stairs. "A friend is picking me up soon—maybe next time."

Marie glared over her shoulder, turning away to watch the movie.

That's it? No, 'What are your plans?' She stopped with her hand on the banister, listening to Matt Damon and Robin Williams have a heart-to-heart, and her long-built-up frustration morphed into something new—bravery.

She turned back to the living room, lips pressed together. "That's it? I'm back for the first time in seven years so I can reconnect with my roots, yet my own parents don't seem willing to reconnect with *me*?"

Both her parents turned to face her. Her father looked uncomfortable and remained quiet, her mother, on the other hand, looked confused.

"Autumn. *You* left *us*."

She felt a mixture of emotions. It was upsetting to hear her mother use her wish to follow her dreams as an excuse for their fallout, and it was disappointing to hear that, after all this time, Marie hadn't dug deeper within herself, missing the reason behind her daughter's decision to leave.

"Leaving this place was one of the most difficult decisions I ever made," Autumn said with tears in her eyes. "You wanted me to be someone I wasn't, Mom. You always compared me to your friends' children, always made me feel like I was never enough. Would you have stayed in a home where you weren't allowed to share your passions?"

Marie scoffed. "You're being ridiculous."

"That's it!" Bill said, standing up as he looked down at Marie. "You're the one being ridiculous. Listen to your daughter for god's sake. She's telling you that you hurt her."

"Are you calling me a bad mother?"

"Marie, listen to yourself. We agreed to be supportive parents and one of our daughters told us she never felt that way. Why are you ignoring this?"

Marie stood up, scowling at her husband. "We raised them to be strong. She's being sensitive and unreasonable!"

Tears were making their way down Autumn's face now. She never wanted to give her mother the satisfaction of seeing her cry. And now they were arguing because of Autumn. She was vulnerable, so she did the one thing she knew how to do.

She ran.

This time, she didn't run too far. She ran to her safe space, to the place where, for some odd reason, she felt protected. She ran to the swing under the big tree.

Autumn sat on the swing, thinking of the years she had spent bottling up her emotions and how it had resulted in her outburst today. Why had it taken her so long to tell her mom how she felt?

It was an odd feeling, because although she had waited years to confront her mother, she never wanted to cause her pain. She looked at the moon shining above her, allowing her tears to stream down her face until they abated, leaving salty streaks in their wake.

"Autumn?" a soft voice said from afar.

She turned to look across the street, watching Emmett walk toward her. He was wearing a deep blue leather jacket and dark-denim jeans. He looked *handsome*. She wiped the last of the tears from her face, hoping it wasn't evident she had been crying.

"Sorry, I didn't realize it was already eight," she said.

He looked at her for a moment. "What's wrong?"

"Nothing. It's been a long day."

He paused and narrowed his eyes. "You're not a good liar."

"I know."

Emmett sat on the grass next to the swing while Autumn looked up at the stars that flickered in and out of existence as the wind pushed at the tree's boughs. There was a long silence, but Emmett didn't seem to mind it. She wondered what was going on in his head, what did he think about the adult woman sitting on the swing, crying like a twelve-year-old?

"Well, if you won't tell me what's wrong, maybe we can talk about why you're upset with me?"

Autumn snorted and tilted her head to the side. "Oh. I am upset with you, am I?"

As he looked at the empty and quiet street in front of them, he took a deep breath. "I wasn't trying to make a fool out of you. You were quick to save Max, and you had such passion for saving her, I didn't want to take that feeling away from you. In this town, everyone knows me as my mother's son, and no one takes the time to get to know me as Emmett. You treated me like a regular patient, and I liked that feeling. When you came in this morning, I knew you would be upset, and I was trying to make light of the situation."

He looked up at her. "After you saved Max, I talked to my mom. She told me she had offered you the job, but you weren't sure if you would stay," he explained. "This town can be a good place to live. I planned to talk to you the night we were at the park and convince you to stay. I know this place holds bad memories for you, but why not try to make better ones?"

Autumn looked back at the night sky. She realized she had been too harsh on Emmett. It wasn't his fault she had lost trust in others, in herself. Autumn had a good feeling about Emmett, maybe this once she should trust herself.

"Sometimes I hate my mom." The words slipped out of her mouth.

She didn't turn to face him, fearing his reaction. Dumping her feelings on someone she didn't know was not something she was used to, and she felt shame for saying such words, but she was also stuck trying to find ways to move on and find the peace she needed. Autumn felt Emmett studying her, feeling his eyes burning into her soul.

"Autumn, I'm not going to tell you how you should feel about your parents, because you are the one person in this world who knows how you feel." He paused. "However, I can share with you how hate can consume you and make you feel so much worse. Your hatred can become an obsession, because you will continue to work on not becoming your parents, but in the end, it will make you more like them."

He placed his hand on hers. "Sometimes parents think they know what's best for their children, but they end up causing more harm than good. It sounds like she's caused you a significant amount of pain. You may disagree, but I don't think you *hate* her."

Again, a heaviness pushed from behind Autumn's eyes as they filled with tears. Emmett Miller was right. She didn't hate her mom. She knew somehow there must be an explanation for Marie's mistreatment toward her, but she also knew it wasn't an excuse for the emotional trauma Autumn had experienced as a child. The reality was there was one person who was responsible for her unhappiness. Autumn didn't hate her dad, she didn't hate her mom, she hated *herself*.

A couple of minutes later, Emmett convinced Autumn to take a walk with him. At first, they walked in silence, but after a couple of blocks they started talking about whatever topic floated on by. He never once stopped to ask Autumn what her mother had done, nor did he push for answers. Emmett helped her forget her worries, even if it was for one night.

"Does this mean you forgive me?" he asked.

Autumn stopped and turned to face him. She had forgotten this was the reason he had come to see her today. She found amusement in teasing Emmett—almost as much amusement as he seemed to get from teasing her.

"I guess I can find it in my heart to forgive you," she said with a faux sigh.

"Thank you. That means we can start over." Emmett extended his arm to her. "Hi, my name is Emmett Miller, but some of my friends call me Em." He stopped, as if remembering something. "Well, the truth is no one calls me that."

Autumn laughed.

He continued, "Anyway, I'm thirty years old, I'm the son of Dr. Elizabeth Pierce and co-owner of the local veterinary clinic in this town. I like long walks, hiking, and I enjoy watching a good comedy."

Autumn giggled, shaking his hand. "Well, it's nice to meet you, Emmett. My name is Autumn Marie Evans. I'm the daughter of the sophisticated Dr. Marie Evans and the Chief of Maplewood Police, Bill Evans. I'm twenty-eight years old, and I left this town years ago so I could be a veterinarian but returned for my sister's wedding. Along the way, I was hired by the local veterinary clinic after saving a golden retriever from her irresponsible owner."

"Hey, I thought you forgave me!"

"I forgave you for not telling me you were a veterinarian. I didn't forgive you for leaving your dog unsupervised."

He sighed, defeated.

"You've learned quite a bit about me and my drama, but I know nothing about you," she said, looking at the ground.

"There's not much for me to say."

"Well, how did you know what to say when I talked about my mother?"

He looked at the homes around them, as if he was debating what to share. "My dad has been trying to get back into my life. For a long time, I tried to reach out, but he never responded to my letters or phone calls. He made it clear he didn't want anything to do with me. Now, he's the one sending me messages, trying to build a relationship. I'm tempted, but ..."

"What's stopping you?"

"I've let it go. I was always so angry at him for leaving us. I'd rather be at peace with that than open the possibility for him to cause more pain."

Autumn nodded. She could understand Emmett's dilemma, and now she also understood why he seemed so easy to talk to. As awful as his predicament was, it was comforting to know that Emmett had a complicated past too.

Sirens pierced the night's air, jolting them apart. Autumn looked up the road to see flashing blue and red lights coming toward them. She pressed her hands to her ears as the ambulance whizzed by but dropped them as it turned right, and a weight landed in her stomach.

"No ... no, no, no." Autumn took off at a sprint back toward her parents' house with Emmett on her heels. Her suspicions were correct, and she watched from afar as paramedics rolled a figure out on a stretcher.

Marie followed it out, eyes wide. Autumn ran the last few feet up the driveway, meeting her mother halfway. "Mom, what's going on?"

"Your father had a heart attack. Call your sister and tell her to meet us at the hospital."

As Autumn watched the ambulance drive away, it felt like someone had ripped her heart out of her chest. And it was all her fault.

5

AUTUMN WATCHED THE AMBULANCE pull away from her home. She wanted to move, but her entire body had gone numb.

"Lil' dove, I can drive you to the hospital if you let me." Emmett tried speaking to her, but she continued to face the direction the ambulance had disappeared into. She had heard him, but she was frozen in place.

He left her side and a moment later pulled up in his car. "Autumn, get in the car now!" he called.

It was all she needed to break from her stupor. She rushed inside his car, and they sped away from her home. Autumn pulled her cellphone out of her pocket and, with shaking hands, dialed her sister's number.

"You're calling me during my honeymoon?" Ortus answered.

"Dad's in the hospital. You need to come home now."

"What? What happened?" Autumn heard some shuffling as Ortus spoke to Jordan, "We need to get back. Dad's in the hospital."

"He had a heart attack." Autumn replied. "How long will you be?"

"I should be there within the next two hours. We're not too far."

"Okay." She hung up the phone, placing it back in her pocket. Streetlights flashed past the windows, but Autumn's eyes weren't focused. She had never felt so much remorse in her life. The last memory her father had of her was of her storming off. For years, she had longed to tell her mother how she felt, but had it been worth it?

Her fingers drummed her thigh for the duration of the short journey until Emmett pulled into the hospital parking lot. Autumn registered her movements as she went from the cool night into the ER, bustling with the sick and injured. Somewhere nearby, a child was screaming.

Autumn wove between people and approached the reception desk where a tired nurse was typing away at a computer. Autumn's foot tapped as she waited for the woman to notice her.

She looked up. "How can I help you?"

"My father was brought here in an ambulance. Would you happen to know where I can find him?"

"Name?"

"Bill Evans."

The nurse tapped away at her computer. "Yes, he arrived minutes ago. Take a right down that corridor. He's in room 23B, but you'll need to wait in the waiting area until he's deemed stable enough to be seen."

Stable enough? "Okay, thank you." Autumn turned, almost colliding with Emmett who had been standing behind her. "This way," she said to him before racing off.

It didn't take long to find the waiting area the nurse had described. It was empty except for a form in a chair in the corner. Marie looked up as Autumn arrived.

"Did you call your sister?" she asked, voice tired. There was no malice to the question this time.

"Yes. She'll be here within the next two hours," Autumn replied. She paused where the seating area began, not daring to sit down. "Is he ... is he going to be okay?"

Marie didn't look at her daughter, focusing on the opposite wall. "I haven't heard from the doctor yet."

She didn't say anything more, leaving Autumn staring at her. A light tug on her hand pulled her attention to Emmett, who encouraged her to sit down.

At almost midnight, frantic footsteps up the corridor made everyone look up, but it wasn't the doctor who appeared around the corner.

Autumn embraced her sister, Jordan following close behind. Ortus was still dressed in swimwear under a light summer dress. As she kept apologizing, Ortus tightened their hug with each word.

Her sister stroked her back. "It's going to be okay."

Autumn broke their embrace. "How could something like this happen? I thought Dad was healthy. I thought ..."

Ortus's eyes flicked over Autumn's shoulder to where Marie sat, observing. Autumn recognized the look. They were hiding something.

"What aren't you telling me?" Autumn asked, stepping back so she could look between her mother and sister.

Marie crossed her arms. "You surprised your father with what you said. According to him, he didn't know how much pain you were in." She scoffed. "He didn't want me to tell you anything, but this was his second heart attack."

Autumn's heart shattered, her worst fear playing out right in front of her. She never wanted to hurt anyone. She never wanted her words to be the reason either of her parents ended up in a hospital. Tears pushed at the backs of her eyes. Emmett reached for her hand and gave it a gentle squeeze.

"Autumn," Ortus muttered. "This is not your fault—"

"How could it not be?" Autumn rounded on her sister. "The moment I find the courage to stand up for myself, I use it to hurt someone I care about."

"Dad's had heart problems for years now."

A flush of anger flowed through Autumn. How could they have kept this from her? But the more her frustration steeped, the more she realized it wasn't toward them, but toward herself. It was Autumn who had chosen to leave her hometown, it was Autumn who had chosen to push her loved ones away, and Autumn was the reason her father was now in the hospital.

"I understand," she said, falling back into the seat behind her.

Her sister gave her a wistful look. "Dad loves us both, right Mom?"

"He does." Marie paused. "Although Autumn has a point."

Autumn's eyes were heavy with sadness, as she turned to her mother "What point is that?"

Her mother scowled. "We wouldn't be here if you hadn't thrown a tantrum."

Autumn remained silent. It seemed no matter where she was, there was always someone wanting to blame her for their unhappiness.

At that moment, a doctor entered the room. "Are you the relatives of Mr. Evans?" she asked.

Marie and Autumn stood at the same time. "Yes, I'm his wife," Marie said.

The doctor nodded, lips pursed. "I'm Dr. Hunt. Mr. Evans is going to be all right, but we would like to keep him in the hospital to monitor his heart for a couple of days."

"When can we see him?" Ortus asked.

"We're going to do everything we can to ensure he is comfortable. He's sleeping now, so it would be best if you go home and get some rest."

A nurse peeked into the waiting room. "Dr. Hunt, you're needed in OR three."

"I'll update you when he's awake," Dr. Hunt said before walking away.

"You should both go home. I'll keep you updated," Marie said, not giving Autumn a second glance.

Jordan held Ortus's hand. "I agree. There's nothing more we can do here."

Ortus nodded, giving Autumn a long hug before leaving.

Autumn stood in the waiting room, consumed with guilt and regret, staring where the doctor had been standing. She wished she'd never said the things she had—at least not in front of her father. She wanted to run into the room and tell her dad how sorry she was. All she could think about was whether he would ever forgive her.

"He'll forgive you, lil' dove," Emmett whispered.

She'd forgotten he was standing next to her. He held her hand, rubbing his thumb up and down it, keeping her grounded.

She met his eyes. "How do you know?"

He gave a comforting smile. "Because I would."

Three days passed since her father's hospitalization, and Autumn hadn't been to visit once. But that wasn't to say she hadn't tried.

Autumn picked up her car keys and beelined for the front door. Today, she would see him.

"Not even going to say goodbye?" Marie asked from the couch in the living room.

Autumn stopped halfway out the door, glancing at her mother over her shoulder. "Goodbye," she said.

Marie looked Autumn up and down. "You better not be going to the hospital."

Damn it. "I *was* planning on stopping by before my shift starts at the clinic."

"Well, don't. I told you your father needs his rest, and you're not a relaxing presence."

Autumn gritted her teeth. "Fine," she muttered and walked out the door, feeling lonelier than she had all week. As she sat in her car, she pulled out her phone before starting the engine. Her texts to her friends had all gone unanswered, and Ortus was gracing her with one-word replies at the best of times. It seemed everyone was already tiring of her presence.

Without giving it a second thought, she drove to the clinic. She was in back-to-back appointments for most of the morning. Autumn found it difficult to focus, her father's condition weighed on her mind.

What if he gets worse?

"Do you think Roofo will be all right?"

Autumn blinked, bringing the world back into focus in her consultation room. On the metal table in front of her was a small mixed terrier, and opposite her, an anxious college student by the name of Alex.

"Roofo doesn't appear to have any physical issues," Autumn said. "How long did you say you leave him alone in your apartment?"

"For most of the day, but I always come back for lunch, and I take him for a walk every evening. But my neighbors have complained about his excessive barking. I love him too much to take him back to a shelter."

Autumn bit the cap of her pen. "And how is Roofo with other dogs?"

Alex grinned. "He's fine. He loves being at the dog park."

"Okay." She nodded. "I think your dog is suffering from separation anxiety."

"That's possible?"

"Yes. You got him from a shelter, which can be a stressful experience for dogs." She leaned toward the counter to scratch Roofo behind the ear. "It's not uncommon for dogs who come from shelters to need extra attention and company during the first few weeks."

Alex's brow contorted. It was common for people to forget that their pets have feelings too.

"Think about it this way," she said. "Roofo is worried you're going to leave and never come back. This makes him anxious, and he doesn't know what to do with himself when you're gone."

Alex nodded. "Poor little dude. So, what's your suggestion?"

She smiled. "If you have any friends who also have dogs, introduce them to Roofo. You can also take him to a dog park more often, it would give him something to look forward to. I would also try leaving some dirty laundry around for him. The scent will help him feel safe until you return."

His eyes widened. "I never thought about leaving dirty laundry out." He looked down at Roofo. "But I'll try it, anything for my pal."

Roofo sat up, wagging his tail, and Autumn laughed.

"If you need anything else, please come back, and if some gentle socialization doesn't work, we can look into giving him some anxiety medication."

After escorting Alex out, Autumn headed back to her office to find Emmett standing at her examination table.

"Oh, er ... hi, Autumn." He rubbed the back of his neck. "Didn't expect to see you here."

She gave him a befuddled look. "This is my office." She hadn't seen Emmett since her father's hospitalization. A part of her wondered whether she had scared him off.

"Oh, right. Well, I brought you a chocolate glazed donut. I figured you would be hungry after the nights you've had."

She studied him, confused by his odd comment.

"But I ate it," he confessed. "I was hungry."

"I don't think I can ever forgive you," she teased.

He shrugged. "I mean, you have before." Emmett placed his hands inside his white coat. "Anyway, it seems your friends are unaware of your stance with surprises, so I thought you should know they've organized one for tonight."

"Oh. It's odd for them to do this when there's nothing to celebrate." A comfortable warmth filled her face. "It was thoughtful of you to share. Thank you."

"I also know you're off in a couple of minutes, but can you cover the rest of my shift?"

"Why?"

Emmett looked at her, flustered. "I—I have a date."

"Oh." Autumn tried to hide her disappointment. She *had* scared him off. Maybe he wasn't the man she believed he was. "Yeah, I guess."

"Thank you." He got to the door and looked over his shoulder, "Happy Birthday." Emmett whispered, leaving the office.

Right, my birthday—at least I won't be alone this year.

He hadn't asked her how she was doing, nor for an update on her father. Maybe he'd realized she was too broken for him. How could she have thought, after a couple of days, that there was a deeper connection between them? They were friends, nothing more.

Right?

On her way home after her extended shift, Autumn wondered who Emmett had chosen to take on a date. Were they tall or petite? Blonde or brunette? A man or a woman? Was the person he had chosen to date into the same movies he was? Did they love animals with the same passion he did?

Get out of your head, Autumn. She mused as she pulled into the driveway, *you shared one moment together, it meant nothing.*

She collected her bag from the car and ambled to the house, where she lingered at her parents' front door. Autumn closed her eyes.

It's just a birthday party. A small celebration with friends.

She took a couple of breaths before opening her eyes once more. Autumn was on the verge of reaching for her keys when she discovered the door was open. Autumn frowned and stepped closer, light on her feet, and listened at the crack for a moment. All was quiet inside, so she pulled back and prodded the door.

It swung open with a loud screech and, again, Autumn stopped. All the lights were off, despite it being sundown. A breeze drifted by, fluttering the flyaways that framed her face and making her shiver.

"Mom?" she called, placing one foot over the threshold. "Ortus?"

No answer.

Where was everyone? Was the party canceled?

What if something went wrong with Dad?

Autumn's heart began to race, and she reached for the handle, ready to lock the door and jump into her car.

If there's no one here, I need to get to the hospital.

A knock.

She froze, her back rigid and eyes wide. Someone was there. She let go of the door handle and stepped inside, casting her eyes about the dark interior for a weapon, but all she found was Dad's umbrella. It would have to do.

Autumn stepped onto the plush carpet in the hall and the door swung closed behind her with an even louder creak. No, not a louder creak, there had been two. One behind her, and the other in the kitchen.

"Who's there?" she whispered, edging ever closer to the arch which led there. She poked her head around first, squinting through the shadows. There was an open packet of chips on the kitchen island and a few half-empty champagne flutes scattered around the many surfaces.

Autumn straightened. "What the—"

"SURPRISE!"

Autumn screamed, throwing the umbrella halfway across the room. Bradley yelled in fear as he batted it away, sending it straight toward his sister's face. Brooke caught it in time, redirecting it across the room to where it landed on the floor and skidded to rest at Ortus's feet.

Bradley tutted. "What was that for?"

Brooke frowned. "An umbrella? Really, Autumn? What use would that have been?"

Autumn, who was now grasping the kitchen island to keep her knees from collapsing under her, shook her head. "What's happening?" She cast her eyes around the now bright room, as someone had turned on the lights. All her friends were crowded around the kitchen island.

"Did you forget it's your birthday?" Ortus asked.

Autumn shook her head. "No, but a lot has happened in the past couple of weeks."

There was a long pause, as if those around her were waiting for her to arrive at a realization. She scanned the room once again. Each face greeted her with a warm smile. When she got to Bradley, he gave her a huge grin and pointed to the corner of the room, where her father stood.

She gasped. "Dad! What are you doing up and out of the hospital?"

"Dr. Hunt said as long as I take it slow, I should be okay to go home." He scowled. "She also said I couldn't go back to work for at least a week."

"It's for your own good," Marie said, embracing her husband, but he shrugged her off to reach for a glass of water.

Ortus placed her hands on her hips. "Well, are you ready to celebrate your birthday with us this year?"

"I am, but please promise no more surprises," Autumn pleaded.

"We promise." J.J. let out a huge sigh of relief. "It got so difficult that at some point, we had to avoid you. Next time we will make sure to run it past you."

After a long pause, Autumn burst into laughter. After all the years she'd spent pushing her friends away, she was determined to focus on rebuilding the relationships she'd lost. The party was split between the home and the backyard, where the trees were still wrapped in the shimmering lights from Ortus's wedding. They talked in the backyard for hours and would have continued talking if, from the corner of her eye, Autumn hadn't noticed a figure standing by the opened gliding patio door.

Autumn excused herself from her friend circle and walked to the kitchen. She breathed a sigh of relief knowing Emmett Miller was here.

"I thought you had a hot date tonight?" She leaned back, placing her hands in her back pockets. *Way to be subtle.*

"I do." He smiled. "I'm where I'm supposed to be."

Autumn's cheeks heated and silence enveloped them. She was glad it was dark out and he couldn't see the impact he had on her. How had she allowed him so close to her heart after so little time? Hadn't she learned her lesson?

"Lost in thought?" Emmett said.

Autumn smiled. "Yeah, silence does that to me ..."

Emmett opened his mouth to respond, but a voice overpowered him. "Hey, Autumn! Emmett!"

When they turned around, Autumn saw Bradley running toward them. On a normal day, she would have been annoyed by Bradley's interruption, but today she was relieved, knowing he'd saved her from elaborating on what she'd said.

"What's going on, Bradley?" she asked.

"Did he tell you what his role was in this surprise?"

She placed her hand in her pockets. "He was just getting to it."

"Oh." Bradley placed his hand over his mouth. "Then I hate to do this but ... there are no more churros left! I suspect Brooke hid them. We need to get to the bottom of it." He grabbed her hand, pulling her back toward the party.

As she was dragged back outside, she turned to look at Emmett as he laughed at her unceremonious exit. Watching him laugh would be one of the many reasons she would keep smiling that night.

After much searching, Bradley's craving for churros was satisfied. She spoke with each of her friends and people who Autumn hadn't seen since she was a teenager. As she bid a couple of her father's colleagues farewell, she noticed her dad wasn't outside. As she made her way back into the house, there was no sign of him until she peaked out the front window. He was sitting on the steps of their front porch, alone. Autumn glanced around, looking for her mother, and found her sitting on their living room couch, reading a book.

She walked to the front porch and sat next to her father. "I'm glad you're out of the hospital."

He gave her a slow smile. "Me too. I thought it was my time to go, but I kept thinking there's so much left for me to do with you girls."

She brought her legs closer to her core. "Are you and Mom okay? After sharing how I felt, you two started arguing. She mentioned you were shocked with how much I was hurting, before—" She paused, unwilling to relive the painful memory.

He looked up at the moon. "I see a lot of violence and abuse in my line of work. I thought being home with my wife and daughters would be my escape from that," he said with a pained stare.

"What do you mean?" her voice low, terrified her father knew parts of her life she didn't want him to know.

"I stood watching while your mother emotionally abused you. When you left home, I thought you were leaving to pursue your career. I never thought you'd be leaving because of your mother. Emotional abuse is one you can miss."

She rubbed her father's arm. "Dad, Mom is tough on me. It's not abuse."

"Oh, sweetheart, you're so pure and innocent." He shook his head. "Your mother wasn't always like this, but I'm not going to stand by anymore and watch her demean you."

Autumn let out a deep breath. "Dad, I don't want to be the reason you fight. I've seen the love you have for each other."

Bill turned to her, giving her an encouraging smile. "Love is about empowering each other to be the best version of yourself. Your mother is stubborn, but we'll work through it. I won't lose you again."

"You're as stubborn as Mom." She smiled. "None of this is your fault, but I won't be able to convince you otherwise."

Her father chuckled as he grabbed something he had hidden next to him. He handed her a small, teal gift bag filled with white tissue paper. "Happy birthday, sweetheart."

She smiled as she took the tissue paper out of the bag and found a small, willow pouch, inside which was a veterinary stethoscope. She read the subtle engraving carved upon the metal ear tubes, "Follow your dreams, not the dreams of others. Love, Dad."

She tightened her grip on the stethoscope and smiled at him. "Thanks, Dad," she said, pulling him into a long hug.

When she returned inside, she partied like she hadn't in years, dancing and singing along to old classics, laughing about forgotten college shenanigans, and opening the occasional gift. By the end of the night, she was exhausted and was zoning out of most of the conversations she found herself in.

"So, do you regret it?" J.J. asked.

Crap.

"Um ... yes?"

J.J. crossed her arms. "You've been zoned out for a good minute."

Autumn rubbed her eyes. "I'm sorry. All this socializing is exhausting."

"I was asking how the new job is going."

"Oh. Yeah, it's good. I'm doing what I enjoy, and Dr. Pierce is a great boss—"

"Oh no," J.J. muttered.

Autumn stopped and looked at her friend, whose eyes were focused on the opened patio door. "What?" She followed J.J.'s eyes, and her heart dropped when her gaze settled on Mason, who had entered the backyard via the path at the side of the house. Her mother greeted him with a broad smile, and Mason planted a kiss on each of her cheeks.

Autumn had feared seeing him when she had wandered into the darkened house and again when she'd spotted Emmett, but now, surrounded by her cherished ones, she felt a flush of irritation. What was he doing here? She was sure he knew she was watching him as he turned to her father, grasping his hand for a firm shake. Mason had always gotten along with her dad. Since they were both involved in police work, they always had something to bond over.

"I need some air," Autumn said.

"But ..." she heard Bradley mutter as she walked away.

She found her way to the swing and sat there, jutting out her bottom lip like a stubborn toddler, eyes unfocused across the road on Emmett's house.

"Excuse me, do you know where Mr. or Mrs. Evans are?" an unfamiliar voice asked.

"They're in the backyard, stabbing me in the back," she said without thinking.

"Oh, okay."

Autumn turned to find a woman around her age, with long brown hair and wearing a burgundy apron over her summer dress. She was backing away, an unsure look on her face.

Autumn sighed. "I'm sorry, I didn't mean to be rude. It's been a long day."

"*El amor es ciego.*"

"Excuse me?"

"Love is blind," the woman explained. "It's a saying my parents use when I'm feeling conflicted. Sometimes we're blinded by all the hate, the grudges, and we forget about love. You're hurting, I can see it in your eyes."

Autumn remained silent.

The woman continued, "Don't let those who have hurt you take over your life but let those who love you show you the way."

Autumn didn't know what to say. She had never seen this woman in her life, and she somehow knew more about Autumn than she knew about herself. Although the phrase had been a genuine effort to make her feel better, she realized she didn't know how to be loved. Love *was* blind.

"I'm sorry, what's your name?" Autumn asked.

"I'm Marisol."

"Nice to meet you, Marisol. I'm Autumn."

Marisol's face lit up. "Oh my gosh, you're the girl I made the cake for! Happy Birthday!"

"Thank you. My parents are round the back. I can help you find them if you want."

"No, it's okay." Marisol nodded over Autumn's head. "Besides, it looks like someone's waiting for you."

Autumn glanced over her shoulder. Emmett was on his way over. He smiled and waved when they met eyes, and she fluttered her fingers back at him.

"Do yourself a favor and say yes."

Autumn looked back at Marisol, who had a wistful smile on her face. She continued, "I had the chance to say yes to someone who loved me, and I hesitated. Don't hesitate. Trust your heart. I'll see you around."

As Marisol walked away, Emmett approached. Autumn looked at the ground, trying to hide the joy it brought her to see him walking toward her.

"What was up with Bradley?" he asked.

She rolled her eyes as he looked up at him. "That was Bradley being Bradley. He acts like he's still twelve years old and has a crazy obsession with food."

Emmett chuckled. "Well, I must confess we all had a role in this." He placed his hands in his front pockets. "Mine was to distract you and to get you here later than usual."

She tucked a strand of hair behind her ear. "So, your date?"

"Was part of the cover up."

It was as if someone had knocked the air out of her. Relief flooded Autumn in the most unexpected way, but so did embarrassment for getting so flustered when he first told her about his non-date.

"I'll admit, I enjoyed seeing you jealous. It was cute," he teased.

Autumn felt her cheeks turn red again. "What do you mean? I wasn't jealous."

"Sure." He looked at the ground, and after a pause glanced back at her. "I ... I like you, and I would be thrilled if you would let me take you on a date."

"Oh, um ..." For a moment, words failed Autumn. She studied the man before her, taken aback by his directness. Although she could feel butterflies in her stomach, she could also feel the fear that had haunted her the past seven years. She hadn't been on a date since she had been with Mason. He had been her first love, after all. The thought of going on a date with Emmett made her nervous. Would he turn out to be like him?

Or ... she could ignore the voice in her head telling her to be afraid. Fear had dictated her whole life so far, so maybe this was the moment she could say *enough*.

As Emmett's smile began to drop, Autumn met his eyes. "Okay," she said.

Emmett's eyes widened. "Okay." His smile returned. "Okay. Okay! I'll call you tomorrow with a plan."

"I look forward to it."

Autumn watched Emmett stride away, back to his home across the road. She stood at the swing, unable to stop smiling. There was something empowering about facing her fears, making a decision she knew Mason would hate. She was beginning to find herself again, and this new excitement gave her hope.

A small breeze blew against her hair, sending a shiver down her spine. Someone was standing behind her.

"Are you considering going on a date with him?"

Autumn scowled and turned. "I can do whatever I want, Mason."

He flared his nostrils. "Does he even know about us?"

"Us?" She crossed her arms. "There *is* no us. What are you even doing here?"

He gave her a smug look. "Your mom invited me. I didn't want to be rude and say no."

"When are you going to leave me alone?"

"When you realize I'm the one for you."

"You hurt me, Mason," she said, feeling her voice crack. "There will *never* be an 'us' again."

She rushed back inside, ran up to her room, and slammed her bedroom door. She didn't care that there were still guests downstairs. She didn't care if people thought she was boring for ending her night now. She needed a moment alone.

Knowing she would be unable to sleep, she went into her bathroom to have a hot shower. She ran the water through her hair and, after a moment, leaned against the wall and slid to the ground. The warm droplets pattered her skin until she became numb.

She desperately wanted to scream.

6

Flowers had begun to bloom across Maplewood. As she walked toward El Café del Poeta, she observed the town and its people. The sidewalk buzzed with conversation as if it were an extension of the cafés and restaurants that let out onto it. It seemed as if it was an expectation for people to be stopped by others in town; everybody had something to say to anybody who would hear it.

"Dr. Evans!" a voice called, causing her to come to an abrupt stop. A sigh of relief escaped her when she looked over her shoulder and found Alex running toward her.

"Hey there, Alex, how's it going?"

"Good!" he said, panting as he stood across from her.

Autumn noticed Alex's red track suit. "Are you training for a marathon or something?"

"There's a 5K our campus hosts, and I've made it my goal to at least run two miles!"

She gave an encouraging smile. "That's a great goal. Good luck!" She turned away, continuing toward the café.

"Dr. Evans?" he whispered.

She paused, turning to face Alex once more.

He cleared his throat. "I wanted to thank you for helping Roofo."

"Oh? How's he doing?"

Alex's face lit up. "It seems his anxiety has gotten so much better since I started taking him to the dog park more often. I left some of my laundry near his bed too, and I haven't received complaints from my neighbors since."

She gave him a satisfied smile. "I'm glad I was able to help. Roofo is lucky to have you."

"Thank you again, Dr. Evans. I need to finish my run but have a great day!" Alex said before running in the opposite direction of where she was headed.

Autumn smiled as she watched him go. She now knew why people enjoyed being stopped by others. It made her feel … at home.

When she arrived at the café, she spotted her friends sitting near the stage. As she walked toward them, she tried not to interrupt the man doing a reading on stage. On Tuesday and Thursday, the townspeople performed their original music and poetry at the café. It wasn't until Autumn got to their table and asked about the current performer that her friends admitted he wasn't good.

"Ethan is trying so hard up there," Bradley said. "But the man doesn't have a way with words."

J.J. frowned across at his friend. "It takes practice, give him a chance. Plus, he's in so much pain. Did you see his face during that last poem?"

"He never grieved the death of his mother," Brooke explained, answering Autumn's confused look. "I'm sure he'll pick himself up again though."

Autumn's foot tapped under the table. She was half-listening to Brooke and Bradley give their commentary on the day's poets. She couldn't stop thinking about her date with Emmett later. What would a date with Emmett Miller be like? Would he take her to a luxurious restaurant, or would they picnic in the park?

"Okay, spit it out."

Autumn twisted the watch on her wrist, "Spit what out?"

Ortus blew on her mug. "You've been acting weird ever since your birthday party. Is everything okay?"

Autumn bit her lip. "Emmett asked me out. We're supposed to go on a date later today."

"He did what?"

"I'm nervous. I haven't been on a date since Mason."

"You don't understand, Autumn, this has to be fate."

"What do you mean?"

"Don't you remember? During your senior year of high school, I was trying to set you up with someone." Ortus placed her tea on the table. "It was Emmett! It was going to be a surprise but—" Ortus paused.

"I refused." Autumn whispered, "I was too focused on college applications."

"It's been so long. If this isn't romance, I don't know what is," Ortus said.

Autumn wondered how her life would have been if she had gone on the date. If she had met Emmett instead of Mason, perhaps her story would've been different, filled with more joy and less fear, more laughter and fewer tears. She didn't know if she believed in fate, but she knew to never bet against her sister.

An hour later, Ortus drove Autumn home so she could get ready. Her sister had agreed to keep her company, but she knew Ortus was there to ensure she didn't run away.

When they got home, their parents were sitting in the living room in profound silence. Their father was reading a book, while their mother flipped through the latest issue of *Doctors Today*. Autumn thought she would be able to sneak past them, but of course that had been an unrealistic expectation.

"Where are you two off to?" her father asked.

"Autumn has a date," Ortus blurted out.

She scowled, nudging her sister. "Thanks for that."

Marie glanced up from her magazine, enthusiasm shining on her face. "Oh, good! You're giving Mason a second chance."

"No, I'm not." Autumn frowned as she crossed her arms. "And can you please stop bringing him up?"

"If it's not Mason, who is it?"

"It's Emmett!" Ortus clapped her hands.

"The veterinarian?" Marie gave a distasteful frown. "You let Mason go for *him*?"

"Emmett is also my friend, so please have more respect for him." Ortus grabbed Autumn's hand. "Now, if you'll excuse us, I'm going to help my sister get ready for her date." She stormed upstairs, pulling Autumn behind her.

After slamming the door in Autumn's room, they laughed. Autumn had never witnessed her sister speak to their mother like she had. There was a sudden comfort in knowing her sister supported her.

As she rifled through her clothing, she wondered whether Emmett had known who she was the whole time. Was their first date going to start off with yet more lies?

"So, you were trying to play matchmaker with Emmett all those years ago?" Autumn asked.

Ortus shrugged. "Listen, I could tell you this story, or you can let Emmett do it. Here, wear this."

Autumn caught the bundle of clothes thrown her way. *What would he say?*

She looked down at the clothes chosen by her sister. "I haven't worn these since college." It was a tan hem sweater, and denim jeans.

Ortus gave Autumn a look that said, "Trust me," and turned around to give Autumn some privacy.

Rolling her eyes, Autumn pulled on the clothes, matched them with some brown leather boots. As she looked at her reflection in the mirror, she grabbed her red lipstick and finished the look.

"I was right. I *should* take Bradley's job." Ortus stood behind Autumn and wrapped her arms around her. The warmth of her sister's embrace made Autumn feel safe, as if nothing or no one could hurt her.

"Promise me you won't run from him?" Ortus said.

"I won't."

"Good." She rubbed Autumn's back. "He's a good man, and you're an amazing woman. Give him a chance to show you who he is." Ortus gave her a gentle smile before walking out of the room.

It seemed everyone who knew Autumn could see how valuable she was. Marisol's words echoed in her head. Love was blind. Her heart would guide her on the right path, but what if she couldn't trust herself to make the right choices?

No. Stop it. You will not talk yourself out of this.

"He's here!" Ortus yelled from downstairs.

"Today will be different. I won't run," Autumn declared, making her way out of the room.

Emmett waited in the car per her request. She wanted to prevent her father from interrogating him, and of course Emmett had laughed at the prospect. He hadn't understood why Bill would treat him any different if he already knew who Emmett was. On the road, Autumn explained how the relationship he once had with her parents was different now that he was taking his daughter on a date.

"Besides, my dad can be protective." Autumn added.

"Bill? He's such a teddy bear though. I used to help fix up his front yard."

Emmett wasn't wrong. Her dad was a teddy bear, it was one of the reasons why Autumn thought her father was good at his job.

"What was it like growing up with a police officer as a dad?" Emmett asked.

She looked out the window as they arrived at a stoplight near Maplewood Park. "Most people assume it's something I adjusted to."

"What do you mean?"

Autumn remained silent for a moment, observing a little girl eating Oreo cookies as she looked up at a man with admiration, presumably her father. Autumn didn't know what he was telling her, but she hoped it was a life lesson like the many she had received growing up.

She sighed. "It wasn't easy. I worried if he would make it back home."

"How did you get past the worry?"

Autumn recalled the exact moment she had. She was sixteen and had walked home from school alone. Ortus hadn't been feeling well, so she had been picked up by their dad earlier in the day. When Autumn got home, she heard crying echoing down the staircase. She was about to knock on her sister's door when she stopped short upon hearing her father's soothing voice.

"Dad, they make fun of me," Ortus whimpered. "They tell me I'm adopted because my skin is darker than Autumn's. They touch and pull my hair too."

"Sweetheart, you're not adopted. I'm sorry this is happening to you."

"Why is it happening? I'm nice to everyone at school, but why are they choosing to pick on me?"

Bill sighed. "Some people harm those who look different than them. It's cruel, and it's unfortunate, but it's the world we both live in. It pains me to say, but I need you to understand how important it is for you to keep your hands visible and never in your pockets if you are ever stopped by a police officer."

"But Dad, you're an officer too. I don't understand." Ortus sniffed, "Are you a bad or good officer?"

"Everyone has different definitions of what is good and bad. I became an officer because I wanted to change the system for people who look like us in our own town. It's a challenging job, but it's worth it when you're the reason someone who looks like us gets to live. I suppose I may be a good cop to some and a bad one to others."

Autumn choked on her words and cleared her throat of the lump that had taken residence there, focusing on the view moving past the car windows. Emmett was patient, waiting for her to finish.

"My dad never needed to have that conversation with me." Autumn began. "Later that night, I begged him to tell me how to help Ortus. He cried as he told me all I could do was open my heart, listen to different perspectives, and educate myself on the obstacles people with different cultural backgrounds face. Regardless, I needed to support my sister *always*."

She continued, "Some of our extended family can be ... ignorant. They look at me and see my mom. When they look at Ortus, somehow the concept of her being my biological sister is ... not understood. I became more vigilant with how others treated Ortus compared to me. My understanding of my own privilege came to me so young, and because I knew my dad was risking his life to make the world a better place for people of color, I learned how to quiet my worries and fears."

"Wow," Emmett said.

"I'm sorry for rambling. This is far too deep for a first date."

Emmett frowned, eyes forward on the road. "Are you kidding? You have nothing to be sorry for. You gave me a real, honest answer, and I'm glad you did. Don't ever apologize for being honest."

"Sor—" Autumn paused, catching herself. "You have a point. I'm used to apologizing for everything, so it might take some time."

It was the first time she had shared with someone the obstacles in being part of a bi-racial home. When she wasn't reviewing her veterinary books, she was trying to grow as a human being. She wanted to keep her promise to her father, so she continued filling her mind with knowledge to create a world with more empathy and understanding.

The sound of Emmett's cellphone ringing cut through the quiet. It was connected to the car's Bluetooth speaker, so she glanced at the center console. It read, "Dad."

Emmett scowled as he reached to the screen and declined the call. He tightened his grip on the steering wheel as he rolled his shoulders, as if trying to shake something off. Autumn knew close to nothing about his father; there had to be more to the story.

A bump in the road snapped Autumn out of her thoughts. When she looked out the window, she noticed they were driving by flat green pastures, away from the city. The sun was making its way toward the horizon, casting hues of pink and orange across the sky. It seemed like they had a long drive ahead of them.

Autumn looked at Emmett again. "Where are we going?"

"If I told you, it would ruin the moment." Emmett teased.

Autumn didn't like surprises, but she had a feeling she would like this one.

It seemed like the entire world was stretched out beneath them. Rows and rows of colorful moonflowers broke up the patches of trees and fields of crops. Mountains poked up on the horizon, reaching to obscure the dipping red sun. The sky was alight with hues of gold, crimson, and orange. She could never find a view like this in Los Angeles, no matter how many rooftop bars she sat at. How had she left all of this behind?

The hot air balloon pilot faced away from them, allowing them the privacy they craved. Emmett stepped in close behind her, wrapping one arm around her waist and placing his free hand on the edge of the basket they stood in. He chuckled. "Close your mouth, there's a plane coming."

Autumn clamped her jaw shut and turned to look at him with a smile disguised as a scowl. Any other day, she would feel embarrassed, but there was something comforting about seeing Emmett laugh, even if she was the reason behind it.

"Growing up, I always dreamed about riding in a hot air balloon, but Ortus is scared of heights, so I never had anyone to go with," Autumn said.

"I know," Emmett said. "Your sister told me."

Autumn turned to him. "Tell me about your childhood. You seem to know so much about mine. What was it like for you to grow up with the astonishing Dr. Elizabeth Pierce?"

He grinned. "Well, my mom is supportive and loving, despite my father not being in the picture. I grew up on the west side of Maplewood for most of my life. I didn't wander to the east side until my mom built the clinic from the ground up."

"As if there wasn't more reason for me to admire your mother."

Emmett nodded. "It wasn't easy, yet she made it work, and it's the reason why I dive into my career. She built a business on her own—all as a single mother. I will always aim to repay her for all she's done for me."

"Your mother is admirable. I'm glad she cares for you," Autumn said, trailing off toward the end. "My mother always wanted me to be a medical doctor. She wasn't as supportive of me becoming a veterinarian. She's the reason I left Maplewood. I couldn't love what I was doing while she was around."

Emmett hesitated, "How's your relationship been since your father's hospitalization?"

"She doesn't speak to me, unless I'm doing something to further her disappointment in me." Autumn crossed her arms, holding on to her shoulders. "She blames me for my dad's heart attack."

"I'm sorry, Autumn, I wish I could help the pain go away."

She wanted to change the subject. There was a long moment of silence as she built the courage to ask Emmett the question she was terrified to ask.

"Emmett, why did you ask me out?" she asked as she watched the view below.

There was a long pause, and for a moment Autumn thought he wasn't going to answer. She wasn't looking for flattery, she was looking for the truth.

"It amazes me how you don't see what I do, but I think you're beautiful, and you have a kind heart." He placed his index finger under her chin, making her face him. "Autumn?" She loved how he said her name. "I don't know what Mason did to you, but I would never hurt you," he said.

Autumn remained silent. Mason had left her feeling she wasn't worthy of love, but when she was with Emmett, time stopped, and she found it difficult to catch her breath. A voice in her mind was telling her to trust Emmett, so instead of debating if she should or not, she took a chance.

She sighed. "When Mason and I were together, he ... didn't treat me right. I always felt alone when I was with him. He—" She paused, correcting herself. "*We* didn't know how to make each other happy."

"You don't have to defend him," he reassured her. "You also don't have to share anything you're not ready to. I'm glad you let me bring you on this date."

Autumn looked away from him and together they admired the horizon in silence. She had been grateful of Emmett's discretion, since most people in her life tried to press for information when she wasn't ready to give it. Emmett had been patient, and although she knew he was wondering what had occurred, she still wasn't ready to talk about it.

"You know, for someone who asks a lot about my past, I know nothing about yours," Autumn teased, leaning toward him.

Emmett smiled. "What do you want to know?"

Autumn thought long and hard about what she wanted to know about Emmett Miller. She went through different questions in her mind. She could ask him about his childhood, where he went to college, his friends. There were so many possibilities, but she narrowed it down to two questions.

"You mentioned your dad isn't around …"

Emmett's demeanor shifted, and his smile flickered. "My father is still not present in my life. I'd rather not talk about him."

Autumn bit her lip. She had made him uneasy so didn't push him any further. Instead, she moved on to her second question.

She parted her lips, "What about your first love?"

He smirked. "Oh, now you're getting into the more interesting parts of my life."

Autumn shrugged. "I'm curious."

Emmett hesitated and took a deep breath. "Her name was Lily. I met her at a bookstore. Our hands touched and it was love at first sight. I know it sounds cheesy, but in the moment, I knew she had to be the one."

"What happened?"

Emmett sighed. "She died."

"I'm sorry, Emmett. How did it happen?"

"Plane crash. They searched so long for her body but it was never found. I remember feeling like my heart had been ripped out of me. I didn't know how to move on for the longest time."

Autumn tilted her head to the side, having a hunch of what had helped him move on. "Let me guess … Max came along?"

Emmett nodded. "After I lost Lily, I moved into the house across from you. I found Max wandering around the neighborhood—in front of your house, to be exact. It reminded me of the first time I saw you."

"What? How?"

"You know the swing in front of your house?"

Autumn nodded.

"It was the summer before college and I was accompanying my mom to some open houses. Of course, I found it boring at the time, so I walked around the neighborhood."

"Naturally." Autumn teased.

Emmett smirked. "You were sitting on the swing looking so at ease. You didn't take your eyes off your book."

Autumn smiled.

"Ortus caught me staring like an idiot. So when I bumped into her at the farmers' market one day, she told me she had the perfect match for me. I believe her exact words were, 'My sister needs to get a life anyway, you two would be perfect together.'" He chuckled.

Autumn laughed, picturing her sister saying this to a stranger. Ortus always did say what was on her mind.

"I didn't object, because I knew it was you," he said.

Autumn took a deep breath. "And…"

"And then I met Lily," Emmett said.

"It was fate for you to be with her and I'm sorry you lost her."

"There's no need to apologize. We're here now, in this moment."

His hand had been brushing against Autumn's the entire time they had been talking. It wasn't until now that she noticed their hands were intertwined. As they looked into each other's eyes, she realized she felt safe, not intimidated. She wondered what it would be like to kiss him. Would she feel butterflies in her stomach? Would she see sparks fly? Or would she feel nothing?

"Emmett … I—" Autumn began.

It all happened so fast. Their lips found their way to each other and the electricity of their kiss flowed through her body. His lips were soft, and he was gentle with her, different from what she was used to. All Autumn wanted was for time to stop, because after days of tormenting herself on whether she would ever feel again…

She had.

After a slow and gentle descent back to Earth, Emmett drove them home. They now stood outside her parents' home with their hands interlocked, unable to stop smiling. Autumn didn't want their date to end.

"I trust you enjoyed today," Emmett said, breaking the silence.

Autumn smiled. "I did. Was it worth the wait?"

"It was. Maybe we can do it again?"

"I would like that," Autumn agreed. Their eyes met once more as they got closer to one another.

"That's never going to happen," a voice interrupted.

Autumn's heart jolted, but not in the same way it had for Emmett. She spun to see Mason standing a few feet away from them on the sidewalk, but it was the anger in his eyes that caused her to freeze as she remembered the terrible nights they'd spent together.

Emmett scowled. "You reek of alcohol, Mason."

"You stay away from her. She's mine, aren't you, my love?" Mason sneered, taking a couple steps closer. Emmett stepped in front of Autumn.

Autumn's shoulders lowered, feeling small again. "Please leave, Mason."

"Are you sleeping with him?" he demanded, looking at Emmett. "She has you wrapped around her little finger, you know? Man, you're going to be disappointed, almost as much as I was."

Emmett crossed his arms. "I doubt that."

Mason glanced at Autumn. His facial expression shifted as her eyes met his. He grinned and pulled something from his jacket, waving around a yellow envelope. She knew what it contained and why Mason had shown up at her home drunk.

"She hasn't told you, has she?" Mason asked Emmett without releasing his stare on Autumn.

"Told me what?" Emmett asked.

Tears pooled in Autumn's eyes. "Mason, please don't."

Mason fixed his eyes on hers. He knew what he was about to say was going to ruin Autumn's night.

He looked at Emmett. "We're married."

On their second wedding anniversary, Autumn made Mason's favorite dinner. She set the table and served the chicken parmesan, fettuccini Alfredo pasta, and a side of Caesar salad on their plates. There was nothing more she wanted than to create the perfect meal for the person she loved. When she finished, she collapsed onto the dining room chair feeling exhausted.

She reached for her phone and noticed she had a text from Mason. It read, "Going to be late, eat without me."

She sighed. *Maybe he's planning a surprise for me. There's no way he forgot, right?*

Autumn stood from her chair and scanned the living room of the apartment, the bluestone walls with picture frames of their wedding, the yellow couch in the center of the room where she often studied. The wooden floor was now covered in the rose petals she'd set down earlier in the evening. It all looked perfect.

Wanting to kill some time, she headed toward the white bookshelf in the corner of the room and reached for the photo album she'd hidden behind it. As she looked through the pages, she couldn't help but miss the friends she'd left behind.

She paused on a page, where a photo of Brooke pushing Bradley off a swing made her giggle. After a moment of hesitation, she reached for her phone and made the call she'd longed to make.

"Well, if it isn't Autumn! To what do I owe the pleasure of this call?" It was Bradley who answered. Autumn was already smiling.

"Autumn?" said Brooke's voice somewhere in the background. "Hey, is that my phone? Give it to me, you dork!"

She giggled, pulling the phone away from her ear to save her eardrums from the subsequent squabbling.

"Autumn! Are you okay?" Brooke asked, her voice clear.

Autumn almost stuttered. No, she wasn't okay. But Brooke couldn't know that. Nobody could. "Can't I give my old friends a call for no reason?" she asked, trying to keep her voice light.

"You don't call much, is all…" she muttered. "Anyway, it's good to hear from you. How have you been?"

"Umm, I'm all right. I'm getting through vet school, nothing too exciting happening," Autumn said.

There was silence on the other end for a moment until Brooke murmured, "Bradley and I miss you, Autumn. When are you visiting?" She paused. "Or we could come visit you?'

"No!" Autumn blurted. "I mean, I'll visit soon. I miss all of you too."

"Bradley has had a hard time adjusting to you being gone for so long. He misses confiding in you ... Oh, and he also says he loves you."

Autumn laughed, knowing Bradley was hovering over his sister's shoulder, but guilt was pouring into her subconscious now. She had called them to feel better, but it was having the opposite effect.

"Tell Bradley I love him too. I'll talk to you later," she said before hanging up the phone. Had she known that would be the last time she would talk to them for the next four years, she would've tried to stay on the line with them longer.

"Who the hell is Bradley?"

Autumn whipped around, dropping her phone onto the couch cushion. "Mason, you scared me," she said, hand on her chest. "Don't you remember my best friend, Bradley?"

"Don't you lie to me, Autumn. You know I don't like it when you lie to me." Mason stepped out of the doorway, toward her. He was still wearing his work suit, the top button of his shirt undone.

"Don't, Mason. I'm tired of this."

Mason stopped, dropping his briefcase onto the floor with a loud clunk. "*You're* tired? I got home from a twelve-hour shift apprehending criminals and solving murders for grieving families, and *you're* tired after reading *books* all day?"

"You know that's not what I meant," Autumn said.

"What did you mean?"

Autumn grit her teeth. She was tired of pretending to be happy when she wasn't, of not being able to see her friends, and of pretending to be the perfect wife.

"I'm tired of your jealousy!" she exclaimed. "I'm tired of seeing you come home drunk. Bradley is my friend! I miss him! I miss all of them!"

He crossed the space between them in a flash. She didn't even see him raise his hand. The sting across her face was intense, but the shock was what left her frozen, supporting herself on the coffee table. Was she having a nightmare? No. This was real.

Something trickled from her forehead, and she reached up to wipe at it. The back of her hand came away red. She stared at it until she heard movement. She looked up and followed Mason with her eyes as he went to sit on the nearest armchair.

"Am I not good enough for you, Autumn?" he asked. His expression was downcast, filled with sorrow, and it took Autumn aback.

"I don't understand how you don't miss our hometown," she said. "Don't you miss your parents?"

He scowled. "My father was an abusive man who beat the shit out of me for no reason. He was cruel. And my mother watched it happen. I don't miss the town that knew what was happening and did nothing, and I do not miss my mother."

Autumn pushed herself up. "You hit me, Mason. How are you any different?"

He raised his hand again, and Autumn flinched. She closed her eyes, waiting for him to hurt her. But nothing happened. When she opened her eyes, his head was buried in his hands.

He sighed. "What else do I have to do to show you I'm the one you need?"

Autumn felt numb as she watched him. He looked up and met her eyes, they shone with unshed tears.

"My love, they don't love you, or else they'd be here too." He reached out and placed a strand of her blonde hair behind her ear. "There is no one else who can love you the way I do." He smiled, staring at her as if she were sunshine on a rainy day. "Come on. I have a something for you, the traditional second-anniversary gift is cotton, you know."

"That's nice," Autumn whispered.

After Mason hit her, everything got worse. He looked through her computer, he went through her social media accounts and deleted them, he disconnected her from those she cared for the most. It became difficult for her to remember the days that went by, they all merged into one vague mass. It was like her brain was protecting her from remembering all the pain she had endured, and a part of her was afraid to open the box of traumatic memories.

"Autumn?" Emmett's voice was gentle from the other side of her bedroom door.

She buried her head in her pillow. She didn't want to see him, she couldn't face his disappointment, the inevitable questions. She should have been honest from the start.

The door opened, but Autumn didn't turn around.

"Oh, Autumn." This time, it wasn't Emmett.

Autumn lifted her head to look across at her sister, who was closing the door behind her.

"Emmett told me what happened," she said, expression filled with pity.

"I—"

Ortus held up her hand. "You don't need to explain yourself to me. Come on, I know someplace that'll help you feel better."

After drying her eyes and removing her cheeks of streaked makeup, Autumn followed Ortus out of her room, thankful to know Emmett had gone home. Outside, J.J., Bradley, and Brooke were waiting by the swing. They sat on the grass and urged Autumn to sit on the wooden plank that swayed soft in the night's breeze.

"I'm sorry I never told you anything. I didn't want you to get involved," she said, voice weak.

"It was your story to tell, Autumn," Bradley said, "whenever you were ready."

"There's more to this, though, isn't there, Autumn?" Ortus said with caution.

Autumn nodded. "Mason is ... abusive. Mentally, physically ..." She stopped herself from finishing the thought.

Brooke slammed her hands on the grass. "I'm going to kill him."

J.J. nodded. "If he thinks he's going to get away with this, he's got another thing coming!"

Brooke took her phone out. "I'm going to call the cops right now."

Autumn shook her head. "You can't do that, Brooke, we're married. They won't do anything. I can't get away from him."

Brooke frowned and looked across at Ortus for confirmation. Ortus sighed and shrugged. "It's true. There are so many of us who want to help but the state laws ... they can bind us in situations like this. He'd be out soon enough for lack of evidence or because of his connections."

"Connections?" Bradley asked.

"He's a detective in LA," Autumn said, staring at the ground. "That's why I couldn't run. I tried ... several times. He always found me. That's why I moved to New Mexico."

Brooke and Bradley shook their heads, wearing matching frowns.

J.J. tilted his head to the side. "When did you move to New Mexico? I thought you were in LA this whole time?"

Autumn looked at the starry sky. "I lived in New Mexico for a year. I got a job as a receptionist for a dental office. It was a small salary, but it's what kept me safe."

"You were a seven-hour drive from us?" Bradley muttered.

"I'm sorry. I was so paranoid he would find me, and I couldn't let any of you know where I was. It was too risky. When I decided to return home, it was with the idea he wouldn't show up. He knew I hated it here and I thought this would be the last place he'd attempt to find me. If I had burned the wedding invitation, he might not have found me."

"Were you going to leave after my wedding?" Ortus whispered.

Autumn nodded. "I came to the quick realization that I couldn't survive if I stayed in one place for long. Every year, I planned to relocate to a different state. I was ready to run for the rest of my life."

Brooke sniffed and cleared her throat. "But you stayed here. Why?"

Autumn's gaze met hers. "Because of you." Her eyes shifted to Bradley, J.J., and Ortus. "Because of all of you. You each reminded me what it's like to be around unconditional love. I thought to myself there is no way he could hurt me, knowing I have people who love me here."

"Why did he show up drunk tonight?" Ortus asked. "I mean, he had those papers prepared. Why?"

"I sent him the divorce papers while I was in New Mexico," Autumn sighed. "When we lived together, he never opened the mail. My guess is he was so focused on finding me, he hadn't thought about the envelope; it's probable it took his lawyer calling him to realize what they were. I was hoping to be gone from the state before he read them."

"Okay, great. Now you can be done with him," Bradley said.

"You don't understand, Bradley," she said. "I knew he wouldn't be happy if I served those papers. That's why I wanted to be far away. But now he's here, and he'll get away with anything he tries, I know it."

Brooke's face dropped. "What happened when you tried to report it?"

"The first time he hit me, I didn't report him because … well, I thought it would be a one-time thing. But when it kept happening, I did report him and told the police what happened. They brought him in for questioning, but he …" She shook her head as hot tears pushed at the backs of her eyes. The detective on her case had informed her that their testimonies didn't match. He'd convinced them he was a little heavy-handed in the bedroom. That night, he hit her again. And worse.

"Er …" Autumn cleared her throat. "When I went to New Mexico, I feared he was stalking me. I was paranoid. They told me they couldn't do anything until he physically hurt me."

Ortus made a fist. "And, of course, he knows that."

"Either way, I lose," Autumn said.

Brooke shook her head. "And what did Emmett say when he found out you were married?"

Autumn looked toward his home. "I don't know. I ran. I wouldn't blame him if he never wanted to speak to me again."

Ortus placed a comforting hand on her sister's knee. "I'm sure he'll understand."

"What can we do to help?" Brooke asked.

"Nothing. I wanted you to know the truth," Autumn said, pushing herself off the swing. "I guess I should go to bed and get some rest."

"I'll walk you inside," Ortus said.

7

WHY *did I stay?*

Two days had passed since Autumn's date with Emmett. She sat in her desk chair, looking out her office window. She often wondered why she hadn't run after the first hit. She had held on to the idea Mason would change. She was alone in California, and he was all she'd had at the time.

On her computer screen, a document was open, "Petition for Restraining Order to Prevent Abuse." Ortus had convinced her to file it the next day. It was a lot of paperwork, and she was sure Mason would contest it, but it was worth a try. She clicked *send* with the knowledge Ortus would do what she could to expedite the process.

Two soft taps captured her attention. Emmett's head poked around the door. "Thinking deep thoughts, lil' dove?"

"Hi, Emmett," she whispered, casting her eyes back to her computer screen.

"We haven't spoken since … well, you know. Are you okay?" he asked. "Was it the hot air balloon? I knew I should have booked the plane."

Autumn looked at him through the corner of her eye. He was smirking, and she shook her head, allowing a small smile onto her lips too. "I'm sorry. I'm sorry for running, I—"

Emmett interjected, "You don't have to apologize, Autumn. But if you're comfortable talking about it, all I want to know is ... why didn't you tell me you were married?"

"Because of that," Autumn was blunt, pointing to his face.

Emmett frowned with genuine concern. "What?"

"I didn't tell you the full story. Mason was an abusive partner who isolated me in believing he was the one person in the world who could love me." Autumn sighed, "And now you're looking at me like I'm broken and need to be fixed. I'm sorry I didn't tell you, okay? I wasn't ready."

Emmett walked over to her and pulled her into a hug. "Stop apologizing, Autumn. This is not your fault, you didn't deserve any of it. You need to know I believe you."

His words surprised her, because all she'd ever wanted to hear, Emmett had said. She believed no one would ever listen, that no one would believe her. The police, her mother ...

"Anyway, I came to give you this," he said, pulling a small box out from behind him. "It's a donut. Promise I didn't eat this one."

Autumn smiled and took the box. "Thanks, Emmett. See you around?"

He clicked his fingers and blasted her with two finger guns as he backed out of the door. Autumn laughed and opened the box to find a jelly-filled donut in the shape of a heart.

By the end of the workday, Autumn was exhausted. Jackie often spent the night at the clinic caring for the animals who were recovering from surgery. Before he started his night shift, Autumn convinced him to go next door and pick up a quick dinner. She knew she was the last one in the office, so it caught her by surprise when she heard the front door open.

"I'm sorry, we're closed!" she called from her office as she finished packing her bag.

She waited for a response, but it never came. She assumed the person had left, so she grabbed her bag, locked her office, and walked to the front of the clinic.

Near the end of the hallway, she slowed, nose lifted. A strong smell permeated the air, making her eyes water.

"What the heck?" she whispered, rushing the last few steps to the waiting area, when she almost slipped, catching herself on one of the shelves on the wall. The floor was wet, slick with something.

There was a clatter at the far end of the waiting area. She looked up and her eyes froze on the gasoline canister lying in the middle of the floor, on the soaked floor and chairs, on the man standing among it all, holding a whiskey bottle down by his thigh.

Their eyes met, blue on what seemed now more black than brown. Goosebumps formed on her arms. She turned and ran.

She was terrified. Mason had done many things, but she had never seen this level of darkness in his eyes.

Footsteps followed her, slapping on the wet floor. Autumn was desperate to open one of the exam rooms, shaking the knob, and trying the next one. She slammed her hands against door after door until she remembered the fire exit through the break room.

As she moved in that direction, a hand grasped a fistful of her hair and pulled back. She lost her balance on the gasoline-covered floor and fell hard, cracking her skull on the tiles. Her vision blurred, but she scrambled to get up. Before she could, Mason grabbed her hair again, slammed her against the wall, and held her there as he leaned down to her ear.

"Mason, please don't do this," she whimpered into the plaster.

He let out a sardonic laugh. "You run away thinking I won't find you, and now you want to keep us apart?"

"What?"

"Don't play stupid," he breathed, breath heavy with liquor. "I know you plan on filing a restraining order against me."

"H-how—"

"You shouldn't leave important documents open on your computer screen. You never know what strangers or patients may—" he kissed the back of her neck "stop by your office."

He let go of her, and she scrambled along the wall, away from him.

He followed her. "You know, I could forgive you for all of this if you would come home."

"I want nothing to do with you!"

He scoffed. "Stop being difficult, do you know how easy it was to find you in New Mexico? All I had to do was call some of my good friends, and there you were, the needle in the haystack. I let you have your freedom, but I followed you every day."

Autumn shook her head. He was standing between her and the fire exit now. "I wanted you to leave me alone. You're the reason why I live out of a suitcase. You've made my life a living hell!"

She got up and ran to her office, pulling her keys out of her pocket as she went. She fumbled with the lock, listening to Mason's calm footsteps approach from behind. He was in no hurry, he knew he had her.

The key turned. She flung the door open and slipped inside, locking it before Mason could follow. Without hesitation, she ran to the window by her desk and pushed it open, but the gap it created was only large enough to fit her arm through. She pushed against the safety mechanism, but it was no use. She was stuck.

Defeated, she slid to the floor, grabbed her phone out of her bag, and called Emmett.

"Emmett, Mason is at the clinic, and he's drenched everything in gasoline. He's going to burn it down." She fought to keep her voice level and understandable despite the heaving breaths wracking through her chest.

"What? Autumn, where are you? Please tell me you're out of there."

"I'm inside. This is what he wants. I wanted to call to tell you how sorry I am."

"Stop. Please don't." He paused. "Mom, I'm turning the car around. Call 911, the clinic is on fire!"

Autumn began to cry. "Emmett, I'm so sorry. I shouldn't have come back to Maplewood. Your mom worked so hard for this place, this is all my fault."

"Autumn, it's okay. I'm on my way."

"Emmett, I'm sorry." She hung up the phone, unable to continue listening.

If she'd known Mason was capable of this, she would've kept driving. She never meant to put the people she cared about in danger.

Mason attempted to turn the doorknob, and when he found it locked, he banged on the door in frustration, "I'm sick and tired of this game. When are you going to get it through that thick head of yours that you're mine!"

He slammed on the wood, causing Autumn to flinch with every impact. Her concentration was fuzzy, she was sure she had a concussion. Her eyes were closing, but she snapped them open when she heard a new voice beyond the door.

"Who are you?" Jackie yelled.

Oh no. Autumn got up, stumbling as she walked toward the door. It took a moment, but she managed to unlock it. She stood at the threshold, watching Jackie's confused face meet hers.

"Jackie, get the animals out of here!" she yelled.

Jackie nodded, running in the opposite direction.

"Oh no, you don't." Mason started walking in Jackie's direction.

"Okay!" Autumn yelled.

Mason spun around.

"Let's go. Now. Me and you, like you want."

A grin erupted on his face. "It's all I've ever wanted, my love."

"She's not your love. When are you going to understand that?"

Both Autumn and Mason turned to see Emmett standing at the end of the hall at the doors to the waiting area.

Mason frowned. "God, you're annoying. She's already chosen me." He reached for Autumn, and in a flash, Emmett was moving. He barreled through Mason, tearing his reaching hand away from her, and both men went tumbling down the hall, crashing into an office door. Emmett came out on top, straddling Mason. He gripped him by the scruff of his shirt and threw punch after punch at his face.

"Run, Autumn!" Emmett yelled without looking at her.

Hands to her mouth, she broke from her frozen state and began a fast limp toward the back room where Jackie was trying to push a cage through the door. She fought through the pain in her head and helped him.

"Is that the last one?" she asked.

"Yes, now hurry, let's get out of here!"

Autumn shook her head. "Emmett's inside, I can't. You need to get yourself and the animals far away from the building. I'll try to buy you some time." She acknowledged Jackie's shocked expression before slamming the back door shut.

She sped through the hall and returned to where she'd left Emmett and Mason. Emmett was on the ground now with Mason on top of him, face bloody and fist raised.

"Enough!" Autumn yelled, grasping the back of her head. Mason froze, giving Emmett the opportunity to push the man off of him. Both men stood and turned to face her.

"Mason, you never treated me right. You *hit* me! I don't know why it's taken me this long to say this, but it was never my fault. I deserve to be with someone who will love me for me, someone who won't try to change me, and that person isn't you." She paused, feeling the distaste in her mouth. "I don't love you. I hate you!"

Mason scowled. "If you don't love me, you can't love anyone else," he said.

Neither Emmett nor Autumn saw the matchbox until it was too late. Emmett lunged at Mason as he struck a match, and the tiny flame fell in what felt like slow motion.

"No!" Emmett yelled as flames burst to life at their feet.

Autumn shielded her face and fell backward, flying into her office. Without thinking, she reached up and slammed it closed. She knew the protection wouldn't last. She was trapped. Pungent smoke began to slither through the crack under the door, filling the room until the opposite wall disappeared in a hazy blur.

In a frantic rush, Autumn reached the open part of the window, "Fire! Someone help us, please!" she screamed.

Autumn tried a couple more times, "Help, someone please!"

No response.

She could hear Emmett yelling beneath the sound of her own coughs. Autumn lowered herself to the ground, right in front of her desk. Her eyes opened and closed every couple of seconds, and for a small moment she lost consciousness. In the hallway now, all was quiet. With any luck, Mason had succumbed to his own crime.

What an awful thing for me to think, Autumn lamented as tears rolled down her cheeks.

Above her, glass shattered, but her eyelids were too heavy to open.

"Autumn?" an unfamiliar voice said.

She mustered a whimper in response. She felt movement and shuffling around her, and she was lifted from her seat, held close to someone's chest, and passed to someone else. Cool, fresh air met her face, jolting a fraction of awareness back into her. She opened her eyes a slither to watch her smashed office window grow farther away. Her eyes fluttered closed again.

"Autumn? Please try to stay awake," the man carrying her spoke. "My name is Liam. Your boyfriend is waiting for you."

"Emmett? He's ... okay?" she whispered.

"Yes," Liam said as more voices emerged around her, though she couldn't understand what any of them were saying. They all blended into one mass, but she heard one over them all.

"Autumn? Oh my god, is she okay?"

Emmett.

The sound of a beeping monitor was loud enough to wake Autumn. The striking smell of antiseptic and bleach made her wrinkle her nose. The hospital light above her was blinding, causing her to squint and tilt her head away from the ceiling as her eyes fluttered open. She faced the glass sliding door of her hospital room, a janitor was cleaning the floors in the hallway. The clock above him read "11:00 P.M."

She sensed someone's light breathing on her hand, and when she glanced down at the blankets covering her body, she couldn't help but smile. Emmett had fallen asleep while holding onto her hand, his head resting by her leg on the mattress. She noticed his right eye had turned purple, beginning to bruise. She couldn't help but feel responsible.

"Oh! You're awake," Marie yelled as she entered the room, Bill following close behind.

Emmett's eyes snapped open, meeting Autumn's. "How long have you been awake?"

With a faint smile, she maneuvered her aching arm out from under the blanket to run her fingers through his hair. "For a couple of seconds."

Marie shook her head. "I can't believe you didn't tell your own parents what was happening."

"Marie—" Bill began.

"I'm her mother. She should've told me the truth about Mason!"

Bill approached the bed on the opposite side of Emmett. "I'm sorry for not noticing. I should've seen the signs, I've been missing a lot of those."

"It's not your fault. I didn't notice them myself." There was a lump in her throat. "What happened to him, to Mason?"

Bill turned to Emmett, who gave him a nod. "Sweetheart ... he ran. When they got the fire under control, we realized he wasn't inside."

Emmett tightened his grip on her hand. "When I saw the fire head your way, I pushed him away from me and rushed outside to find your office window. The firefighters were already breaking into it."

Bill glanced at Emmett. "I'm grateful for that." Emmett smiled as Bill continued, "They were able to follow him to the next town over before losing him."

"He's gone?"

"Yes. When we looked through the surveillance cameras, we saw him arrive in a grey 2015 Ford Fusion Hybrid. He'd removed the license plates, so we have the description of the car he was in." Bill laid his hand on her shoulder. "Honey, I won't stop looking until he's arrested and pays for what he did to you."

Marie rubbed her temple. "I thought he would be the one for you, Autumn. What did you do to upset him so much?"

Emmett scowled as he stood up. "Mrs. Evans, I think it's best if you go home and let Autumn rest."

Marie placed her hands on her hips. "How dare you—"

"Marie, let's give them some privacy." Bill kissed Autumn's forehead. "We'll see you at home."

As her father nudged her mother out the door, Autumn said nothing.

"How are you feeling?" Emmett asked once the sliding door clicked shut.

Autumn rested her eyes on the opposite wall. There was a door there, leading to a bathroom. Her voice was monotone as she said, "Although Mason hasn't been arrested, there's a comfort in knowing he's no longer in Maplewood."

Emmett sat on the edge of the bed. "We'll find him, I promise."

She sighed and looked at him. "This is the perfect opportunity for me to run in the opposite direction he did. I can start over, and the probability of him finding me will be even less."

His forehead furrowed, expression torn. He leaned toward her, placing his forehead against hers. "Autumn, I ... I've enjoyed getting to know you," he whispered. "And I would love the privilege of continuing to know you. But I understand if ..." He trailed off.

"I need to start over," she said, eyes focused on the folds of white fabric covering her chest.

"Maybe the safest place to be is near your loved ones," Emmett said, pulling away. He met her eyes, "I think you should stay in Maplewood."

"What are you two talking about?" Bradley pulled open the sliding door. Ortus, Brooke, and J.J. stood behind him in the hallway. Emmett's hand dropped.

Autumn smiled as her friends entered the room. In this moment, she didn't know whether she would stay, but what she did know was whenever she was around those, she cared for ...

She felt *safe*.

8

Three months later, in mid-October, Autumn walked into her new apartment. Unpacked boxes covered the cherry wood floors, and large windows brightened the white walls, providing a view of the downtown park, surrounded by oak trees whose leaves were changing color. It was perfect, and though her belongings were sparse for having to flee Mason, it was *hers*.

She walked over to her refrigerator and grabbed the jar of fresh squeezed lemonade she had made earlier.

"Thank you for helping me move in," she said, setting glasses of lemonade on the table.

Brooke placed a heavy box on the floor, letting out an exhausted breath. "It's what friends are for, right?"

"All this moving has made me hungry and thirsty," Bradley said, gulping down an entire glass of lemonade in what seemed to be one mouthful.

"Shocking," Brooke said in a sardonic tone, as she reached for a glass herself, but Bradley swiped it from under her nose and downed that one too. Autumn chuckled and offered her glass to Brooke instead.

Ortus fell onto the couch. "How do you feel about being out of our parents' place?"

With all the moving, Autumn hadn't given much thought to how she felt. She glanced over at her friends who each gave her an encouraging smile. She hadn't had the heart to let go of the friendships she had rebuilt and the new ones she had started. If she'd moved to a new location, she would've had to start over. No family, no friends, and no Emmett.

"It feels good." Autumn sat on the couch, laying her head on Ortus's shoulder.

"You look different too." Brooke flicked Autumn's hair as she sat on Autumn's other side. "You look happy."

Ortus studied her sister. "It's the hair."

Autumn giggled. She had chopped her long hair off in the hopes it would help her feel like a new person. Now, she had shoulder-length hair, styled into a lob, where the front pieces of her hair were longer than the back. She had held on to the past for so long, and for the first time in a long time, it was Autumn before anyone else. A fresh look, a fresh place, and a new beginning.

"Ugh! I can't take it anymore, I need food!" Bradley yelled. Before they could stop him, he had already run out the door, leaving enough space for Emmett to enter the apartment.

"Let me guess—food?" Emmett asked.

Ortus nodded.

Brooke shrugged. "We'd better go follow him before he ambushes someone," she said as all three women got up.

As Ortus and Brooke headed toward the door, Ortus looked back at Autumn, whose attention was now on Emmett.

Ortus smiled. "We'll see you later," she said, locking the door behind her. Neither Autumn nor Emmett moved, both locked into the other's gaze. She still couldn't believe he was a part of her life now.

He pulled a red rose from behind his back. "Happy two-month anniversary," he said, stepping in close as he held it out for her.

Autumn took it and closed her eyes as she smelled the soft petals. The aroma brought her comfort. It pleased her to know she had been on Emmett's mind. "Why does it feel like we've been together longer?"

He pulled her into his arms. "If someone would've told me the woman who saved Max would end up being my girlfriend, I wouldn't have believed them. Well ... maybe I would've. My queen in shining armor."

Autumn scoffed. "Don't remind me. I thought you were so irresponsible."

Emmett shrugged. "Nobody's perfect."

Her heart skipped a beat as Emmett drew close to her. He cupped her face in his hands and met her lips with his. Her heart pounded through her chest as her body became weak, overwhelmed by how addicted she was to his touch, and he hers. Their energy bounced between them both as they sank onto the couch.

Emmett moved over her, one hand at the back of her neck and the other supporting himself on the back of the couch. As their kissing intensified, his fingers made their way up her shirt, to the back of her bra. She gasped for air. All she wanted in this moment was to give herself to him.

The door swung open. "Hey, neighbor, long time no see!"

Emmett sprang from Autumn, who tucked her hair back into shape. Blood flushed her face. "Oh, hey, J.J. How did you get a key?"

"I didn't, but your doorknob has issues. It doesn't lock all the way."

She sighed. "I'll have to fix that."

Emmett chuckled. "I'll pick you up later tonight for the fundraiser gala." He gave her a peck on her cheek before leaving the apartment.

Autumn turned to J.J., folding her arms across her chest. "You are the worst."

"Hmmm...what did I do?"

She didn't answer him but walked over to the boxes on the floor. J.J. put the pieces together.

"Oh ... Yeah, you should get that lock fixed."

Autumn rolled her eyes, tossing him a red cleaning cloth. "Since you ruined the moment, can you at least help me unpack some of these boxes?"

J.J. nodded as he sat on the couch. She pulled photo frames out of the boxes and handed them to him. Each frame contained a memory of her sister and friends. She stopped when she noticed a white photo frame with a photograph taken at their college campus carnival. Her friends stood in the center, a Ferris wheel in the distance and an endless row of game booths shining bright on both sides of where they stood. Ortus, Autumn, Brooke, and J.J. had been caught laughing and pointing at Bradley who had dropped his snow cone on his shirt.

Bradley's distraught face made her smile. "I haven't seen this photo in a long time." She turned the frame toward J.J. "Our lives have changed so much."

"I know," he whispered. "I'm not around as much."

She scoffed, handing him the frame. "That's because you're traveling the world. You're a well-known movie critic *and* you're managing a film studio that helps underprivileged youth get filmmaking experience. I don't blame you for not being in Maplewood as much."

"You make me sound like a hero."

Autumn walked toward her kitchen, where plates and bowls were scattered on the counter. She grabbed a pink cloth and a plate and wiped it clean as she turned to face J.J. again.

"Do you not think you're a hero to the kids you're helping?"

J.J. grabbed the boxcutter and broke down the now empty boxes in front of him. "I'm sure I am, but I travel the world critiquing all these films when I could be dedicating more time to the studio." He placed the broken-down boxes next to the others by the door. "A hero would've known his friend was in danger."

Autumn placed the cloth down. "Don't you dare blame yourself for what happened to me. Mason is the one to blame. At least that's what I'm trying to convince myself…"

J.J. nodded his head, changing the subject. "Are you excited about the gala?"

"Yeah, it's the least I can do," Autumn said. "It's my fault Mason wanted to burn the clinic down in the first place." She paused, staring at the shining counter, lost in a memory. The smell of gasoline was engrained in her nostrils. She shook her head and continued, "The gala should help us raise enough money to fix the remaining damage."

"You better have a ball gown ready to impress lover boy."

She rolled her eyes. "Of course I do. What do you take me for?"

"I like this newfound confidence you've discovered in yourself. I missed seeing this glow on you." He stepped away from the frames on the wall. "Well, that's the last of them."

They both walked to the door and scanned the apartment. For the first time in over seven years, she had a place she could settle in.

A home.

After J.J. left, Autumn took a long, warm shower and changed into a red gown with lace sleeves. A couple of months ago, she had been terrified of getting close to Emmett and now she couldn't wait to be in his arms again. Right on cue, there was a knock on the door.

She stood from her vanity and brushed her thighs of nonexistent lint. When she opened the door, Emmett froze.

"Whoa," he said, looking at her from crown to toe.

Autumn giggled. She knew what she was doing to Emmett, and she enjoyed every moment of it. "You like?" she teased.

Emmett rubbed the back of his neck. "I do. In fact—" he pulled her closer to him, "what would you say to spending the night here instead?"

Every time their lips touched, a spark shot through Autumn, a spark symbolic of not lust, but warmth and security.

"Your mother is expecting us at the gala," she said, pushing him away.

"I suppose you're right." He stepped to the side and motioned his hand toward the door. "After you, Autumn."

The gala was being held at The Maple, a local venue known to host the most sophisticated events in town. When they arrived, they walked through an arch made of woven branches and covered in fairy lights. The room was decorated with artificial blossoming trees in each corner. Long and high-top tables with cherry blossoms as centerpieces dotted the area. Autumn spotted Emmett's mother, who looked overwhelmed beneath a canopy of white flowers.

"Autumn, Emmett! I'm so glad you're here." Dr. Pierce called them over.

"The place looks great, Dr. Pierce," Autumn said.

"Thank you," Dr. Pierce sighed. "Emmett, there's something we need to discuss in private. Sorry, Autumn, please excuse us," she said, pulling Emmett away from her.

"Mom, I can't leave Autumn alone for too long," Emmett said as his mother hauled him through the hallway. "You know these types of events stress her out."

"I'm sorry Emmett, but this is important. How much does she know about your father?"

He scowled. "Not much. What's this about?" They paused in front of a large white door. Emmett crossed his arms. "What is going on?"

"Please don't be mad. I need you to listen."

Before he could question her, she opened the door they stood before. As it creaked open, a figure in the middle of the room turned to face them. Henry rubbed the back of his neck.

"Hello, son."

Henry's hair had turned winter white in the years since Emmett last saw him. His eyes were blood-flecked, and bags hung beneath them. Aside from looking older, he looked ashen and shaken.

Emmett stood behind the door, not daring to enter. "Henry," was all he said.

His mother placed her hand on his shoulder. "Honey, I think you and your father need to talk."

"There is nothing I have to say to this man."

"Please, son," Henry whispered.

Emmett turned to go back to the gala, glancing over his shoulder at Henry. "I stopped being your son when you walked out on me."

He stomped down the hallway with his frantic mother following behind him.

"Emmett, your father needs to speak to you," she called.

Emmett stopped, turning to face her. "Why are you defending him?"

Dr. Pierce sighed. "Please, do this for me. I'm begging you."

Emmett's face fell. Why was his mother being so persistent? He studied her. Her shoulders had slumped, and her eyes were telling him there was more she wasn't sharing. He glanced behind her to where Henry now stood in the doorway, looking out at him. Henry gave Emmett a smile, a final plea.

"I'll think about it, but I'm not making any promises," he said, storming away from them.

Autumn stood in the middle of the room with her arms crossed, a tight knot forming at the pit of her stomach as people walked by, eyeing her. It's possible they blamed her for the fire. Her own mother had, so why wouldn't the rest of the town?

She brushed the thoughts away and scanned the room in hopes she would find someone she knew. There were a lot of different people at the gala, including owners of local businesses, members of the police force, and some of the firefighters from Station Thirteen. Her eyes landed on a group of men in fancy tuxes speaking to some of the firefighters. A man in a velvet blue tux whose hair was in a manbun stood in front of them. She couldn't see his face until he turned in her direction. The brown eyes that met hers reminded her of Mason. Out of habit and instinct, she turned away.

After a breath, she turned toward the man, but he was no longer there. Her heart skipped a beat as she scanned from face to face in the room, trying to hide the panic rising within her. Each met her gaze with a gentle smile, but it wasn't until she spotted her sister and friends standing in a corner that she felt a moment of relief. Her friends were snickering, mocking the people around them.

"What was that all about?" Ortus asked as Autumn approached them.

"What do you mean?"

"Emmett's mom taking him away from you."

"Oh, I have no idea." Autumn grabbed a champagne flute from a passing server. "Guess they need to talk in private."

Bradley was focusing on the guests walking by them. "There are a lot of attractive doctors here."

"You got that right. Ooh, look at that silver fox." Brooke turned toward a suave, elder gentleman with a trimmed grey beard and a strong jawline.

"Brooke, you're engaged!" Bradley objected.

"Oh, relax! I can still be fascinated from a distance."

While her friends bickered, Autumn sipped at her champagne, Dr. Pierce's concerned face etched into her mind's eye. She pursed her lips. Did Dr. Pierce blame her for the incident at the clinic too?

Brooke placed her water on a nearby high-top. "Well, I have to go. I have a late-night shift at the hospital."

Autumn tilted her head in surprise. "You're working at the hospital again?"

"I am. I've missed helping my patients since opening the gallery, so I've been taking a few shifts here and there."

"That's amazing, Brooke."

Brooke shrugged. "Every artist needs a break. I'll see you all later." She grabbed her purse and hugged them all goodbye.

As they watched her go, Autumn caught the eyes of a few other guests. These didn't smile, breaking eye contact with her to whisper something to their friends. Autumn dropped her eyes to her glass.

"Are you okay?" Bradley asked.

"No. Emmett is taking longer than I thought." She glanced over her shoulder. "I'm worried."

Ortus rubbed her back. "I'm sure he'll tell you what's wrong after he's done talking to her."

"You're his partner in crime, why are you so worried?" Bradley asked.

She looked around the room. "Ever since the fire, it feels like everyone is blaming and judging me for what happened. It's making me feel like staying in Maplewood wasn't the right choice."

Bradley moved closer and nudged her. "The town respects you, Autumn."

She scoffed. "Yeah, right."

"It's true. What you endured with Mason was beyond traumatic. The people of Maplewood don't know how to support you. Not much happens here besides petty drama."

"That's why they sent all those flowers to our parents' house," Ortus added.

Autumn's eyes widened. "I assumed those were from Emmett."

Bradley shook his head. "It's a town tradition. When someone goes through a tough time—illness, maybe loss of a loved one—sometimes words aren't enough."

"Wow." Autumn shook her head and placed her glass on a nearby table. "I need to get some fresh air."

She walked through the building and found a staircase that led her to a balcony. Down below, Maplewood sparkled under scattered lights and, above, the shining moon, obscured by the occasional cloud. She leaned on the stone banister as a small breeze blew by, pushing her hair up around her ears.

Over the past couple of months, Autumn had changed. It was all so surreal to her. Had she gone from the girl who hated Maplewood to the girl who never wanted to leave? The town had shown her kindness when she had assumed the worst in them. It was a habit she had, thinking the worst of people to protect herself. Having Emmett and her friends in her life had begun to change that, but it didn't mean her lack of trust in people would go away overnight.

Emmett.

He'd made her feel loved the past couple of months. This new chapter in her life was unfamiliar to her. Emmett wasn't Mason by a long shot but being with such a cruel man had messed with her. The first month after the fire and as an official couple with Emmett had been difficult. Autumn had flinched every time he touched her, jumped whenever she heard a fire truck, and could no longer work late shifts at the clinic.

However, as time went on, she became more comfortable with Emmett's touch. He had been gentle with her, asked for permission anytime he was near, and held her hand every time Autumn felt like she was on the verge of a panic attack. Emmett cared for her.

"What are you thinking about?"

She didn't jump this time as Emmett wrapped his arms around her waist.

"Nothing." She placed her hands above his and leaned toward his chest. "Is everything okay?"

"Yeah. My mom…" He paused, taking a deep breath. "My father is back in town."

"I don't think I've ever heard you talk much about him before."

"Yeah. There's a reason for that."

She turned in his arms so she was facing him. "Do you want to get out of here and talk about it?"

He nodded, "Later. For now, let's network for the clinic."

"For the clinic." Autumn agreed.

They spent the hours that followed mingling with important donors who had flown into Maplewood for this event.

"She built an empire for Maplewood, it's impressive." J.J. spoke of Dr. Pierce to Autumn and Emmett.

"She has presented at several worldwide conferences." Emmett observed his mother shake hands with multiple other veterinarians. "Because of those presentations she has met so many people. I've got a lot to learn from her still."

"As do I." Autumn agreed.

By the end of the evening, Emmett and Autumn had met more people than they bargained for. Every donor who had flown in donated, raising $200,000 dollars for the clinic and bringing great relief to Dr. Pierce.

"I can't believe it," Dr. Pierce expressed, embracing both Autumn and Emmett. "We have enough to pay the debt of the clinic and more!"

"Congrats Mom," Emmett exclaimed.

"Now, you two head home, you look exhausted." Dr. Pierce savored the last of her champagne. "I'll clean up here."

"Are you sure?" Autumn asked. "I don't want to leave you here alone."

"Oh, hush I won't be. I'll grab Jackie to help, besides the vendor takes care of most of the takedown."

Without another word, hand in hand, they said their goodbyes to those at the gala and made their way back to Autumn's apartment. There, Autumn changed into a comfortable tank top and sweats and texted J.J. to let Emmett borrow something to wear. While he changed, she prepared two mugs of hot chocolate.

"Well, you look comfy," Autumn said as Emmett entered the living area wearing a burgundy tank top with grey sweats.

"Guess I'm lucky J.J. is your neighbor, huh?"

Autumn rolled her eyes. "He owes me after barging into my apartment this morning." There was a long pause before she spoke again. "You were saying about your father?" she asked as she handed him a mug.

He accepted the hot chocolate with a gracious nod and brought the mug to his lips, looking down at it. She hadn't known Emmett for all that long, but she could see the hurt he was trying to hide in his eyes. The story she was about to hear was not going to be one with a happy ending.

"He left us when I was ten years old," he started. "He came back years later trying to be part of my life, but I pushed him away. His name is Henry, and he's also a veterinarian."

"Why do you think he's back in town?"

He sighed and put his drink down on the coffee table. "I don't know. He's persistent. The last time I saw him was when I was a kid. When I saw him at the gala tonight—"

"Wait, what? He was there?"

Emmett nodded. "When my mom took me away from you, she brought me to meet him. I was so furious that I left." He frowned, eyes on the blank television screen. "But there was something different about tonight."

"What do you mean?"

"She ran after me, begging me to give him a chance." His voice deepened. "She's never asked me to do that before."

Autumn placed her mug down to focus on Emmett. She tilted her head in concern. "Are you going to?"

"I ... I don't know. I'm nervous, maybe even afraid." He looked at her. "Is that weird?"

Autumn never thought she would see Emmett afraid, let alone admit to it. Ever since he came to her rescue that night at the clinic, she'd pictured him as a hero, fearless—but even the best heroes can have tragic pasts. He had gone out of his way to protect her, and now she wanted to protect him.

She placed her hand on his. "You should go see him. If you don't, you'll wonder what would've happened if you did. I'll go with you if you want."

Emmett looked down at her hand over his. He didn't move, and for a moment, Autumn wondered if she'd said the wrong thing. But when he looked up at her, his lips were curved into a sad smile.

"I'll think about it," he said, raising his hand to her cheek and pulling her to him.

He started kissing her, taking her by surprise, but she kissed him back. His touch sent electric currents through her body. Every time they kissed it felt like the first time, and it was a feeling she hoped would never change. She had never wanted someone as much as she wanted him that night. In the two months they had been a couple, they had never spent the night together, but that night was different. It was magical.

The next morning, Emmett made Autumn breakfast, and to her surprise, he was a great cook. She hated cooking during her time with Mason. He had always expected her to prepare every meal for him. With Emmett, it was different. He enjoyed making her breakfast. This morning, he'd made her favorite combo of pancakes, scrambled eggs, and potatoes.

"This was so good," Autumn said, dabbing her lips with a napkin.

He smiled from opposite her. "Thank you."

"We should hurry or we're going to be late for work." She got up from her seat and placed their dishes in the sink. "I don't want to upset your mom."

"My mom likes you. No need to try to impress her."

She giggled. "Yeah, but I'm also a responsible adult who likes to be on time."

"All right," he sighed. "I'm going to head home to change. I'll see you at work." He kissed her cheek before leaving.

Once Emmett was gone, she stood in her kitchen in silence. Last night had been electrifying. She hadn't been intimate with anyone in a long time. Emmett had been gentle with her, he had checked in on her and made her feel safe.

After getting ready, she decided it was a great day to walk to the clinic. On her way there, she couldn't stop smiling. She noticed the people around her laughing and enjoying their time together, greeting acquaintances and strangers alike with a joyful hello. When she had walked in California, she always avoided eye contact, worried someone would see through her confident facade and question her secret suffering.

Today, she looked at the faces who made up this town. She wanted to share her happiness and wanted the people in the town to know she wasn't as broken as she once was.

The enticing scent of fresh baked bread made her come to an abrupt stop. She stood in front of Marisol's bakery. Autumn glanced at her watch, deciding she had enough time to pick up some bread for lunch later today.

The bell above the door jingled as she entered. Inside, the smell was much more intense, and despite having eaten a full breakfast, her mouth watered in response. The cream-colored walls were lined with shelves filled with different types of *pan dulce*. It all looked and smelled delicious.

"Autumn, fancy seeing you here!" Marisol, who had her long brown hair up in a bun, stepped out from behind the cash register. "I missed you at the gala last night."

Autumn ran to hug her. "Oh, my boyfriend and I had to go…"

Marisol smiled. "Well, I'm glad you stopped by. Welcome to El Corazon del Pan. It means 'The Heart of Bread.' This bakery has been standing for generations."

"Well, its aesthetic is mesmerizing." Autumn turned to eye the shelves filled with fresh bread. "I can't decide what to get."

"Here, let me help you." Marisol grabbed a tray and some tongs and began selecting buns.

Autumn paused, biting her lip. "I've been wanting to thank you. The advice you gave me on my birthday has stayed with me."

Marisol looked sideways at her. "Oh? I'm guessing you said yes to the guy?"

Autumn laughed. "Yes, I did. We've been together two months now."

"I'm glad you listened. Does he make you happy?"

"He does." Autumn's voice softened, "What about you? Did you end up going to find the guy you said no to?"

Marisol smiled. "No. We're friends now because I met someone else. His name is Ethan, he challenges me to be the best version of myself. We bicker, but our differences bring us together."

"Wait ... is Ethan a poet?"

"Yeah. He performs at the café down the street, but he's not—"

"Very good," they both said.

Marisol laughed. "Ah, so you know who he is?"

"I don't know him, but my friends Brooke and Bradley do."

"Oh, the famous Knight twins. Bradley is always buying most of our bread." Autumn laughed. "I bet he makes your life difficult."

"Nah, if anything, he's one of the main reasons we're still in business. Come on, let's get these wrapped up for you."

Autumn glanced at her watch. *Just in time too.* "Thanks, what do I owe you?"

"Nothing," Marisol said as she shoved the box of breads into Autumn's hands.

"What? No, no. I can't take all this for free."

"Yes, you can, and you will. Come to me when you need a wedding cake, and we'll be even."

Autumn sighed but smiled as she relented and took the box. "Thank you, Marisol. I will."

Autumn rushed to the clinic and, as she reached the front door, so did Emmett. They both looked at each other, unable to stop smiling. They could have remained standing there for the whole day if Emmett's growling stomach hadn't made them laugh.

"Are you already hungry?" Autumn asked.

"It's the bread you're carrying, it smells so good!"

"Well, let's get inside, and I'll put some in the break room," she said as Emmett opened the door.

When they entered the clinic, Dr. Pierce looked up from where she was flipping through documents at the front desk. "Nice of both of you to show up."

"I'm sorry we're late, Dr. Pierce," Autumn said with a nervous smile.

Dr. Pierce grabbed the box of bread from Autumn. "Don't worry, I'm sure last night tired both of you out."

Blood rushed to Autumn's face. Emmett wouldn't tell his mother about their night, right? She glanced at Emmett, who looked as uncomfortable as she did.

"Uhh ..." she began.

"The gala took a lot of energy out of me too." Dr. Pierce took a bite of *pan dulce*. "I stayed up too late last night. Although, I was able to hire a new doctor after you left."

Emmett took a bun from the box, earning him a smirk from Autumn. "Why? There're more than enough of us here," he said.

"I'm getting old, Emmett, and if there's someone willing to help, I'll take it." Dr. Pierce grinned. "Besides, I have a feeling you'll like this specific veterinarian."

"Dr. Pierce, I was wondering if—"

Autumn and Emmett both turned to see who had walked through the door. A handsome man wearing sunglasses, a black leather jacket, and holding a motorcycle helmet in his hand stood in front of them.

The man recovered from his surprise and smiled, walking to stand next to Dr. Pierce. "Good morning, doctors," he said.

Autumn watched Emmett's face light up. "Jayden?" he said.

Jayden chuckled as he embraced Emmett. "It's been a long time, Emmett."

"What are you doing here?"

"I moved back to Maplewood, I'm living in my parents' old house."

Emmett tucked his hands into his pockets. "I'm surprised the place is still standing."

"Well, the folks I was renting the house to just left." Jayden rubbed his chin. "I figured it was about time I came back home."

"And he returned at the most convenient time." Dr. Pierce raised both of her hands. "I hired him as our new veterinarian!"

Jayden pulled his sunglasses down his nose and looked at Autumn over them. "My oh my, and who is this beautiful woman?"

Emmett rolled his eyes. "Back off, Jayden. This is my girlfriend, Autumn Evans. Autumn, this is my childhood best friend, Jayden Rose."

"It's nice to meet you." She extended her hand to shake his, but instead Jayden embraced her, squeezing her tight.

A memory flashed through Autumn's mind, her body colliding with a wall, Mason's hand wrapped around her forearm. Her heart rate accelerated and a deep tremor erupted in her torso. Jayden's grip on her relaxed.

"Are you okay?" he said as he let her go.

She became unsteady and held on to the ledge of the reception desk. "I need a minute…"

"Lil' dove, look at me." Emmett turned her toward him. "Focus on me and your breathing. You're here with my mom, Jayden, and me. No one else is here."

Breathe.

Inhale. Exhale.

Inhale. Exhale.

After a couple of breaths, her heart rate returned to normal.

She turned to face Jayden. "I'm quick to get startled, I'm working on it—"

"*We're* working on it," Emmett corrected her as he held her hand.

"I'm sorry, I shouldn't hug strangers…" Jayden paused at the placating smile Autumn gave him, and shifted gear, slapping Emmett on the arm. "Well, I'm glad you found someone, man."

There was a long silence, as if the two men were having a telepathic conversation. Autumn glanced at Dr. Pierce too, noting the odd half-smile on her face. There was a history between these two men that Autumn wasn't privy to.

"Jayden, let's get you started on your training, shall we?" Dr. Pierce interrupted.

Jayden nodded. "Sure, although I did spend a lot of time here as a teen."

"It's been a couple of years, things change," Dr. Pierce said, walking toward her office.

Jayden glanced at Emmett and Autumn for a moment before following Dr. Pierce. Once he was out of earshot, Autumn turned to Emmett, ready to question him, but Emmett clapped his hands together and entered the waiting area to greet his first patient. Autumn hummed and followed. Her curiosity would have to wait.

Dr. Pierce spent most of the time training Jayden, who turned out to be a quick learner. After Autumn saw her last patient, she stayed to speak to Jackie and Emmett for a minute.

"How are your studies for the national licensing exam going, Jackie?" Emmett asked.

Jackie sighed. "It's difficult, but I'm trying."

"I may have my old notecards."

Emmett kissed Autumn's forehead. "Of course, you do."

"Autumn, I'm glad you're still here," Dr. Pierce called. "Would you mind spending some time walking Jayden through the files? I have a patient coming in soon," she said, approaching them with Jayden walking close behind.

"Of course." Autumn nodded, "Do you want to join us, Emmett?"

Emmett rubbed the back of his neck. "Eh, I think you got this honey. You know paperwork isn't my favorite thing in the world."

Autumn rolled her eyes. "C'mon, Jayden, the files are in the back office."

Jayden smirked. "Perfect place for us to get some quality time together."

As she walked into the room, she saw Emmett through the window roll his eyes. He stood with his arms crossed, studying them together. Was he jealous?

Autumn spent half an hour walking Jayden through some of the patient files, explaining to him the needs of the patients he would be seeing.

"And then there's Fern. She's a ten-year-old Siamese cat who doesn't like strangers touching her. I recommend you sit on the floor and let her wander to you, you'll have to wait a couple minutes before you can examine her."

Jayden grinned. "Sounds easy enough."

"What brought you back to Maplewood?" Autumn asked, closing and locking the filing cabinet.

"I left about two years ago. I needed to escape and—"

"Have a fresh start," she said.

Jayden nodded. "I went to New York City, but it's such a busy place. I couldn't keep up most of the time."

"It's not as easy to connect with others, right?" Autumn said. "Almost makes you feel even worse."

He cocked his head to the side. "You've tried the city life before?"

"Oh yeah." She walked toward the door to reception. "I'm glad I'm back, though. I think I was destined to come home to Maplewood."

Jayden leaned against the wall. "Emmett is a great guy. I'm glad he found you. I was beginning to worry about him."

"How come?"

He looked at the ground. "He's ... been through a lot."

Jayden was charming and yet genuine, which made Autumn question why Emmett had never brought him up. Was there more to their story? If so, why had he kept it from her?

Emmett watched Autumn walk out the door after her shift. He closed his eyes, feeling a sudden lightness as the tension he was feeling escaped his body.

Jayden Rose, back in Maplewood? He left so suddenly the last time Emmett had seen him, and Emmett never understood why.

"What are you looking at?"

He flinched at the voice that crept up from behind him, Jayden's. Emmett had tried to avoid him most of the afternoon; he knew it was a matter of time before his old best friend found him.

"I'm making sure Autumn left before you bombarded her with questions," Emmett said, walking toward his office.

"A little too late for that. Although, she's the one who asked me questions, and not even about you. She seemed interested in me," he said, following close behind.

"It's what Autumn does. She's invested in getting to know the people around her, anything she can do to help others."

"She seems like a great woman, she has a fire similar to Lily."

Hearing her name come out of Jayden's mouth was enough to make Emmett's heart sink. As he walked to his desk, he shuffled through some old papers, avoiding eye contact.

"Why are you back?" he asked.

Jayden collapsed in the chair patients would sit in. "I got tired of New York, it wasn't for me. I don't know why my sister wanted to live there."

Emmett crossed his arms, knowing there was more to it.

Jayden glanced at Emmett and let out a heavy sigh. "Fine. I couldn't stop thinking about my sister. When I left, I was in so much pain. I lost my best friend, I lost my father, and well, I never had my mother."

Emmett slammed his hands on his desk. "But you had me. We were best friends, and you left without so much as a goodbye." He glared at Jayden. "I thought it was something I'd done."

"No, it wasn't you." Jayden rubbed the back of his neck. "You reminded me of my sister too much. You two were inseparable, and it was too much for me. She went on that trip—"

"Because she wanted us to move," Emmett continued for him. "She wanted to branch out, open a business of her own. I should've stopped her—"

"Stop." Jayden shook his head, as if he knew what he was about to say. "It wasn't our fault. It was never our fault. Even if we had tried to stop her from getting on that plane, she wouldn't have listened. She's Lily."

"Was Lily," Emmett corrected him.

"Right."

Emmett sat at his desk, processing how his old best friend was sitting in front of him. They'd continued along different paths and their lives were different now, but perhaps the friendship they once had wasn't lost.

"So," Jayden said, perking up a bit, "I think Autumn might like me."

Emmett crumpled up a Post-it and threw it across the table at Jayden, whose head fell back with laughter.

After her morning shift, Autumn agreed to meet Ortus, Bradley, and Brooke at the farmers' market in town. As she drove, the radiant spring weather shone down on Maplewood. The red Maple trees bloomed over beds of yellow pansies, giving life and color to the center of town. It was the perfect day to be outside.

The car chimed, reminding her to fill the gas tank. She turned up the radio, listening to her favorite Beatles song, "Here Comes the Sun." It had been years since she'd last listened to it. She'd stopped once she realized the sun in her life didn't seem to be returning.

But now, it sent her into a moment of personal bliss.

She sang along, recalling the last time she had been to a farmers' market. She was seventeen when her first boyfriend, Oliver Walker, had broken up with her. She'd been determined to spend the day crying in her room, but her sister and friends had a different plan.

"We need candy apples *stat!*" Bradley said after one look at Autumn's morbid expression.

Autumn sighed. "We were doing so well. I don't know what I did wrong."

"Oliver is a jerk. Breaking the hearts of the pure is like a hobby for him," Brooke said with a sneer.

After grabbing their candy apples, they found a bench to sit on. Within minutes, Autumn was near tears of laughter as she and Ortus helped remove a grumpy Brooke's hair from Bradley's candy apple, which he'd been animatedly waving around. Disaster averted, they chatted about their weeks, giggled at awkward couples on first dates, and spent time making fun of Oliver.

It became Autumn's favorite place to be in her spare time.

She parked her car and went in search of her friends, walking between the rows of vendors, many of whom owned local businesses in town. Large crowds of shoppers surrounded the handmade jewelry stands, children clustered around the candy apple vendor, and fresh produce sellers called out to passersby, advertising their stock. Parents walked hand in hand with their children, teens wandered with their friends, while pets pranced by with their owners. Many chatted with the sellers as friends rather than customers.

Autumn spotted Ortus waving at her from next to a large barrel of apples.

"About Jayden ... Emmett didn't tell you more about him?" Ortus asked as she placed some apples in her shopping bag.

"Emmett didn't say anything about him. I wanted to catch him at the end of my shift, but he seemed busy. I feel like there's more to their story."

"Maybe he has a crush on you, and Emmett doesn't like that?" Bradley said through a mouthful of his candy apple. A drop of juice dribbled down his jaw.

"You need to listen." Autumn handed him a napkin. "They have a sibling relationship. I don't think that's it."

While Ortus and Bradley both shrugged and diverted their attentions to the vendors surrounding them, Autumn noticed Brooke was silent beside her, intent on avoiding eye contact as she stared in fascination at a piece of gravel on the sidewalk.

"All right, spit it out, what do you know?" Autumn demanded.

Brooke looked across at her. "Me? What makes you think I know something?"

At that, Bradley whirled around, mouth full and chewing. He stared at his sister for a moment, who met his eyes with a frown, looking at Autumn. "Yep, she knows something."

Brooke tutted, "Traitor," looping her arm through Autumn's and pulling her toward an empty white bench under a tree, isolated from everyone else. Bradley followed close behind, munching on his candy apple. Ortus caught on a moment later, dragging herself away from a stand selling cakes.

Brooke sighed. "Jayden and Emmett both went to schools on the west side of town growing up. You remember my rebellious stage, right?"

Autumn nodded. "Oh yeah. There was a good part of high school when we didn't see you."

"I'll admit, I didn't handle my parents' death the best. I did some things I wasn't proud of, but one day I was smoking a cigarette—"

Autumn gawked. "Brooke! Are you serious? Cigarettes?"

"It's not one of my proudest moments." She grimaced. "Anyway, I was smoking a cigarette on the other side of town, and Jayden caught me. He pulled the cigarette out of my mouth and told me I would die if I continued to smoke. I remember thinking he was such a prude." She laughed, shaking her head.

Autumn pulled her mouth to the side. "I mean, I agree, but that's rich coming from someone who rides a motorcycle."

"I'll get to that." Brooke grinned. "We became friends, and he helped me process a lot of things, helped me find my way back to all of you. He was the secret friend I never told you about. We grew up so fast, and before I knew it, we each had gone our separate ways."

"What happened next?"

Brooke looked at her fingertips. "His sister died in a plane crash."

Autumn tilted her head. "That sounds like the story Emmett told me about—"

"Lily," Brooke finished her thought. "Lily Rose was Jayden's twin sister."

"That explains why Emmett might not have shared much," said Ortus as she cleaned an apple with her skirt. "He might not have wanted to be insensitive to you by talking about his ex, and also didn't want to bring the pain up again for Jayden."

"Jayden was never the same," Brooke whispered. "I reached out to him when I found out and supported him as best I could. Loss can break a person."

Autumn touched her stomach. "I can imagine." She sighed, getting up from the bench. "I'm going to go look for some mangos, I'll be right back."

While she did intend to search for her favorite fruit, she needed a moment alone to think. She began to consider why Emmett had never talked about Jayden before. Maybe Jayden reminded him of the pain and loss he had experienced. After all, it had been easier for Emmett to help those around him than deal with what he was feeling. They were similar in that way. With Jayden's reappearance and Emmett's father trying to make contact, it looked like his past was creeping up on him, and Autumn would make sure to be there for him as he was for her.

Someone tapped her shoulder. "Excuse me, are you okay?"

Autumn jumped and turned around, surprised to see the poet from the café. He had his brown hair brushed back, making his freckles more evident, and was wearing a yellow apron.

"Ethan, right?" Autumn asked.

He nodded. "Yeah! I'm surprised you remember me. You're a friend of the twins, right?"

"I am. I saw you at open mic night. Your poem was ... *deep*."

He laughed. "Thanks, but I'm well aware I'm not good at it."

"If you're proud of your work, that's all that matters."

"Thanks," he said, restocking the box of mangos in front of him. "Are you okay? I know a look like that on a person. You're not sure about something."

Autumn smirked. *Like boyfriend, like girlfriend.* "Yeah, I'm fine. My boyfriend is keeping something from me, and I'm wondering why."

"Is that a bad thing? For him not to tell you things?"

"No," Autumn said, picking up one of the mangos to inspect its flesh. "I was always the one with secrets, it's weird being on the other side."

Ethan shrugged. "Talk to him about it but be patient."

"It's not that easy."

"Why not? If you want your relationship to work, all you have to do is talk. Trust me when I say that hiding how you feel is the worst thing you can do. Trust your gut, but above all, trust your heart."

Autumn placed one hand on her hip, using the other to hold out the mango she'd selected to Ethan. "You know, you're the second person who's told me that? Almost word for word."

He smirked and took the mango, placing it in a bag for her. "It sounds like you've met my fiancé, Marisol."

She nodded. "Hard working woman, she is."

"I'm glad you've already met her. She's amazing," he said, rubbing the back of his neck. His cheeks adopted a pink tinge above his smile.

Autumn laughed and handed him payment for the mango.

"Good luck with your conversation," Ethan said as she waved goodbye.

Autumn knew he was right. If she wanted to know why Emmett had never brought up Jayden, she would need to ask him.

After a moment, she found herself laughing at the thought of asking Emmett not to run away from his past when it would be hypocritical of her to do so. After all she'd been doing the past couple of months. She had at one point been too afraid to fill up her car's tank, for the stink of gasoline and the scary memories it brought up.

Back at the white bench, Autumn found Ortus and Bradley.

"Where's Brooke?" she asked.

"She had to go cover for a friend at the hospital," Ortus said.

"Yeah, she's so lame," Bradley said, now halfway through a tub of strawberries.

Autumn shot a sardonic look, "So, what's your job again?"

"Real estate. I've said this so many times, you never listen." He let out a heavy sigh, ate another strawberry (leaves and all), and got up. "I'm getting another candy apple," he said.

Both Ortus and Autumn laughed as they watched Bradley walk away. It was in moments like these she knew remaining in Maplewood had been the right choice.

9

On her way home from work the next evening, Autumn came to an abrupt stop in front of a wedding dress shop. A cluster of women sat inside, drinking champagne as they ogled the bride who twirled in a white dress in front of them. Autumn couldn't help but think of Mason. She had locked her most hurtful memories in a box inside her mind, but there were moments the box would burst open when she least expected it to.

In the glass of the storefront, her reflection looked back at her, content on the outside, but still hurting behind her soft eyes. Over her shoulder, the opposite side of the street glowed—and a hard silhouette moved along it.

The hairs on the back of her neck stood on end, and she whirled around. The other sidewalk was empty, aside from Marisol, who was packing up the sandwich board in front of her bakery.

"Hey, Autumn."

Autumn jumped and turned, hands flying up, but stopped and sighed when she saw who it was. "You scared the bejesus out of me."

"Bejesus? What are you, five?" Brooke said.

"Whatever." Autumn rolled her eyes, noticing her friend was still in scrubs. "It's been a long day."

Brooke scoffed. "I get that."

Autumn's head tilted. "You sound like you need to vent."

Brooke sighed, hiking her bag farther up her shoulder. "It was a long and dreadful shift with one of my patients. It's so sad."

"We can walk home together and talk more about it?" Autumn suggested, stepping away from the shop window.

A slight smile graced Brooke's face. "Sure, that'd be nice."

They started down the street, passing shops as they closed for the night. The sidewalk darkened the longer they walked until the streetlamps and the moon above lit their way.

With a calm composure, Autumn waited for Brooke, whose gaze was fixed on her shoes as her purple hair fell over her eyes, until she looked up, face to the stars.

"I love my job, but sometimes it sucks."

Autumn could empathize. She loved helping the animals that came to the clinic but seeing them in pain was hard at the best of times.

"There is a patient who was unconscious when she was found, but she's fallen into a coma since."

Autumn brought her hand to her mouth. "That's terrible!"

"Yeah …" Brooke nodded. "I'm glad they found her when they did, she's stable now."

"Well, that's good news, isn't it?"

They crossed the road, entering the street where Autumn's apartment block was located. She slowed their walk, not wanting to rush Brooke to finish.

"It should be, but we don't know if she'll wake up. Plus, she's a Jane Doe. Her loved ones must be worried." Brooke shook her head.

"I can't even imagine the worry." Autumn said.

"Yeah. I wish there was a way I could help."

"Maybe you could read to her and keep her company?" she suggested. "I'm sure it'll make her feel better to see someone when she wakes up."

"*If* she wakes up." Brooke sighed. "You're right. I know she'd be a lot happier if she saw a face she knew instead."

They stopped, bathed in the warm glow that seeped through the glass doors of the apartment block lobby. Autumn turned to her friend. "You have a good heart, Brooke, but you can't control everything. Sometimes we have to let things play out."

"When did you become so wise?"

Autumn scoffed, almost offended. "I've always been wise. I needed to come home to be reminded."

Brooke sighed. "Why did we choose these career paths again?"

"Because whether we like it or not, we love helping others."

Autumn's phone buzzed, a message from Emmett displaying on her screen,

Hi Lil' dove, I'm waiting for you in your apartment. I want to ask you something, take your time getting home!

She texted back,

I'll be there soon.

Autumn slipped the phone in her pocket. "I better get home, Emmett's waiting for me."

Brooke smirked, walking away, "Have fun with lover boy."

As they went their separate ways, Autumn headed inside. She felt terrible for not being able to better support her friend, but now she understood the reason behind Brooke's investment in her art studio, it helped her cope and find joy in life. Autumn's joy came from making crochet animals.

Her footsteps echoed out across the lit lobby. A porter sat behind the reception desk, watching a football game on his phone. The armchairs and sofas by the front windows were empty, except for one person. Autumn stopped when she realized who it was.

"Jayden?" she said.

He glanced up from his book. "Oh! Hey, Autumn."

"What are you reading?" she asked, walking toward him.

Pride and Prejudice. He grinned, raising the book to show her the cover. "Got to love the classics."

"You're full of surprises, aren't you?"

He smirked. "It's not on purpose."

For a moment, they both maintained eye contact. As Autumn looked into his caramel eyes, she noticed the dark bags below them and knew this man was struggling.

"Are you doing all right? You look ... exhausted."

He gave a feeble smile. "I'm dealing with some personal things."

For a moment, they remained silent. She wanted to help him, but if he wasn't ready, she wouldn't push. "What are you doing here?" she asked.

"I bumped into Bradley at Marisol's bakery. I mentioned I wanted to chat with you and he shared where you lived." He closed his book and got up from his chair.

Autumn stepped back. "Well, you found me, what do you want to talk about?"

"Emmett. I'm sure he's told you about my sister?"

She gave a comforting smile. "I wish I could've met her."

"That's how I know you'll be good for him. The biggest regret I have is running away and not being there for him."

"You needed time to heal."

He nodded. "Yeah, I did. You know I haven't seen him smile in a long time, and you're the reason behind that." With a timid smile, Autumn tucked her hair behind her ear, and Jayden continued, "I wanted to say ... don't break his heart. It's what my sister would've wanted me to say to you. I think she would've liked you."

"I can't think of a scenario where I could break his heart."

"Considering you're the first woman he's been with since Lily, I expect you won't. You're special to him."

She looked at him, dumbfounded. She had met this man yesterday.

His phone rang. "Sorry, I have to take this. I'll see you around," he said, hurrying out of the lobby.

Autumn knew what it was like to push away those closest to you. It had taken her time to rebuild the relationships she'd let go of, and she wished Emmett would be able to do the same.

She walked into her apartment, her feet dragging on the floor and her knees about to give out from exhaustion.

"Emmett? You here?" Autumn called.

"Yup, in your bedroom."

She placed her bag on her sofa and grabbed a glass of water before heading into her room.

The bedside light was on, and sure enough, there on her bed lay Emmett in an Eden flannel shirt, looking uneasy.

"You look comfortable," she said, turning around to change out of her dirty clothes and, once she pulled on a nightgown, she joined him. He lay on top of the covers, while Autumn tucked herself underneath. She turned on her pillow to look at him, her arm tucked under her head. His face was placid as he stared up at her ceiling. She placed a hand on his chest, and he looked over at her.

"Emmett, are you all right?" she asked.

"Yeah, why?"

"Well, for one, you haven't kissed me yet." She smirked, triggering a chuckle from him. "But ever since you found out Jayden was going to work at the clinic, you've been acting different."

Emmett sighed. "Yeah ... his return has me shaken up."

"Brooke told me he's a twin too."

He nodded. "It brings back so much pain and sadness. The three of us were best friends—like you and your set of twins."

"They're great."

He smiled. "Things changed when we lost Lily. He left, and he never looked back. I try to trust people to the best of my ability, but I lost my dad at a young age, my girlfriend died, and I lost my best friend."

She reached for Emmett's hand and shuffled under the covers so she could rest her head on his shoulder. "That's a lot to handle all at once."

He sighed. "Maybe I'm more broken than I realize."

She lifted her head and with the tip of her thumb and index finger, she moved his face toward her. "And that's okay. It's okay to be broken. You and I are together for a reason, it's so we can pick up the pieces of our pasts *together*."

"That might take a while."

"That's okay. It could take a lifetime, all I care is that I'm spending it with you."

Emmett kissed Autumn, and they sank into each other's embrace. There was a comfort Autumn had never experienced in knowing they both understood each other's pain. They had both been hurt, and they would heal together.

Emmett pulled off his shirt and pants, throwing them to the floor, and slipped under the covers. He wrapped his arms around Autumn, pulling her close, but didn't kiss her again. Instead, he hovered over her face, smiling.

"There's something I came here to ask you."

Autumn giggled as his hand snaked up her torso, tickling her. "Oh?"

"I was wondering how you would feel about a little getaway this weekend?"

"I would love that. Where are we going?"

Emmett grinned, sinking down to trail kisses from her neck to her ear. "It's a surprise."

10

The next morning, Emmett and Autumn headed out of town. He still hadn't told her where they were going, but this trip seemed different. He hadn't been as talkative in the car, a clear indicator that there was something bothering him. She didn't question him, believing he would tell her when he was ready.

The environment whizzing past them changed. Farmlands disappeared, replaced by seas of pine trees. In the distance, mountains erupted from the horizon. The road they traveled on became thinner as they wove through the pines. A dirt track led through the trees, stopping at a secluded cabin. They passed several of these modest homes until Emmett pulled up to a similar cabin. A fire pit sat in front, and behind, a beautiful sky-blue lake glittered in the midday sun.

"How did you find this place?" Autumn asked, unloading the car.

"My parents would bring me here as a kid. I've never brought anyone here before," he admitted.

"Well, don't I feel special." She kissed his cheek.

"That's because you are."

Inside the cabin was a kitchen, a fireplace, two bedrooms each connected to a bathroom, and a nice outdoor porch presenting a view of the lake. The idea of sharing this entire place with Emmett made Autumn blush.

After getting settled in, she changed into something more comfortable. When she entered the living area, Emmett was nowhere to be seen, but she soon found him on the back porch, leaning his forearms on the banister, staring out over the water. His expression was faraway, lost in thought. Autumn crept up behind him and wrapped her arms around his chest, placing her head against his back.

"Is there something you're not telling me?" she asked.

Next to her ear, his heartbeat increased.

"My father lives ten minutes from here," he said. Autumn pulled back as he turned, but he kept his eyes down. "I'm thinking about taking you up on your offer to join me when I see him. If it's still on the table?"

"Of course. I'd do anything for you."

His hand came up to cup her jaw, and he pulled her to him. The kiss was gentle, but as his hand snaked to the small of her back, more warmth slipped into it. She lifted her arms, placing one behind his head, and lifted her from the floor.

She giggled through their kiss as he carried her to the master bedroom and laid her on the bed, where they continued to kiss. Every time his soft lips touched her, from her mouth to her neck to her chest to her stomach, electricity shot through her body. Being in his arms made her feel alive.

The next morning, the pile of clothes on the bed grew as Autumn tried to choose an outfit. She wanted to leave a great first impression. After digging through her luggage, she settled on a simple, grey long-sleeved sweater and denim jeans.

"What do you think?" she asked, turning away from the mirror.

Emmett leaned against the bedroom doorframe and took a sip of his morning coffee. "You look beautiful."

She went to him. "I know you're saying that because you don't want me to go through my luggage a third time."

"Can you blame me?"

She rolled her eyes. "All right, let's get going."

On the road, Emmett remained silent. She knew he was apprehensive, so she held his hand as they drove. Following the guidance of their navigation system, they pulled up outside a cabin with two rocking chairs on its front porch. Weeds and grass had been left to grow untamed, taking over the entirety of the path to the front door and snaking up the stairs. Emmett hadn't told his father he was coming. Autumn guessed that was so he'd have an opportunity to change his mind.

He turned the engine off, and they sat in the car in silence.

"Are you ready?" Autumn whispered.

Emmett sighed. "It's now or never, right?"

"I'll be next to you the whole time," she said, still holding his hand.

Emmett's face shifted, the stress falling from it and being replaced with a smile. They got out of the car and walked to the front door, knocking a couple of times.

No answer.

Emmett walked around to the edge of the porch and looked in through the dark window. "Doesn't look like he's around." He walked back to Autumn. "Maybe we should—"

Autumn smiled as she opened the front door, which had been left unlocked. "You're not off the hook just yet."

Emmett gave her a shy smile. "You're smart." He poked his head through the open door. "Henry?"

Still no response.

They walked through the living room, which was cleaner than the outside. The walls were made of natural wood, red carpet covered the floor, and old pictures of Emmett with his father hung on the walls. Emmett walked to the table across from the brown couch and found a bowl of chicken noodle soup, still warm. He glanced at Autumn.

She shrugged. "Maybe he's in the kitchen."

As they walked into the kitchen, they found his father holding on to the edge of the sink and looking out the back window. His white hair was messy, long enough to cover his ears, as if he hadn't seen a barber in some time.

"Hey, Henry?" Emmett said.

No answer.

"Henry," he said again, but it wasn't until the third time he called his father's name that he turned around.

"Son? What are you doing here?"

"You wanted to see me ..." Emmett said, voice level, emotionless. "We were in town, and I thought—"

Henry's coughs erupted beyond his control. Autumn poured him a glass of water while Emmett studied his father's demeanor from the doorway, almost as if he was too afraid to come any closer. Henry continued to cough but tried to speak.

"I missed you, son. I'm sorry, I—" Henry said as Autumn handed him the water. Before the glass touched his lips, it slipped through his fingers, shattering on the ground. A moment later, Henry followed.

"Henry?" Emmett ran to his father, crouching next to him. "Henry!"

Autumn grabbed her phone and called 911, wishing Emmett wouldn't regret not visiting sooner.

"Will my dad be okay?" Emmett asked Dr. Lopez, who had walked out of his father's bedroom. Emmett and the paramedics had moved Henry from the floor to his bed while Autumn had called the doctor after finding a note stuck to the refrigerator. The paramedics remained on standby outside, ready to transport Henry if Dr. Lopez deemed it necessary.

"He should be okay. It's a side effect of the treatment he's receiving," Dr. Lopez said, placing her stethoscope in her bag.

Emmett clenched his jaw. "What treatment? What are you talking about?"

"Sorry, Emmett, doctor-patient confidentiality. You'll have to ask your father. Call me if you need anything else." Dr. Lopez handed him her card before walking away.

Autumn held on to his arm. "It's going to be okay, Emmett. We'll have to ask your dad about it."

Emmett nodded.

Upon entering Henry's bedroom, she spotted a covered corkboard on the far wall with newspaper clippings. As she neared, she realized the photos were cut-out articles of Emmett's success as a veterinarian. Henry had kept up-to-date with everything Emmett had accomplished over the years.

Henry lay on the bed, covered in his red sheets. He had regained consciousness.

"Henry, what's going on?" Emmett demanded.

"I felt a bit dizzy, nothing too serious."

Emmett sneered. "For once in your life, stop lying to me! Dr. Lopez said something about treatment. Tell me the truth."

Henry took a deep breath and after a long pause said, "I have cancer."

Though Emmet's face remained stoic, his hands balled into fists. His Adam's apple bobbed as he swallowed. "When I decided to come see you, it was so I could demand answers as to why you gave up on Mom and me. Now I can't even do that," he whispered, storming out of the room.

Autumn was about to chase after him when she stopped at the threshold of the room. She looked over her shoulder and noticed Henry's gaze lowered to his chest, avoiding eye contact with her. In that moment, she decided to give Emmett his space and instead walked over to Henry.

"Are you feeling better, Dr. Miller?" she asked.

"You can call me Henry, dear," he sighed. "I knew he would be angry. I don't want him to pity me because this isn't his fault."

"If you mean what you say, he deserves the answers to his questions. I can't tell you what he's thinking right now because I don't know, but I do know your son. He's genuine, caring, and he told me about you."

Henry rubbed his temples. "I bet he had some bad things to say about me, huh?"

"He doesn't understand a lot of the things you did, and that's what brought him here. He's hurting right now, but something I've learned is that Emmett needs his space to think."

"He's much like me in that way. The difference was I ended up pushing people away for it."

Autumn remained silent, at a loss for words, but after a moment she said, "I'm going to check on him, okay? I'll be right back."

She called for Emmett in the house, went into every room, but she couldn't find him. Looking out the window from the living room, she saw his car was still there.

He can't have gone far.

It had become dark outside, but the stars were shining brighter than ever. She walked out of the house to the front yard, where she found Emmett sitting on the grass, obscured by tall weeds. His head tilted to the sky as he took in deep breaths, eyes closed.

Hearing her step down from the porch, he looked up at her. "It's cold out here, you should grab your sweater."

She crossed her arms. "Emmett, talk to me."

He dropped his gaze to look out onto the dirt track that led back to the main road. "I don't understand how this could've happened. I wanted to come here and yell at him. Now ... I'm not sure what to do."

"I think he looked for you so he could apologize. He knows what he did was wrong and can't repair the years lost. I told him how you opened up to me about him, and he mentioned you two were a lot alike and—"

"You did what?" Emmett's head snapped back to look at her, eyes narrowed. "You told him about our conversation?"

"No, I didn't, I—"

He got up, smacking dirt from his jeans. "I trusted you. How could you do that?"

Autumn stepped back, palms raised. "I was trying to help, I—"

"I didn't ask you for that!"

"That's enough!" She pursed her lips and balled her fists, keeping the distance between them. "I'm trying to help you come to peace with what's tearing you apart. Why won't you let me help you, Emmett?"

"Because it's none of your business!" he yelled, but clamped his mouth shut squeezing his eyes closed. He groaned and raised a fist to his forehead.

Tears pushed at the backs of Autumn's eyes, but she held them back. She had to be strong for Mason.

Emmett. This is Emmett, not Mason.

Emmett was looking at her now, pain of many kinds showing in his expression. He took a deep breath and lowered his hand, holding it out to her.

"I'm sorry for shouting," he said, taking a step toward her.

But Autumn took another step back, despite the hurt in his eyes. Emmett was speaking to her the same way Mason had. Her utter disappointment showed on her face. She had vowed to herself that she wouldn't let anyone else speak to her that way again.

She let out a shaky breath. "I thought we were in this together. I guess I was wrong," she whispered, walking away from him.

"Autumn, I'm sorry, I—"

"No. You know what, Emmett?" She swung to face him, her face flaring red with anger. "You don't get to talk to me that way. You're angry and frustrated, but I will not be someone's punching bag again!"

She stormed off, away from Emmett and into the woods.

11

Autumn trekked through the forest using the light of her cellphone to guide her. She had walked around the same fallen trees for what felt like hours. She couldn't be too far from the cabin, but her sense of direction had never been her strong suit. Autumn was lost, but she was also losing sensation in her fingers and could feel her lips turning blue. She had made dumb decisions before, but walking outside in cold weather, without a sweater, had made the top of the list.

She started walking slower, trying to stop thinking about the cold and instead focus on her argument with Emmett. He had been upset, but was he right to be? Had it been none of her business? Did this mean he didn't see a future with her?

Leaves rustled. Autumn froze.

She lifted her phone to dispel the shadows from around her, peering between the trees.

Crack.

She spun, darting the light around, up, down, left, right. A shadow protruded from a distant tree. Something moved, shifting leaves underfoot. Autumn's heart rate sky-rocketed, it sounded like it was moving toward her. She stumbled back, catching her foot on a tree root, causing her to trip. Her back hit a hard trunk as a quick creature slinked by, trundling back into the shadows—a raccoon.

She took a couple of deep breaths to calm herself, but the moment of respite was short-lived when footsteps replaced the silence—heavy ones that cracked over bracken. They were walking in her direction.

"Hello? Is anyone out there?" she cried out in a panic, flashing her phone in the direction she'd heard the footsteps.

No response.

She took a couple of steps forward, and the stranger's steps mimicked her own. Someone was following her.

Don't panic. There was no reason for her to be afraid. What could she be afraid of right now?

She chuckled to herself. Mountain lions, coyotes, bobcats, bears … Mason.

What if he was out here? Would he be foolish enough to still be following her?

She continued for a few more miles before she came to an abrupt stop. As she suspected, the footsteps behind her continued for a beat longer, unsuspecting of her actions. Fear crawled up Autumn's spine, goosebumps on her arms and legs. *Run.*

Following her instincts, she sprinted into the forest, leaping over logs and ditches, pushing aside branches and bushes, but that didn't stop twigs from snagging at her clothes and scratching her skin, like fingers reaching to keep her in this moment of panic. She had no clue where she was running toward, but she needed to get out of the forest. She needed to get home.

An intense pressure developed in her chest as she pulled in fruitless breaths of air. Her chest ached. The cold was getting to her, freezing her from the inside. A protruding branch snagged at her shirt. She turned to dislodge it, but her foot twisted under her, and she lost her balance.

She let out a shriek as she tumbled over the uneven ground, rolling over soft moss and hard rocks until she came to a stop when her side crashed into a tree.

She lay shivering on the ground, staring up at the night sky, body pained by scratches and bruises. The footsteps had stopped, it seemed like she'd gotten away from whomever it was, but judging by the darkness, she'd be lucky if she was found by people she *wanted* to see again.

Emmett surfaced in her thoughts. She wanted things to be okay between them.

A heavy shiver shook her, making her groan as she agitated her bruised ribs. She didn't think anything was broken, but the cold was getting to her. She tried to reach for the trunk beside her, but her hand flew through the air and slapped the wood, pointless and numb. Above, the leaves silhouetted by the moonlight spun in slow, dizzying circles. *I'm going to die out here.*

Drowsiness began to pull at her eyelids as something emerged from the silence—footsteps.

"He ... llo?" she slurred, lips too cold to enunciate.

The footsteps continued by, somewhere above, near where Autumn had fallen. With each passing moment, they began to fade.

No! She summoned her last ounce of strength, inhaling a painful breath of air, and shouted, "HERE!"

The footsteps stopped as Autumn closed her eyes, letting her head fall back. The shout had made everything spin, she couldn't focus anymore.

But the person was coming closer, their steps echoing off the trees. They kneeled beside her. "Did you think you could run from me?"

She yanked her eyes open to see a figure hovering over her. Her blurry vision couldn't make out who it was. Her eyes fluttered closed once more as a pair of lips found her ear, breathing down her neck. "I'll follow you until the end of time."

"No ..." she moaned, pulling her eyes open once more.

But there was nobody there. The forest was empty and silent except for her labored breathing.

Darkness descended once again. Her thoughts slowed, and time became nonexistent. She could no longer open her eyes, even when strong arms jostled her, lifting her from the ground, taking her who knew where.

When Autumn woke up, she did so with a scream. The blanket that had been covering her had slipped off, pooling on the floor. She was back at the cabin and was on a rocking chair in front of a fireplace.

Emmett sprinted toward her from the kitchen, "Autumn, are you all right?"

"I-I thought—" She shook her head. "I was so scared."

"You were ice cold when I found you." He went back to the kitchen to grab a couple of mugs, the enticing scent of hot chocolate drifting toward Autumn. "You'll be okay, you need to warm up. Here, drink this." He handed her the mug before sitting in the chair next to her. He stared into the fireplace as he said, "I'm sorry. I shouldn't have said the things I did."

Autumn gazed into her mug with an empty expression, noting how her side ached as she lifted her right arm. "Your words hurt me."

"I know."

"No, you don't." She scowled. "You know what he put me through. I promised myself I would never let anyone else make me feel weak. I promised myself I wouldn't love anyone ever again, but you changed that. You saved me from a life alone, so it hurt a lot more than you realize."

Emmett remained silent for a moment. "You're right. I was a jerk. I lashed out at the wrong person, and all you were trying to do was help. I know you're not Lily, but at times I feel like you're going to leave me like she did." He sighed. "Every relationship has its hurdles—even ours."

Autumn lowered her hot chocolate to her thighs, warming them. "Where does that leave us?"

"We're going to love each other, we're going to support each other, and sometimes we're going to argue." He grinned. "But we'll get through it together."

"I like that," she said as a shiver rippled from her arms down to her legs.

Emmett lifted the blanket from the floor and draped it over her knees. "Will you forgive me, lil' dove?"

"Why do you have to make things so difficult?" She pulled the blanket over her reddening face. "You know I love it when you call me that."

He placed his mug on the coffee table and kneeled in front of her, placing his hands on her knees. She let out a heavy sigh and placed her hands over his.

"I'm sorry for being a jerk." He paused, looking up at her like a puppy. "I'm all in, lil' dove."

"I guess I can find it in my heart to forgive you," she teased, leaning down to kiss him, despite her bruises.

Emmett returned to Henry's home the next day. Autumn had agreed to wait in the living room while Emmett made his way to Henry's bedroom. Instead of directing his anger toward Autumn, he needed to tackle the root of the problem.

He walked into his father's bedroom, where Henry was looking through some old newspaper clippings.

"How long?" Emmett demanded while he stood by the door.

Henry placed one of the newspaper articles down. "I've known for a couple of months. I have stage three prostate cancer."

"I want to be mad at you."

His father glanced up at him. "I know."

Emmett shook his head. "No, you don't. I lived my whole childhood thinking about what it would be like to have my father around. Do you know what it's like to see your friends with both their parents and wonder what you did to make one of them leave?"

He entered the room and began to pace, "And now, when I was ready to tell you how I felt, I find out that you're leaving me again." His voice was starting to strain against the blockage in his throat, so he stopped and swallowed.

"I'm sorry, Emmett," Henry said. "I don't expect you to forgive me, and I don't want you to pity me. Leaving you was the hardest thing I ever did."

"Why did you do it?"

Henry took a deep breath. "When I was in high school my mother left my father and me. My father found himself in a dark place and became an alcoholic. He didn't want me to go to veterinary school because he didn't want to be left alone. My goal was to make some money to get us off the ground, but he didn't see it that way. He believed that was his responsibility. Every time I walked in the house, he reeked of alcohol, and I remember arriving late so I wouldn't have to see him."

Henry continued, "He pushed me away, so I pushed people away too. Elizabeth tried to remind me it wasn't my fault and shielded you from ever seeing me in a vulnerable state. Having you was the best thing that ever happened to me, but I was already falling into my father's footsteps. I am a recovering alcoholic, Emmett."

Emmett studied his father, connecting the dots from his past. He remembered coming home and his dad locking himself in his home office, and never understanding why. His mom would say Henry didn't feel well, and there was a point when Emmett started to feel like Henry didn't love him. Could Emmett blame Henry for falling into the same footsteps as his father? In a sense, Henry had tried to protect Emmett from seeing him at his worst, but that still didn't make up for the time he had been left without a dad.

"I can't forget all those years of abandonment, but I want to try to forgive you," Emmett whispered.

"I know it won't happen overnight, but thank you, Emmett." Henry paused for a moment. "But I don't want you to make the same mistakes I did."

"What do you mean?"

"Where's your girlfriend, son?"

Emmett looked out the bedroom window, avoiding his father's gaze. "She's waiting in the living room. I said some horrible things to her last night."

"Do you love her?"

What was there not to love about Autumn? She was perfect. She was beautiful, smart, and down to earth. She never let her scars define who she was, but she let them shape her into who she wanted to be. There was a moment in his life when he thought he would never love again, but she had changed that. Did he love her? The answer was—

"Yes."

"If she's here, it's because she's already forgiven you." Henry stood, while Emmett supported his balance, "and it will be your actions that prove whether you were worth forgiving."

"Is this your attempt to give me fatherly advice?"

Henry chuckled. "Emphasis on the 'attempt.'"

With a cunning smile, Emmett watched his father walk toward the living room, until he whispered, "Not bad."

Autumn had already set out cups of coffee for Emmett and Henry by the time they joined her in the living room. As she took a seat across the coffee table from them, Emmett and Henry alternated between thoughtful silence and small talk, which indicated to Autumn that their father-son relationship would take some time to rebuild.

"How are you feeling today?" Emmett asked Henry.

"I'm feeling better. The chemotherapy drains me, but I'm optimistic." Henry stirred his coffee. "When are you headed back?" Henry asked.

"Tomorrow, but I wanted to stop by before we left."

Autumn spotted an orange photo album underneath the coffee table. "Maybe you can tell us some stories," she suggested.

Henry nodded. "I've got plenty."

When Autumn opened the album, the first set of photos showed Henry in his football jersey and photos of him at a football game. It prompted Henry to spend most of the time talking about his favorite football team and the time he won the state football championships.

"Do you like sports?" Emmett teased, his tone sarcastic.

Henry chuckled. "You could say that."

As Autumn flipped through the next few pages, Autumn spotted a photograph of a young Henry, holding a girl's hands. She had long, ginger hair, freckles, and hazel eyes. She was beautiful.

"That doesn't look like Elizabeth," she observed.

Henry grinned, "That's because it isn't."

"Who is it?" Emmett asked, glancing over at the photo.

Henry adjusted his glasses. "We all have a first love, and Katherine was mine," he began. "We were friends, but it became something much deeper. Since we both had screwed up families, one day she convinced me to run away. She bought the train tickets, and we agreed to meet at the station one night."

Autumn smiled. "Sounds romantic."

Henry nodded but didn't smile. "It should have been. I had to go home and pick up some things the night we were leaving. On my way, I was robbed and beaten. I was at the hospital for two days, and when I woke up, I tried to get a hold of Katherine, but she was gone. I never saw her again."

Autumn's fingers covered her mouth. "I'm sorry, Henry."

"I'm not. The incident led me to meet Emmett's mom in college. I might not have been there all those years, but Emmett was the best thing that ever happened to me."

A ghost of a smile snuck onto Emmett's face at that, but he didn't address the comment. Instead, he asked, "Do you ever wonder what happened to her?"

"I do," Henry nodded, gazing at the photo. "I hurt her by not showing up that night. I would give anything to at least apologize to her."

Autumn looked at Emmett, who was studying his father. She couldn't imagine what it would be like to lose someone you care about over something you couldn't control. In her heart, she knew she never wanted to lose Emmett.

Later in the evening, after saying their goodbyes to Henry, they decided to go on an evening hike. Autumn had a head start and got to the top of the hill first, where she admired the view of the forest as the sun began to set. It had been the longest weekend of her life. What was intended to be a romantic getaway had turned out to be an interesting adventure. Through it all, she knew one thing—Emmett had let her in. Though he had built walls around his heart, he had let *her* in. She wondered why, what had changed?

"Thinking about me?" Emmett whispered into her ear.

Autumn jumped but calmed. She was getting used to Emmett's surprises. His presence, however, continued to have a soothing effect on her.

"How did you know?" she asked, feeling her cheeks turn pink.

Emmett smiled. "I always wish I'm one of the people you like to think about."

"Well, someone seems to have a big ego."

"It shows when I'm around you."

"And why is that?" Autumn teased, turning to face him. She wrapped her arms around his neck as Emmett looked into her eyes. As the sun dipped behind the mountains, fireflies began to awaken from the bushes, taking flight to surround them where they stood.

Autumn tiptoed to kiss his soft lips. There was something different about this kiss. In the past, their kisses had sent an electric current through her body, but now they flooded her senses with an all-encompassing warmth.

"I love you," Emmett said.

Autumn grinned. "Took you long enough."

Emmett brought her closer to him, kissing her once more, neither of them wanting their trip to come to an end.

12

"HE SAID WHAT?" Ortus exclaimed.

Brooke took a sip of her hazelnut latte. "That's so adorable."

"Don't you think it's too soon?" Ortus said.

"How long did it take Jordan to say I love you?" Autumn asked.

Ortus picked at her banana bread muffin. "Two days."

Both Autumn and Brooke rolled their eyes. Autumn had arrived back in Maplewood that morning, and her friends hadn't even given her time to unpack before they demanded she meet them at the café for all the latest gossip.

"Anyway, what did he say when you said it back?" Ortus asked, gliding her cherry flavored ChapStick to her lips.

Autumn's smile vanished from her face. "Oh my gosh."

There was a beat of silence before Brooke's mouth dropped open. "You didn't say it back?"

Autumn covered her face. "Does saying, 'took you long enough' not count?"

"No!" Brooke and Ortus exclaimed.

"I kissed him back! Doesn't that make it obvious?"

Ortus shook her head. "Good thing men don't overthink this stuff."

"I beg to differ. Have you met my brother?" Brooke said.

Ortus hummed. "Good point."

Autumn bit her lip, drumming her fingers on the side of her mug. "What am I supposed to do now?"

Ortus shrugged. "If you don't feel it, you should never fake that you do."

"I guess the question is ..." Brooke leveled Autumn with a hard stare, "do you love him?"

Did she love Emmett Miller? He looked at her like she was the sole woman in the world. He reminded her how strong she was. Sure, he wasn't perfect, but to Autumn, he didn't have to be. So, did Autumn love Emmett Miller?

She looked up at them and smiled. "I do."

"Then why do you look like you're about to barf?" Brooke asked.

Ortus rubbed the back of Autumn's back. "You're green, are you all right?"

"I'm fine, I..." Autumn trailed off, letting out a slow breath as a lump appeared in her throat, her muffin finding its way back up. She covered her mouth and sprinted from their table.

"When people say it's great to be lovesick, they don't mean literally, you know?" Ortus called out as Autumn pushed through the crowd of people waiting in line for coffee.

"Watch where you're going!" a teenage girl yelled after her.

Autumn would apologize later, because in this moment, she needed to get to the restroom, and she didn't care who stood in her way.

"I walked through my front door a couple of minutes ago, why does it have to be now?" Emmett spoke into his phone. Bradley had called almost as soon as Emmett had gotten off the phone with Autumn, who wasn't feeling well, demanding they meet at Maplewood Park.

"Because I'm making a conscious effort to improve my health and fitness?"

"Okay, and what's the real reason?"

Bradley let out a frustrated sigh. "Brooke bet Ortus I couldn't commit to working out at the park without being tempted by the cotton candy stand. I need to prove her wrong. Get over here now!"

Emmett couldn't remember the last time he'd seen Bradley attempt to work out, and what's more, he couldn't remember the last time Bradley had said no to food.

He sighed. "Okay, I'll be right over."

Once he was able to find his sweats and sweater, he headed to the park. A heavy overcast hung over Maplewood. He knew their training wouldn't last long before the rain caught them. In the middle of the open grass, he found Bradley, also dressed in sweats and a sweater, struggling to do burpees.

"Your form is all wrong," Emmett pointed out as he dropped his bag and water bottle onto the ground.

"We're not all as ripped as you," Bradley said as he wiped the sweat off his forehead.

"You're one of the lucky ones who has a fast metabolism. All you need to do is start training at least three times a week and you'll be in better shape."

Bradley rolled his eyes.

"Hey, Emmett! Bradley, I didn't expect to see you here."

Bradley and Emmett both turned to see Ethan striding up to them in maroon sweats and a hoodie, a water bottle on a string dangling from his wrist and a towel draped over his shoulder.

Bradley scowled. "Why not Emmett?"

Ethan grasped Emmett's hand and slapped him on the shoulder with his other. "Emmett and I have worked out together a few times. Mind if I join you?"

"Not, not at all," Bradley mumbled, turning back to Emmett. "Anyway, how was your trip?"

"Fine."

"Uh-oh, what happened?" Bradley sank onto the grass, beginning his sit-ups.

"Nothing, I had a great time with Autumn."

Emmett and Ethan joined Bradley on the ground. While Emmett went at his own speed, Ethan started slow, but picked up his pace as soon as he realized

Bradley was trying to compete with him. Bradley let out a heavy grunt of exhaustion and flopped back onto the grass.

"Maybe you shouldn't try to compete with me," Ethan said, looking down at Bradley.

"I'm not trying to compete with you."

Ethan rolled his eyes and turned to look at Emmett. "What's up with you?"

Emmett paused mid sit-up. "What do you mean?"

"I know that look. What's on your mind, Emmett?"

Emmett pursed his lips and sat up, relaxing back on his hands. "I told Autumn I love her, and I'm not sure if she said it back."

Bradley shot upright. "She didn't say it back?"

"Does saying, 'took you long enough' count?" he asked, shameless.

Bradley rolled his eyes in frustration. "No!"

Emmett had felt confident when he told Autumn he loved her, but her response had him questioning whether she felt the same. She wouldn't have spent the whole weekend with him if she didn't, right? One thing was for sure, he didn't want her to feel pressured to say it back if she wasn't ready.

"Do you think she feels the same way, even if she didn't say it?" Emmett asked.

"Er ... yeah, sure," Bradley muttered, avoiding eye contact.

Emmett faced Ethan, who had started his set of burpees. He seemed to be invested in working out.

"What do you think?" Emmett asked him.

Ethan paused and grabbed his water bottle, taking a couple of sips before responding. "Stop overthinking it. She loves you. If she didn't, she wouldn't be with you right now. It *is* a little odd she didn't say it back, but maybe that was her special way of saying it."

"You're wise."

"That's what I tell him," Bradley said, cotton candy in hand.

Emmett's jaw dropped. "When did you even leave?"

"When Ethan decided to throw you his words of wisdom."

Ethan shrugged and returned to his workout. Emmett, on the other hand, laughed as his shoulders dropped, feeling more at ease. He knew Autumn struggled to let people in too, but she had chosen him, and he wasn't going to take that for granted. Even if she didn't say it back, he believed she felt something for him, and whether or not she would call it love didn't matter.

After their exercise session and being drenched by the rain, they headed to El Corazon del Pan. When they arrived, Ethan walked around the counter to the woman there, wrapped his arm around her waist, and gave her a peck on her cheek.

"Bradley, back for your usual?" the woman said, letting go of Ethan.

Bradley nodded. "You know it."

"Honey, this is Emmett," Ethan said. "Emmett, this is Marisol."

"Nice to meet you." She grabbed a plate of bread and handed it to Bradley.

"You made Autumn's birthday cake," Emmett remembered.

Marisol smiled, walking out from behind the counter to stand next to Ethan. "Yes. And you must be the guy she said yes to."

"Oh, is this the boyfriend that likes to keep secrets?" Ethan teased. Emmett felt his ears turn red, and Ethan chuckled. "It's all right. We all struggle to trust others at first. I think what matters in the end is being able to trust the person you've chosen to be in love with." He eyed Marisol, nudging her.

"It's still a sore spot for Emmett, though," Bradley said, mouth half-filled with coffee cake.

Emmett rolled his eyes, glaring at Bradley, as an inquisitive look crossed Marisol's face. "What does he mean?" she asked.

"Nothing," Emmett grumbled.

"Oh, it's something," Ethan began. "Emmett told Autumn he loved her, and she didn't say it back."

Marisol's mouth fell open. "Did she say anything?"

"She said, 'took you long enough,'" Emmett muttered.

Marisol shook her head. "She loves you back, you idiot. If I know her, she's beating herself up about it too."

"I was thinking it might be hard for her to say because of what she's been through," Emmett said as he raised his water bottle to his mouth.

"I mean it could be ... granted I base my opinion off of what I've heard in town," she warned. "She also might think you already know."

"When are you going to get married?" Bradley asked.

Emmett spit out his water, making a mess on the counter but causing Marisol and Ethan to laugh. "Why are you asking that now?" He paused. "Wait, has Autumn said something?"

Bradley chortled. "No. I knew you'd freak."

"What's stopping you from asking, though?" Marisol asked.

Emmett cast an incredulous look at each of them. "We've known each other for like six months. It's too soon ... right?"

Ethan shrugged. "That's about the amount of time it took me to propose to Marisol."

Marisol flashed her ring. "I thought it was soon too, but you don't have to wait for love when you know it's right in front of you."

Emmett scoffed. "I ... I don't think she's ready."

Marisol crossed her arms. "I think she might be. The question is, are you?"

Marriage had crossed Emmett's mind once. The month before Lily's accident, he had gone with Jayden to look at rings. He had wanted an estimate on how much he needed to save up for one. It shocked him to know the cost, but he didn't care, he wanted to be with her. After she died, marriage had never crossed his mind. What was stopping him? He knew he was in love with Autumn.

He grabbed some bread for the road, leaving Marisol's question unanswered. Outside, rain had started pummeling the sidewalk. He ran to his car as the water soaked through his jacket and was on the verge of pressing the ignition button when he received a call from Autumn.

"How are you feeling?" he asked.

She drew in a deep breath. "A lot better. I've stopped vomiting."

"I'm glad to hear that."

"Listen ..." She hesitated. Emmett could picture her biting her lip. "If ... if you don't have plans for tonight, I would love to see you. There's something I need to tell you."

His heart skipped a beat. "I need to go shower, but I'll be there."

"Shower? Where did you go?"

"Bradley took me to the park to work out, but it resulted in him doing like three push-ups and walking away with cotton candy."

Autumn started to laugh. He hadn't heard her laugh in what felt like ages. The pure sound filled him with joy, it was like hearing his favorite song.

"I know, I was as surprised as you are," he said.

She giggled. "I'll see you tonight," she said as he hung up the phone.

As he drove back to his place, he thought of Autumn. He believed she loved him back, but she had been through so much with Mason, he wanted her to tell him when she was ready.

Lost in thought, he arrived at an intersection. He felt a presence, as if someone were watching him. He glanced to the car on his left, where he saw a man in a brown hoodie turn toward him. Through the shadows and the rain making its way down the windows, Emmett could make out a smirk beneath the man's hood and a manilla envelope on his dashboard.

Emmett's stomach dropped.

It was sudden, but the car sped away, and following his instincts, Emmett followed. He was confident the man was Mason. His breathing deepened as the car accelerated, and he tightened his grip on the steering wheel. He wouldn't let that man get to Autumn again.

As Mason made a sharp turn, Emmett followed, almost flipping his car on the slippery road. Mason turned again into a residential area. Fear took over Emmett's body.

Shit. He knows where she lives.

But the thought had distracted him. He turned his wheel at the last second to follow, skidding with the speed. Rain swiped across his windshield, obscuring his vision as the car drifted over a puddle. The wheels left the road, hydroplaning. He'd lost control. A lamppost approached. Emmett lifted his arms as the side of his truck crumpled. Pain consumed his entire right side as the windows shattered, scattering broken glass over him.

All went quiet besides the hissing of the smoke erupting from the hood in front of him. Through the haze, he could make out the fading break lights of Mason's car.

He groaned through gritted teeth and turned his head right, then left. His door had caved in toward him. He moved his legs, feeling pain, but wasn't sure where it was coming from. The important part was that he could move.

Swiping away the fabric of the airbag, he undid his seatbelt and twisted left, grimacing with every movement. He pulled himself onto the passenger seat, opened the door and spilled onto the road with another painful grunt. There he remained, catching his breath. Blood trailed down his forehead to his nose, and onto the ground, forming a small, red puddle. The single thought on his mind was to get back to Autumn. If Mason was in town, she was in danger.

The rain was getting heavier, washing the blood from his face and soaking his clothes, freezing him. His eyelids lowered.

"Hey, are you all right?" a woman's voice said.

Emmett opened his eyes and, for a short moment, they remained open. He couldn't believe who was standing over him. A woman with long brown hair and caramel-colored eyes met his.

"Lily?" Emmett whispered.

The woman leaned closer to him, concerned. "No, I'm sorry, hon. My name is Alice. Please try to stay awake."

It was for a small moment when he opened his eyes again, realizing the woman standing over him was older and looked nothing like the woman he once loved.

"Please find Autumn," he whispered.

Somebody was patting his face. He opened his eyes. A man was leaning over him, shining a flashlight in them. Nearby, red and blue lights flashed, lighting up the street.

"He's awake," the man said to someone over his shoulder, before redirecting back down to Emmett. "What's your name?"

"Em ... Emmett ... Miller," he replied as a shroud cloaked his thoughts once again.

"Try to stay with us, Emmett."

He yanked his eyes open again. Bright lights surrounded him, pushing into his pupils, making his head pound even more than it already was. He groaned. He was so tired.

The cool hospital air hit his body as his clothes were cut away. Someone pulled on his eyelid, flashing a light in it. The brightness hurt, and Emmett lifted his hand to swat it away, but it didn't rise farther than his waist.

"You'll be okay, Emmett," someone said. "Your wife is on her way."

"Wife?" he muttered.

"Your girlfriend is on her way." The medic clarified, "Please stay awake, don't close your eyes."

But it was too late.

Braving the rain, Autumn drove to the local grocery store to grab items for dinner. She knew he would be surprised to see her cook, but she owed him after not saying the three words she knew he wanted to hear. She figured cooking would help ease her into telling him she loved him.

"Hey there, gorgeous," Jayden said, approaching her.

Autumn rolled her eyes and bagged a few carrots. "Always a pleasure running into you, isn't it?"

Jayden smirked. "Why do you refuse to acknowledge that you enjoy my company?"

"Maybe because I don't know anything about you." She moved along to the potatoes, ignoring Jayden but expecting he would follow.

"Oh, come on. You know I'm a veterinarian, you know I like classic books…"

Autumn hummed. "Superficial stuff."

"Well, what else would you want to know?"

She turned to him as she placed a bag of potatoes into her shopping cart. "You always act like you have everything under control, but your eyes tell me something different. I see pain and sorrow. I'm wondering what brought you back to Maplewood."

Jayden's chin jutted back, creating a fold beneath it. He opened his mouth, closed it, raised a finger, then dropped it. "I don't think you're interested in knowing my life problems, Autumn."

"So, you admit there are problems ..." she remarked, and he clamped his lips shut. "But I am interested," she continued. "I know we're still strangers to one another, but I want to help you. I don't like seeing someone suffer the way you seem to be. I've been there. It's ..." She sighed and shook her head, moving along to select some pasta.

Jayden followed in silence, chewing on the inside of his cheek. As Autumn selected a packet of noodles, he took a deep breath.

"My father died at the end of my senior year," he began.

Autumn looked at him over the noodles. "I'm sorry to hear that."

Jayden nodded. "A friend had taken me to a graduation party, which I'd been hesitant to go to. I was an awkward teenager, so party scenes weren't my thing. I had too many drinks that night, and the friend who brought me disappeared, leaving me behind."

He continued, "I had to call my dad to come pick me up. He wasn't happy, but he was like my best friend, so I didn't think it would be such a big deal. He came to pick me up and, on the way back ..." He paused, clearing his throat. "We skidded off the road."

Jayden sighed. "Losing him was the most difficult thing I had to go through. My sister and Emmett helped me through that pain. When my sister died, I ran away from everything, but I could never run away from the pain. It was destroying me from the inside. I came back to Maplewood because I knew she wouldn't want me to be alone."

"You know," Autumn said, placing the noodles into her cart, "I've learned that it's never too late to reconnect with old friends. I pushed them all away, and it took some time, but we've rebuilt what we lost. You can too."

He shrugged. "I still feel out of place, but I'm optimistic."

She studied Jayden, his expression revealed the guilt he held within him. It was something she was all too accustomed to, and it never got her anywhere. It had taken her time to forgive herself, and when she had, she realized there was nothing she had to forgive herself for, because she hadn't done anything wrong. Mason had.

"You're still hurting, Jayden. You're blaming yourself for something you couldn't control. That guilt can consume your whole life and prevent you from living a good one. Is that something your dad or your sister would want?"

Before he could respond, Autumn's phone buzzed. She pulled it from her pocket with an apologetic look at Jayden, but he waved his hand that it was fine.

"Hey, Brooke," Autumn answered, paused, and frowned. "Slow down, what are you saying?"

She dropped the canned tomatoes she'd been holding, feeling her heart go numb. Brooke's voice faded into the background.

"Autumn, what's wrong?" Jayden placed a hand on her shoulder.

"It's Emmett ... he—" But she couldn't get the words out. Everything around her started to spin. Jayden's voice beside her sounded like it was miles away. Around her, the grocery aisles blurred as she lost her balance, dropping like a stone.

13

Maplewood's bookstore wasn't a place to buy books, it was a place to meet with friends for a coffee, relax into a story, or study for a test. Comfortable red sofas decorated the front of the store. The walls were rustic red brick, the floors brown wood, and a spiral staircase led to the upper level where the fiction books and the café were located. Emmett closed his eyes as he entered and took a moment to breathe in the smell of coffee that flowed through the store, intermingling with the nostalgic scent of hardcovers.

The bookstore was his safe space, where he often hid from the town. Already knowing where he needed to go, he walked up the staircase to the second floor. As he navigated the shelves, he found himself stepping over bodies with books in their laps, engrossed in their stories. It was comforting to know he wasn't alone in viewing the bookstore as an escape.

He had spent the last couple of days searching for the new edition of his favorite book, *Pride and Prejudice*. After requesting the book to be stocked at the Maplewood bookstore, he had rushed over to find it. He scanned the shelf, finding the book in the middle—it was the last copy—and as he reached for it, his hand touched another's.

"Oh!" the person whispered.

Emmett followed the other hand up to a face, somewhat hidden by a head of long, brown hair. The woman swept it aside, revealing caramel eyes and a shy smile. She looked down at the book they both still held.

"I'm sorry, I believe this is mine," she said, tugging it a little closer to her.

"I got to it first, though," Emmett replied, pulling it back.

She tilted her head. "Listen, it's for my brother. I'm always telling him about how great this book is, and I need him to read it. Besides, his birthday is coming up."

Emmett studied her, trying to determine if she was lying. After a long pause, he let go. "Fine, but you'll have to tell me your name."

"Lily." She smirked and tucked the book under her arm. "My name is Lily Rose."

"Rose? Are you related to Jayden?"

Her eyebrows lifted. "Yes! He's, my brother. Do you know each other?"

Emmett chuckled and rubbed the back of his neck. "He's sort of my best friend."

"Ah, so you must be the famous Emmett Miller I've been hearing so much about?"

This time, Emmett's eyebrows rose. "All good things?"

She giggled. "Sure. Hey, how about we split the cost on this thing?" She pulled out the book. "It can be a gift from both of us."

"Sounds like a plan." Emmett grinned and followed her to the cashier. A warmth emanated from her that made his heart squeeze in his chest. He couldn't take his eyes off her, her smile, her twinkling eyes.

As he handed her a couple of bills to pay for his half, he said, "Do you want to grab an ice cream after this?"

Her smile fell. She turned away from the cashier to face Emmett, looking up at him through shining eyes filled with ... pity?

"Aren't you forgetting about someone, Emmett?"

"Er ..." Emmett stuttered, stopped, and slapped his forehead. "Of course. Jayden. I'm sorry, I shouldn't have asked—"

She shook her head. "No, not my brother. Autumn."

Emmett froze. Reality rushed at him. Color seeped from the environment, dripping away until everything turned white—the floor, the walls, the shelves, even the books themselves. The cashier disappeared, as did everyone on the street outside. Emmett and Lily remained.

Something tickled his forehead. He lifted his hand, touching the wetness there. When he pulled it in front of his eyes, it shone with bright, fresh blood.

"The accident …" he whispered, keeping his eyes on her. "Lily? Where am I?"

"You're in the hospital, Em. Listen …" She fell silent and looked up to the sky.

Emmett did as he was told and listened—for what, he wasn't quite sure. Until he heard it—a muffled, unfamiliar voice, as if somebody were speaking to him from behind a thick wall.

"Stay with us, Emmett. You're going to be okay. Your wife is on her way."

He refocused on Lily. "What are you doing here?"

"Well, you did something stupid, and I'm here to make sure you don't do it again."

He grinned. "You're always trying to keep me out of trouble."

She shook her head. "You idiot. You didn't even know if that was Mason."

"I couldn't risk it."

"You were reckless. If you die, you'd be leaving her unprotected from Mason." She shifted to sit on the cashier's counter, swinging her legs.

He sat beside her. "I know."

She studied him. "You love her, don't you?"

Emmett nodded.

"Why haven't you asked her to marry you?" She nudged him. "Afraid of commitment?"

He shook his head. "This is weird. I'm not going to talk to you in detail about this. Besides, you seem to know so much already."

"I'm a figment of your memories, Em. Of course, I know everything." She placed her hand on his shoulder. "It's okay to move on. You can let me go."

"I didn't even get to say goodbye to you," he whispered.

She pouted in disapproval, "You know how I feel about goodbyes."

He looked at his hands. "I didn't want to lose her too. That's why I didn't think twice about speeding. It was stupid, you're right. I wasn't even sure if it was him."

"We do a lot of stupid things for love. Don't let her go Emmett, she's a good one."

How can this be happening?

Against doctors' orders, Autumn wandered out of her hospital room in search of Emmett. As she walked through the hospital wings, doctors, nurses, and patients watched her with concern. She looked in every room she passed, but there was no sign of Emmett. Autumn somehow ended up in pediatrics and found herself observing the newborn babies.

It seemed like no matter what she and Emmett did, life continued to try to keep them apart. Yet they somehow always found their way back to each other.

"They're cute, aren't they?" Jayden said, approaching her from behind. "How far along are you?"

"How did you—"

"You have the pregnancy glow, it's real you know?"

She sighed, her focus still on the babies. "The doctor said I'm about a month along."

"Congratulations!" he said with enthusiasm, but Autumn remained silent. He gave her a thoughtful look. "Why don't you look more excited?"

She turned to him, biting her lip to hold back the tears. "What if Emmett doesn't wake up?"

"Hey…" Jayden reached out to rub Autumn's shoulder. "It's going to be okay. You need to take care of yourself—for the little one you're carrying. You have to think about them now."

She nodded, dragging the back of her hand across her cheeks to dry them. "I want to see him. Will you help me find his room?"

"Sure," Jayden said. "But let's get a snack for you and the little one first."

After asking a nurse where they could find Emmett, they walked to a vending machine and grabbed a pack of the M&M's Autumn had been craving.

When they arrived at Emmett's room, they found him in a hospital gown, surrounded by monitors. He was breathing on his own, but his face was covered in crusting scratches. There was a long silence, and Autumn burst into tears.

She laid her head on his bed and held his hand. "You have to wake up, my love. For me, for us. We're going to be parents," she said through her tears.

"Autumn?"

Her gaze shifted upward, "Emmett, you're awake!" She said, kissing him. "How are you feeling?"

He scrunched his eyes closed as he shook his head. "I'm okay … I—"

"Easy bud, don't overdo it. You were in a horrific accident," Jayden warned.

He nodded, turning to face Autumn, cringing as he did. "I'm glad you're okay."

She looked at him, placing her hand on his cheek. "Why wouldn't I be?"

Emmett's mouth opened and closed. He looked over her shoulder, in Jayden's direction. Autumn frowned and withdrew her hand.

"Emmett, why where you speeding?" she asked.

"I—" He hesitated again, looking between her and Jayden. Autumn turned to see a peculiar expression on Jayden's face, as if he and Emmett were having another silent conversation.

"I was excited to see you," Emmett said, bringing Autumn's eyes back to him. "You're my world."

Autumn smiled. "Next time be patient, please. You can't leave us."

"Us?"

She stood up and rubbed her stomach. Jayden stood behind her with a huge smile on his face. It took a moment for Emmett to put the pieces together, and when he did his eyes widened.

"No way. Are you serious?" He almost leaped from his bed, when he was reminded to stay put by the wires connected to him. Instead, he cringed through the pain and shuffled until he was sitting up. Autumn propped up the pillows behind him as he did.

She giggled. "We're going to be parents."

"I'm going to be a dad," he said, a little out of breath. After a long pause, he dropped his gaze to the blanket covering his legs. "I'm going to be a father."

Jayden was gentle and patted him on the shoulder. "Congrats, man."

Autumn went to visit Emmett at the hospital every day. They read through a couple of baby books together, preparing for what the coming months would bring them. Their friends visited Emmett daily, and before they knew it, Dr. Alvarez gave the approval to discharge him.

As Autumn packed Emmett's belongings and he walked into the bathroom to change, she heard someone open the door behind her.

"Autumn Marie Evans, when were you going to tell me you were pregnant?"

Autumn flinched and sighed. "I haven't even made it out of the hospital with Emmett. When would I have had time?"

Marie walked to the other side of the bed, hands on her hips. "You're not married. You're not even living under the same roof, and you're going to have a baby."

"Mom, I'm happy. Does that not matter to you at all?"

"Of course it does, but you're not going to be fully happy until you do things the way we planned. You already ruined being a doctor—" Marie pointed at her ring finger "—so you might as well try to get Emmett to put a ring on it."

Emmett walked out of the bathroom. "We found out Autumn was pregnant a couple of days ago. We have plenty of time to plan our futures. This is our plan now, not anybody else's."

Autumn grabbed Emmett's bag as the nurse brought in his wheelchair. Emmett sat in the chair, and the nurse began to wheel him away. Autumn walked to the threshold of the door and looked over her shoulder at Marie. "This is our life now. You won't dictate how we'll live it or how we'll raise our child."

Before Marie could respond, Autumn was already out the door and following close behind the father of her child.

Later in the evening, in Autumn's apartment, Emmett was lying on the couch, sore and stiff from his injuries. Her sister and friends overwhelmed them with attention since they'd left the hospital.

"What did the doctor say about your injuries?" J.J. asked.

"To get some rest. They kept saying how lucky I was." He turned to Autumn. "Which I agreed with. I'm lucky to be here with you and our little one."

Autumn smiled.

"Did you know that babies can hear music from inside the womb?" Bradley said, flipping through the baby book he was reading. He had been excited to hear Autumn was carrying a child and was now calling himself a baby whisperer.

Brooke sat on the rug in front of them, rolling her eyes. "Yes. That's the fifth time you've said that today."

"Bradley, I think we've got this," Autumn said as she sat beside Emmett, careful not to jostle him.

Emmett chuckled. "Don't spoil his fun. He's going to be the godfather, after all," he said.

Bradley gasped while Brooke's hand flew to her forehead.

"Oh no, you didn't ..." Ortus said.

Bradley got up and grabbed his car keys. "I'm going to be the best godfather, I promise!"

"Where are you going?" J.J. asked as Bradley got up from the floor.

"I'm going to go buy baby clothes!" Bradley clapped with genuine excitement.

Brooke tugged Bradley's arm, bringing him back to the floor. "Calm yourself and sit down."

Emmett rubbed the back of his head. "He knows I was joking, right?" He whispered.

"Nope," Brooke and Autumn said.

As the six of them laughed, Autumn couldn't help but think what a nightmare the past few weeks had been, but somehow, she was filled with happiness knowing the love of her life was alive and that soon they'd be brought together by a bundle of joy.

"Well, I need a proper shower." Autumn looked over at Bradley. "Please don't destroy my apartment looking for food, I haven't had time to go grocery shopping."

As Autumn walked into the bathroom, she heard her friends' laughter echo toward her, but by the time she'd had a hot shower, dried her hair, and changed into comfortable sweater and sweatpants, all was quiet.

Autumn walked out of the bedroom barefoot and paused as something soft touched her toes. When she glanced down, she noticed a trail of rose petals leading from the room.

With a smile, she followed them into the hallway, which was now lit by candles. Their warm glow led her to the kitchen, where a wooden dove had been placed on the dining table.

As she walked closer to the dove, a rush of thoughts engulfed her, reflecting on how different her life was now. She'd almost lost the love of her life, she was now expecting a child, and through thick and thin, Emmett and Autumn always found their way back to each other. How could their lives get any better?

"Lil' dove, I love you," Emmett said, embracing her from behind.

She lay the back of her head against his chest. "I love you too, Emmett."

"Since the first day I met you, I've wanted you. You healed my broken heart, and I don't want to spend a second away from you."

After a short pause, she turned around to face him, but he wasn't standing behind her anymore. Instead, she saw her friends gathered around the sofa, and when she looked down, Emmett was on one knee, and she let out a low gasp.

He looked into Autumn's eyes and asked, "Autumn Evans, will you marry me?"

14

Five months after Emmett's accident, five months after his proposal, six months of carrying their child, and Autumn was about to lose it.

"Autumn, Bradley Jr. needs to eat," Bradley said, rubbing her tummy.

Ortus scoffed. "The fact that you think she is going to call her baby Bradley Jr. is ridiculous."

"Enough! You're both driving me crazy," Autumn groaned.

Bradley hid his hands behind his back. "We want to make sure Bradley Jr. is okay."

"We don't even know if it's a boy or a girl," Autumn said, shaking her head.

"I can't believe you're waiting until the day you give birth."

"I already want to spoil the kid," Ortus said.

Why do I even try? Autumn turned, walking away from them.

"Where are you going?" Ortus called out.

She ignored her and walked to a nearby playground where a few children were playing on the slide and swings. Autumn sat on a brown bench, where she had agreed to meet Emmett. She noticed across from her a little girl who had brown curly hair, beautiful brown skin, and light-brown eyes. The little girl was working on a sandcastle by herself.

Autumn closed her eyes, enjoying the breeze and the silence that followed. The sun warmed her skin, making her feel at ease. She knew her friends had her best interests in mind, but she couldn't deny feeling a small amount of relief getting some space from them. It was the first time in months she had been able to get a moment to herself.

Her small moment of bliss was interrupted by two little girls arguing. She opened her eyes and realized it was the same girl who had been working on her sandcastle, except now it had been destroyed by a similar-looking girl—perhaps her younger sister. Autumn observed as the mother approached them. She couldn't hear what she said, but soon enough, the two girls hugged while the mother looked on, smiling in approval.

Autumn had always feared being a parent. Growing up, she faced the pressure of becoming someone she didn't want to be. She looked at her palms, her posture slumping as she realized her mother hadn't spoken to her since Autumn's remark at the hospital. It was as if she wanted nothing to do with her.

Autumn didn't want her child to ever feel as if she didn't love them. Children are fragile, anything you do can jeopardize who they grow up to be. What if she hurts them, and they don't feel comfortable telling her? What if they become distant and never want to hear from her? How do parents deal with such pressure? She was terrified of making the same mistakes her mother made, she didn't want to lose precious time with her children.

"What are you thinking about?" Emmett asked, sitting next to her.

She turned to glance at him and looked at the ring on her hand. She was still in disbelief that they were engaged. She had jumped into his arms after he had proposed and after many tears, she had said yes. Autumn was in love with Emmett Miller, and she couldn't wait to spend the rest of her life with him and their baby. Being reminded she didn't have to face this alone gave her the bravery to be a mother who would love her child with absolute devotion.

"Thinking about this little one," she said, glancing at her tummy.

"I'm excited to meet them. Have you thought about a name yet?"

"No, but it will not be Bradley Jr."

Emmett crossed his arms. "He's being persistent, isn't he?"

Autumn sighed. "Yes. I guess it's a good thing we don't know the sex."

"It's for the best, trust me. Now, is my fiancé ready to go give back to the community?" He extended his hand to her. She reached for it, the word fiancé still making her blush.

As they walked to the outdoor plaza where the community fair was being held, they encountered endless rows of booths wrapped with balloons and streamers. The whole community was raising funds for their individual businesses and charities. The fire station, for instance, was selling "acts of service" tickets, where if someone paid twenty dollars, they would be able to call the station for any help they needed, from gardening to packing moving boxes. The veterinary clinic had chosen to sell batches of cupcakes— with each purchase customers were entered into a raffle for a discounted dental treatment for their pets.

Autumn glanced over to the police department's booth, where her parents were talking to the owners of the local café. She closed her eyes, took a calming breath, and started walking toward them. Emmett, who was still holding on to her hand, paused.

She looked back at him, "What's wrong?"

He narrowed his eyes. "Your dad's uniform is intimidating."

"You've known him for most of your life. Why are you afraid of him?"

"He's not a fan of me getting his daughter pregnant."

Autumn rolled her eyes and dragged him toward her parents. They were going to have to get along now that they had one thing in common—their love for Autumn and her unborn child.

Both her parents glanced at her as she approached them. Her mother's stare was absent of emotion and her father's lingered on Emmett, who tensed in Autumn's hand.

"Hi, sweetheart," her father said.

"Hi, Dad."

Emmett extended his arm. "Good afternoon, Mr. and Mrs. Evans."

Bill took Emmett's hand, "Hello, Emmett."

"I'm so glad to see you!" Marie exclaimed. "You'll appreciate my advice, right? I am the grandmother, after all." She glared at Autumn—again.

Autumn rubbed her baby bump. "I still don't want you controlling my life, nor my baby's."

Emmett kissed Autumn's forehead. "And I support whatever the mother of my child wants."

Marie crossed her arms. "That's a tad overdramatic, don't you think?"

"No. It's what you do, Mom."

Marie shrugged. "I'm trying to provide wisdom to you Autumn, and you'll soon do the same for your child."

Autumn felt a sudden ache in her stomach as the pressure resurfaced with that one comment. The truth was, she didn't want to know it all. She wanted to show her child parents can be wrong and make mistakes. Autumn didn't want to be perfect.

Emmett squeezed her hand. "I think we'll be good parents. After all, our priority is for our child to feel loved by those around them, including their grandparents."

Bill loosened his posture. "I agree," he said, smiling at them.

Marie cleared her throat. "Where are you two thinking of living? I'm assuming across the street from us, it'll be easier for us to help."

Emmett had suggested his home a couple months prior, but Autumn voted against the idea. She preferred keeping a little distance between her and her parents. The lack of privacy they would have would drive them both mad.

Autumn rubbed the side of her arm. "For now, we've settled in my apartment. It's big enough for us."

Her mother crossed her arms, "Don't you have a dog?"

"Yes, but—"

"An apartment isn't a place for two adults, a newborn baby, and a dog."

Autumn didn't respond, now focusing on the pain in her abdomen. She rubbed her stomach until it disappeared.

Emmett let out a gentle cough. "You're right, Mrs. Evans." Autumn looked at him, shocked, but he continued, "We need to go talk to my father, Henry. He seems to be calling us over."

They looked at Emmett's father, who was invested in a conversation with a firefighter. Autumn grinned, realizing what Emmett was doing.

"Talk to you later, bye!" Autumn said as she was pulled away from her parents.

As they walked toward the fire station's booth, she started laughing. "Thank you for that."

He grinned. "Anytime. Hey, Henry!" Emmett called out as they approached Henry.

Henry's face lit up. "Hi, Emmett! How is planning for the baby going?"

"We've read a lot of books, and I took your advice to indulge in all of Autumn's pregnancy cravings."

With a gentle squeeze, "Fried pickles have been popular this week," Autumn said.

Henry adjusted his glasses, adding, "Will I get the privilege of meeting the baby when they're here?"

With a smile, Emmett brought about a peaceful pause in the conversation. Over the past months, Emmett and Henry had grown closer, yet the conversation of introducing the baby to Henry had never been brought up.

Henry cleared his throat, shifting the subject, "Oh, I'd like you both to meet Liam."

"Nice to see you again, Autumn!" Liam exclaimed as he walked toward her and embraced her. "I'm so glad you're doing better."

Emmett scoffed.

"I've been meaning to thank you for saving me that night," Autumn said.

He chuckled. "Not a problem. All in a day's work."

"Have you met my fiancé, Emmett?" She glanced at Emmett. "You remember Liam, right, Emmett? He pulled me from the fire at the clinic."

Emmett, not looking away from Liam, said, "Yeah, I remember him. Nice to see you again. How do you know Henry?"

Henry placed his hand on Liam's shoulder. "Liam visits me when he can. I almost set my house on fire once, and this young man was there in a matter of minutes."

"You give me too much credit, it's part of the job Henry," Liam said, cheeks turning pink.

Autumn tilted her head to the side. "I didn't know you lived in the middle of the woods."

Liam shrugged. "I rent my cabin out there, I live in town."

"Are you living with your girlfriend?" Emmett asked.

Liam smiled as he looked at the ground. "No, I don't have a girlfriend." An awkward grin crossed his face, "I should go check in with my chief. It was nice to see you again."

After Liam left, Emmett turned to his father. "How are you doing, Henry?"

"I'm fine, Emmett. The treatment seems to be working. I feel tired, but it's nothing I can't handle."

"I worry about you."

"It makes me happy knowing you're here and that you stop by every Sunday. Besides, I'm not alone all the time. Liam stops by when he can too."

Emmett gave a skeptical look, "I don't trust him."

Autumn rolled her eyes. "Emmett, he's a friend."

Henry sighed. "He's been nothing but a good man." He paused, looking over at the veterinarian booth. "I need to go talk to your mother. I'll see you in a bit," he said, walking away from them.

Autumn turned around, placing her arms around Emmett's neck. "Are you jealous?" she teased.

"The man saved your life and looks out for Henry. How can I not be?"

She kissed his cheek. "Don't worry. You're the one I want to be with. Plus, if I remember, you came to my aid that night too."

He sighed. "Do we need to go help Jackie and Jayden?"

Autumn looked over at them. They were flashing their charming smiles at four women who surrounded them. "Oh, yeah. If they're going to stand there getting attention, they also better be selling those cupcakes."

Emmett chuckled.

They spent most of the afternoon helping at the booth and were able to sell all the cupcakes they had made—no thanks to Jackie and Jayden.

Autumn and Emmett felt the consequences of a day on their feet later that evening when they returned to her apartment. She sat on her bed, playing with the ring on her finger while Emmett remained on his laptop.

"You've been on your laptop since we got home," she observed, attempting to sneak a peek. "What are you looking at?"

Emmett snapped his laptop close. "Oh, I'm finalizing a purchase."

Autumn narrowed her eyes, "A purchase for what?"

"Eh … the clinic. Mom wanted me to buy new equipment." He kissed her forehead. "Enough about work, how are your feet?"

"I'm so exhausted." She reached for his hand, "I'm also wondering why you were cold to Liam."

He studied her and after a deep breath said, "His interaction with Henry is so natural, whereas mine is like walking on eggshells."

"Why do you think that is?"

He avoided her gaze, "It might have something to do with me waiting for him to make a mistake and giving me a reason to cut him off."

Autumn placed her head on his shoulder. "Making mistakes is part of being human. What have the past months with him shown you?"

"That he's not the same man he was years ago." He placed his head on top of hers. "This version of Henry wants to be involved in my life, even wants to meet our baby."

"And will you let him?"

"Time will tell, I'm not sure yet." He sighed, "I'm sorry about my jealousy earlier. I'm also scared," he confessed.

"And why is that?"

"I know you love me as much as I love you. There is a need I feel to care for you and our child."

Autumn pulled Emmett into a hug. "I have the same worries, love, but you know what helps keep me calm? Knowing I have you and that we're going to do this together."

"This is one of the many reasons I proposed to you. It wasn't because you got pregnant, and it was the 'right thing to do.' It's because I love you. You're everything I've ever needed in my life."

"I love you too. You're all I want," she said, kissing his lips.

As they stood nose to nose, Emmett whispered, "I've got something to show you."

Autumn pulled her head back to smirk at him. "Oh?"

"Tomorrow," he said, pecking her on the tip of her nose.

Autumn's jaw dropped. "Hey!"

But Emmett jumped away before she could grab him, chuckling his way to the bathroom.

The next morning, Emmett made Autumn breakfast and looked in horror as she ate pickles with peanut butter instead.

"But I made you such a warm breakfast," he declared.

"This combination is so good!" She exclaimed. "Are you going to question the woman carrying your child?"

He opened his mouth but closed it. Autumn enjoyed pulling the pregnancy card on him, and she would continue to do so while she still could. After breakfast, Emmett drove her to a surprise location. He parked a couple of blocks away from their destination.

"Hurry up, slowpoke," he called as she trailed behind.

"I'm not sure if you've noticed, but I'm pregnant!" Autumn yelled.

"I know, I like teasing you." Emmett came to an abrupt stop, allowing her to catch up to him.

"Where are we going at this hour in the morning?"

"I lied to you last night."

"About?"

"Finalizing a purchase for the clinic." He averted his eyes. "I sold my old home."

"Why, what's going on?"

"What do you think of this?" He smiled, redirecting his gaze toward the house ahead.

Autumn turned to look at the home they were in front of. It was a stunning, white, two-story home with an open porch and a well-kept front yard. There was no doubt in her mind the people living there were happy.

"It's remarkable, but who lives here?" she asked.

Emmett held both her hands. "We will."

Autumn's mouth fell open. "What?"

"For the past couple of months, I searched for the perfect home for us and our baby. When I saw this house last month, I couldn't help but envision us on the front porch. So, after selling my house, I worked with the real estate agent to put an offer in for this one. We need you to cosign," he confessed, with a self-conscious hand rubbing his neck. "I know I was hasty in my decision, I would understand if you're mad."

It dawned on Autumn how hesitant she had been in returning to this town, and now here she was, in love with her best friend, carrying their child, and being asked if she would stay in Maplewood forever. Marisol had told her to trust her heart. Taking her advice had somehow led her to him and this moment.

Autumn placed her hand on Emmett's cheek. "You know I love you, right?"

"I do."

She took a moment to look at the home again. She studied the open porch with the swinging bench. For a moment, Autumn closed her eyes, visualizing herself sitting on the porch with Emmett and their child. She pictured herself growing old in the house and sitting on the bench with Emmett and her friends. This house was their home, but there was one thing missing.

"Okay," she said. "But we'll need to add something there." She pointed at the tree in front of the home.

He grinned. "A swing, maybe?"

"You read my mind," she whispered into his ear and kissed him on the cheek.

When they returned home, Emmett called the real estate agent to discuss next steps, while Autumn rested. Her sister and friends soon joined her after a message to the group chat. Bradley and Ortus sat next to Autumn on the couch, while Brooke and J.J. sat on the soft rug in front of them.

"Wait, you're moving?" J.J. exclaimed.

Brooke stared down at her hands. "Is it far from us?"

"Are you sure about this?" Ortus asked.

She knew her friends would question her decision to move into a quieter area—knowing Autumn's isolated history. But she knew it would be different this time. She wouldn't cut them out of her life like before.

"I love you all," she began, "but I'm engaged now. I'm pregnant, we have a dog, and my apartment isn't big enough for all of us."

"Did Mom tell you that?" Ortus questioned.

Autumn pursed her lips, feeling a small cramp form in her abdomen. "Well, yes, but—"

Bradley sat on the floor next to Brooke. "You can't take Bradley Jr. with you," he said, leaning against his sister. Autumn began rubbing her stomach, trying to ease the cramp she was feeling.

Brooke sighed in her brother's direction. "I once again have to question how we're related."

Ortus studied Autumn. "I know this is what's best for you. You've come a long way, sis. It's... things are changing so fast."

Autumn scowled. "Why are you against this?"

"I love Emmett, but I worry. The last time you went this fast, it didn't end well."

"Ortus, I love him. I trust myself this time, and I don't think I'm making a mistake."

Brooke and Bradley glanced at one another. After a long pause, Brooke asked, "When are you moving?"

"Emmett is speaking with the real estate agent, but he's thinking in two months."

"So soon?" J.J. blurted.

"That's impressive..." Bradley murmured.

Autumn rolled her eyes. "Can you all be supportive of me?"

"It's not that, Autumn," Bradley said. "The real estate agent knows what they're doing."

"Do you work in real estate or something?" Ortus teased.

Bradley scoffed. "Yeah, I've told you this before. Does nobody pay any attention?"

J.J. shrugged. "All you do is talk about food."

Autumn giggled. "Emmett has been working with the agent for the past couple of months now. He sold his old home and is sending over the documents with my signature for the new one. The previous owner has been trying to sell the home and hasn't had any takers—which is surprising."

"It does sound a little odd," Brooke sighed, "but I'll support you wherever you go."

"It's a twenty-minute drive, everyone. It's going to be okay!" Autumn said and slumped back onto the sofa. Concerned friends were exhausting.

"At least let us help you pack," Bradley offered.

Autumn smirked. "That's why I invited you over. I need to go to the clinic, but would you all mind packing some of my things?" She pointed to the kitchen, which was dotted with multicolored paper squares. "I've already started labeling things with sticky notes."

Ortus rolled her eyes. "You're so lucky you're pregnant."

"I love you!" Autumn teased. "Now, help me get up so I can get to the door."

Ortus sighed as she got up from the couch and pulled Autumn up. "Please, be careful. You can't be running around like you used to."

Autumn grinned and grabbed her keys from the wooden key holder near the door. "I'll be fine."

She took a moment to glance back at her friends, who had already moved from the living area. Brooke pushed Bradley out of her way while he ate some of the chips Autumn had left for him on the kitchen counter. As she had suspected, the packing would come down to Brooke and Ortus, while J.J. watched and entertained them. He turned to look up at Autumn and smiled at her. She smiled back, leaving the apartment and closing the door behind her.

A small breeze turned the page of the *Fashion Weekly* magazine open on Hope's thighs. The sun was vibrant and shining on her brown skin as she lay on a pool lounge chair in her pink polka-dot swimsuit. She blew air into her bubble gum as she eyed a particular chic suit.

Pop.

"I'd look great in that."

Hope's phone rang from the garden table, where she had also left her laptop. She ran to the table and picked it up, tapping the *accept* button with her French-tipped finger.

"This is Hope."

"Hi, Hope, it's Emmett Miller. I showed my fiancé the place, and she loves it. I sent over the documents to purchase the home. It includes my fiancé's signature, so everything should be set to send an offer?"

Hope's eyes moved to her computer screen as she navigated to her inbox with her free hand. "Ah yes, I see that's come through. Wonderful!" Hope smirked. "Like I told you before, Mr. Miller, the seller is desperate and wants to sell this house. I know I said I could give you the keys in two months but I'm thinking within the next month you'll be new homeowners."

"That sounds amazing, thank you. My fiancé and I are excited."

"Not a problem, Mr. Miller. I'll give you a call when everything is finalized. Take care," she said, hanging up the phone. Without delay, she dialed a new number. "Hey, the Millers have agreed to purchase. I'm finalizing the sale now. You owe me for this."

The voice on the other end hummed in satisfaction. "Good, good. I'll make sure to be nearby. You should be too."

Hope lowered her phone as the call disconnected, "Guess I'd better pack."

Throughout the morning, Autumn saw many patients, but one was her favorite.

"Mira should be fine," Autumn told Dani, who had brought her cat in for a checkup.

Mira was a sweet, ten-year-old tuxedo cat. She was vocal and purred at the sight of anyone who would give her attention. Every time Autumn treated her, Mira would force her head under Autumn's hand, demanding attention.

"The two small bumps on her back aren't cancerous?"

Autumn shook her head. "They're small bumps that show up on some cats. You could remove them, but it would be for cosmetic reasons. They can grow, but it's not harmful to them."

Dani sighed in relief. "Thank goodness. She's my best friend. I can't imagine my life without her."

Autumn smiled as she walked to open the door. "I know the feeling. Have a good day, Dani."

She followed close behind Dani, back to the reception area. As she glanced around at the waiting faces—human and otherwise—she couldn't help but feel proud of the work she was doing in this town. It was far more rewarding than working as a dental receptionist.

She turned to Jackie, who had been filing away Mira's paperwork. "What else do we have?"

Jackie grinned. "You're done for the day. You got through your patients faster than Jayden today, it has to be some sort of record."

"Speaking of Jayden, where is he?"

"Ah, he's finishing up some paperwork in his office." Jackie's voice lowered, "Which is his least favorite thing to do; he likes to hide so he can complain about it on his own."

"I feel like I could be doing a lot more."

Jackie snorted. "You're doing amazing. I, on the other hand, am halfway through this pile." He tapped a mountain of folders on the desk next to him. "But hey, who'd have thought all our paper records would get burned up, eh?"

Autumn's smile faltered, but she kept it in place as she looked over Jackie's computer screen. The night of the fire, half of the patient records were lost, so Jackie had been hard at work since digitizing every word of every remaining file and the backups.

"I still can't believe it happened." He turned to look up at Autumn. "It must've been terrifying for you."

Autumn looked down at her stomach. "It was."

And it still haunted her. The burn of a cigarette could get her heart racing. She had nightmares about him too—about Mason. It had been months, and they still hadn't caught him. Was he still out there watching her?

A faint throb pushed through Autumn's abdomen. She frowned down at it, rubbing it. "You okay in—?" she whispered, but before she could finish, the throb magnified, sending a shooting pain through her abdomen.

"Ouch!" she screamed.

"Autumn?" Jackie said, getting up and calling for Jayden. "Jayden, we need some help!"

What's going on? She took a sudden deep breath as dizziness crept up on her out of nowhere.

In the past couple of months, her baby had kicked, she had felt it move, but she had never felt this type of pain. Her rapid breaths where quick—too quick. Darkness was creeping in at the edges of her vision. Jackie wheeled his chair behind her and sat her down before crouching in front of her and looking into her eyes. "You'll be okay."

After a moment, Autumn felt her shoulders shake. She let out a gentle groan as she opened her eyes. *When did I close them?* Once her vision adjusted, she saw Jayden standing above her.

"What happened?" she whispered.

"Jackie said you fainted. Has this happened before?"

Jackie handed Autumn a bottled water. "You gave me quite the scare."

Autumn chugged the water, she was parched. "I've felt a sharp pain a couple of times, once at my apartment and the other at the fundraiser event."

Jayden nodded. "Let's get you to the hospital. I'll drive."

"I can get myself there," she objected as she attempted to get up, assisted by Jackie.

"Emmett will kill me if I let you go anywhere by yourself." Jayden held a set of keys in his hand. "Besides, I already have your keys."

Autumn rolled her eyes. "Fine."

As Jayden drove to the doctor's office, Autumn pulled her phone out to call Emmett.

"But are you okay, Autumn? Did the fall hurt you or the baby?" His frantic voice made her heart drop. She didn't like being the reason behind his distress.

"I'm not sure, but Jayden is driving so slow that by the time I get to the hospital, I'll be in labor."

Jayden scoffed. "I'm driving at the speed limit. Besides, we don't want to risk an accident."

"Meet me at the hospital, please," Autumn said.

"Of course. I love you, lil' dove."

Autumn glanced down to her pregnant stomach. "I love you too."

Once in an examination room, Jayden placed his hand on her shoulder.

"The baby will be okay," he said.

"How do you know? What if I hurt him?" she asked.

"Him? You're sure it's a boy?"

"Yes." Autumn nodded. "I'm sure of it."

Before Jayden could speak again, Dr. Rodriquez returned. "I've got your results back."

Autumn was terrified. "Is my baby, okay?"

"The baby is okay, but—"

Autumn almost stood, but Jayden held her back. "But what?"

Dr. Rodriguez sighed. "You need to take care of yourself, Autumn. Your stress levels are also causing stress on the baby. This means no more work, no more strenuous activity, no more sudden movements, and no arguments either. Your focus should be on resting and taking care of the baby. Got it?"

Jayden crossed his arms and nodded in agreement. "I'll make sure of it," he said.

As Dr. Rodriguez left the room, Emmett ran in, out of breath. "Autumn, are you all right? I got here as fast as I could. How's our baby?"

With the help of Jayden, she got off the exam table. "Our baby is okay. I fainted. If Jayden hadn't been so quick, I don't know what would've happened," she said, embracing Emmett.

Emmett sighed, looking up at Jayden over Autumn's shoulder. "Thank you for bringing her here and not leaving her alone."

Autumn broke their embrace and gave both men a wide smile. "Look at you both, talking like old times."

Emmett grinned. "We're best friends, that's never changed."

She looked over at Jayden, satisfied that she had been right. Old friends can be lost, but they can always find their way back to one another, no matter how much time has passed.

15

As Hope promised, Emmett collected the keys to their new home within a month. With the help of Bradley, Brooke, J.J., and Ortus, they made the move. After a long day of lifting boxes, Autumn prepared lemonade for everyone to enjoy on blankets in the backyard.

"Oh!" Autumn exclaimed, placing a hand on her belly.

Emmett almost threw his lemonade to the grass as he jumped to Autumn's side. "What is it? Are you okay?"

She giggled. "The baby is kicking."

His posture relaxed, and he rested his hand next to hers, feeling the little feet press into his palm. "This is perfect. Our little bundle of joy will be happy here."

"You're not moving that far, but Bradley Jr.—" Bradley began.

Brooke rolled her eyes. "If you want a Bradley Jr. so bad, go make one."

"That's such a great idea Brooke, wow, why didn't I think of that?" he said, flicking the top of his sister's head.

Emmett laughed, but Ortus sniffed, drawing his gaze. He saw a tear escape her eye before she wiped it away. He nudged Autumn and was subtle in directing her attention to her sister before raising his lemonade glass to his lips. Autumn was quick to catch on.

"What's wrong, Ortus?"

Ortus shrugged, cradling her lemonade glass. "You've come so far. I mean, look at you," she said, motioning her hand up, down, and all around Autumn. "You hated being in Maplewood and now you're engaged, a homeowner, and carrying a little one in there." She sniffed and rubbed at her eyes with the back of her wrist. "I'm so happy for you."

Emmett glanced at Autumn, who had tears in her eyes. He knew the tears were influenced by her pregnancy hormones, but that didn't change the fact she had embraced her self-worth. Emmett pulled her into a hug.

"It's okay, don't cry."

"I don't know why I'm crying. This is so nice."

Emmett's phone buzzed, prompting him to answer.

"Hi Emmett!" Hope began on the other end of the phone, "I'm here with your keys, do you think you can meet me outside? I'm in a bit of a hurry."

"Sure thing, I'll be out in a second." He said hanging up the phone.

Emmett excused himself from the group, leaving them to enjoy themselves in the backyard. As he turned the doorknob and opened the front door, he was met with a dark-haired woman leaning against a sleek, ruby-red car. He closed the door behind him and walked in her direction.

"Hi, Mr. Miller," she said.

"It's nice to meet you in person." Emmett offered a genuine smile and extended his arm, offering a handshake.

Hope accepted the handshake. "You're handsome in person."

"Um, thanks..." Emmett said, releasing his hand. "And thank you for working on getting us to move in so fast. You've made everything easy."

Hope touched his arm. "Of course. I've been wanting to sell this old home for some time now. There are a lot of old memories here, so I'm happy we get to leave it to such a loving couple."

Emmett cocked his head. "Oh, I didn't realize this was your place."

"Mine?" Hope's rubbed her hands together. "Oh, I misspoke, I apologize. I've been working with the seller for a long time now, so their words sometimes become mine." She laughed, but her eyes drifted to the trees surrounding the home.

Emmett cleared his throat and rubbed his hands together. "Well, I bet you're dying to meet Autumn. I can call her over," Emmett said, walking toward the front door.

"No!"

Emmett stumbled to silence, turning to see Hope standing wide-eyed by the car. She backed toward the driver door as she said, "I mean, I wish I could, but I have another client to see. I wanted to drop off the rest of the keys." She pulled a jangling ring of keys from her pocket and handed them to him. "See you around!"

And she was gone.

Emmett retreated to the home, venturing into the backyard. "Autumn, could you join me for a moment?" he called.

Autumn groaned. "It should be a crime to force me to walk all the way over there," she said as Bradley helped her stand. "You know it takes me six hours to get off the ground now, right?"

They walked into the living room. Emmett turned and wrapped his arm around Autumn's waist. "I have all the keys to our home."

Autumn released a smile. "The real estate agent stopped by?"

"Yeah, I wanted to introduce you to her, but she ... left in a hurry." He frowned back at the door. "What a strange woman ..."

"Maybe another time," Autumn said, looking down at her stomach. She sighed, looked up again. "I hate to sound like Bradley, but I'm hungry."

Emmett chuckled. "All right, let's go make everyone some food," he said, holding her hand as they turned to the kitchen to find Bradley with his head deep in the fridge. "You don't think they're going to be here all the time, right?" Emmett whispered, and Autumn giggled.

Hope watched rain fall onto the windshield of her car as she waited outside the cabin. How had she ended up in this predicament? If she'd known introducing them to one another would change her life, she would never have done it. She had lost too much already.

She reflected on the moment she met Autumn. Her parents had passed away a couple of months before she started college, and it had broken her. They couldn't help Hope move in, they wouldn't see her graduate, and they would never see her get married. The day she moved into her dorm, she had been sitting on the floor in the hallway, contemplating leaving as she watched all the moms and dads beam with excitement at helping their kids transition through life. Most of the new students shrugged off their parents, rolling their eyes as Mom gushed about her baby's success or Dad critiqued the furniture and light fixtures.

"Hey, are you all right?"

Hope narrowed her eyes on the feet that had stopped beside her. "I'm fine. What do you want?" she snapped, not taking her eyes off the floor.

"If you don't want to talk that's fine, but you don't have to be rude about it …"

Hope sighed. "You're right, I'm sorry." She looked up to find a girl with long, blonde hair looking down at her. "I'm Hope."

"I'm Autumn. Are you Hope Taylor?" she asked.

"Yeah. Do I know you?"

"I'm your roommate. I was out with my parents most of the day."

A sharp pain pierced her chest. Hope envied Autumn for being surrounded by relatives who would support her success throughout the next four years. Hope, on the other hand, had the odds stacked against her. She had no one. The two girls studied one another, neither of them saying a word.

"You don't have to tell me what's wrong." Autumn pulled in a deep breath, "But I refuse to leave my roommate by herself. C'mon, let's go get some ice cream," she said as she turned to walk away.

Hope scoffed.

"Don't make me come back for you," Autumn warned.

Hope, reluctant, got up and followed Autumn to the ice-cream shop on College Avenue. Once they had their ice cream, they sat down and ate in silence. That was what Hope liked about Autumn, she didn't push her to talk, and although they'd remained silent, it had been the beginning of their friendship. Of course, the silence had lasted for a short time.

"Are you from Maplewood?" Autumn asked.

Hope shook her head. "No. I'm from California."

"Why did you choose Maplewood?"

She let out a heavy sigh. "My parents grew up here. They still own a house here..."

Autumn hummed in interest and licked her ice cream. "It must have been nice for them to bring you today."

Once again, tears pushed at Hope's eyes. "They passed away a few months ago."

"Oh..." Autumn lowered her ice cream. "Hope, I'm so sorry."

"Thanks."

"Do you ... have any other relatives?"

She shook her head. "Not in Maplewood. My cousin and I left this town before we started high school. California became our home, but my parents' deaths drew me back."

"Well, no one should experience college on their own. I promise you I'll be here for you until you tell me not to be."

Autumn had kept her promise. They remained roommates for the rest of their time in college and became close friends. Hope got to know the rest of Autumn's friends, and although Hope wasn't always around them, they had always been welcoming of her.

During the fall semester of their final year, Autumn returned to their dorm room after taking her last exam.

"I'm so exhausted, I could sleep until graduation day." Autumn threw her bag on her bed. "But I can't wait to go to veterinary school."

Hope flipped a page of the book she was reading. "Have you even told your mom about going to California?"

"No. I'm waiting until I graduate."

Hope rolled her eyes. "Yeah, that's going to work out great."

"You never know, she might be supportive." Autumn groaned. "I haven't even found an apartment to live in."

Hope got off her bed. "My cousin is on his way up here. He's been a detective down in California for almost a year. I can ask him to help you find a good apartment?"

Autumn narrowed her eyes and crossed her arms. "What's the catch?"

"No catch. We're friends. This is the least I can do for you."

"You know, I wouldn't have survived these past couple of years without you, right?"

Hope flipped her hair. "Tell me something I don't know."

There was a knock on their door. If Hope could go back in time, she would take back her offer. She would've asked Mason to meet her somewhere else, but there he was at the door to their dorm.

"Autumn, this is my cousin Mason," she said.

The way Mason had looked at Autumn, the way she had blushed as he flirted with her, it had been her two favorite people coming together. It was the reason why she hadn't objected to Autumn joining them back in California after graduation.

Hope stared at her phone in her lap, listening to the rain patter the metal over her head. The screen showed the texts she'd shared with Emmett. She had never wanted to sell her parents' old home, but Mason had threatened her life and the life of the person she loved most. Every time Mason contacted her, she agreed to meet him wherever he wanted.

Before she'd sold the house to Emmett and Autumn, he demanded a copy of the keys so he could install microphones in the home. Mason was waiting for the right moment to act on his plan to get Autumn alone. He had everything he needed to spy on them, so why had he asked her to come pick him up at this cabin?

The passenger door swung open, making her jump.

"Didn't mean to scare you, cousin." Mason sat in the passenger seat, soaked in rain.

"Yeah, sure." She rolled her eyes. "What do you need?"

"I need you to stay in Maplewood a little longer and go about your business." He smirked.

"What? No!" She slammed her hands on the steering wheel. "You said I would be done after selling the house."

"Well, I changed my mind!" He snapped.

She looked away from him. "You're a monster," she whispered.

"Oh, Hope, please stop."

"Why are you so obsessed with her? Why can't you move on?"

Mason glared at her. "You know, earlier today I was sitting at the park reading the newspaper. A little girl hit me with her ball, her eyes reminded me of yours."

"Mason, stay away from her."

He scowled. "Don't test me, Hope."

Hope glared at him in disbelief. "Answer my question. Why are you so obsessed with her?"

Mason looked down his nose at her. "I wouldn't expect a single whore of a mother to understand."

Hope's jaw dropped, but he silenced her retort with a finger. "I let my emotions get the best of me. I got messy, and I made mistakes," he said, voice low. "But I am the right man for Autumn. She needs to see that."

Hope sighed, resting her forehead against the steering wheel. "What are you going to do?"

"That's for me to know." He sneered. "I'm going to lay low, so I'll need you to keep tabs on them. Keep an eye on her and make sure that she is the happiest she can be."

16

In September, Autumn and Emmett had finished the nursery for their child. The room had been painted a light-vanilla color, and they had placed the crib next to the large window where Autumn and their baby would enjoy the snow falling in the winter and the blossoms blooming in the spring.

She stood in front of the crib, rubbing her now nine-month pregnant stomach. She was lost in thought when she noticed the sun highlighting an unfamiliar teddy bear in the crib.

"Did you get this bear?" she asked Emmett as he walked into the nursery.

"No." He shrugged. "My guess would be it was Bradley?"

She held his hand as they observed the crib in silence. She enjoyed these moments because he never asked what she was thinking. Autumn hugged one of the bears, still struggling to believe she was one week away from becoming a mother. She was terrified, to protect an innocent life from this cruel world was a lot of responsibility. Autumn knew she wasn't alone, but she couldn't push away the fear she had.

Emmett squeezed her hand as if he knew what she was thinking. She leaned her head against his arm, feeling comfort in knowing they would love and protect their baby together.

Later in the evening, Autumn dug through her closet for an outfit to wear to Brooke's rehearsal dinner. It had taken her an hour to find her favorite purple maternity dress. When Emmett walked into the room, he was horrified by the mess she had made. He got to work picking up the clothing she had dropped on the floor.

"You sure know how to destroy a room," he said.

Autumn was struggling to straighten the back of her now medium-length hair. "I'm sorry, I feel the most comfortable in this dress."

He walked up behind her, grabbed the flat iron from her hand, and ran it through her hair. "Well, you look stunning."

She smiled at him through the mirror. "Thanks, love."

He turned off the flat iron and placed his hands on her shoulders. "Are you excited about tomorrow?"

"I can't believe Brooke is getting married." She let out a deep sigh. "It feels like it was yesterday that we were college students getting into trouble."

Emmett laughed.

She tilted her head to the side. "What's so funny?"

"I can't imagine a world where you're a troublemaker."

She laid a gentle kiss on his lips before heading out. "I guess you're right."

The rehearsal dinner was in the back room of Brooke's favorite sushi restaurant located in the heart of Maplewood. The room was decorated with peonies, and a tall candlelit centerpiece filled the middle of the long table, surrounded by sushi. Brooke had never been one to enjoy luxurious locations.

Brooke stood from her seat as Emmett and Autumn approached. "Thank you for joining us tonight."

"We can't wait to share our special day with you tomorrow," Neil added.

Ortus, in her long-sleeved lavender dress, arrived next to Autumn and nudged her to follow her. Autumn excused herself and allowed her sister to guide her to the bathroom at the back of the restaurant, where Ortus proceeded to open each stall, checking for occupants.

"Ortus, what's going—"

Ortus spun around, her voice deepening. "The police are calling off the search. They believe that because Mason has been off the radar for so long, he's no longer interested in you. They're keeping the warrant out for his arrest, but they're no longer looking for him."

"I was afraid of this."

"He has no other criminal record. They don't believe him to be a threat to anybody else. It makes me so angry but—" Ortus placed her hand over Autumn's "maybe they're right. He hasn't shown up. Mason might be done with you now that you're pregnant. He's a lot of things, but somehow, I don't see him capable of hurting a baby."

Autumn twisted the ring on her finger. "Perhaps you're right," she whispered.

The knot in Autumn's stomach tightened. Something was telling her this wasn't over, even though she longed for it to be. She craved to be free. Maybe one day she would be.

Ortus and Autumn returned to the rehearsal dinner. Autumn scanned the room.

"Where's Bradley?"

Ortus rolled her eyes. "You know Bradley, he's always late."

"I thought that was J.J.?" Autumn noted as they walked over to sit next to Emmett and Jordan.

J.J. leaned on the table, "It is, but I came for the sushi and—" Brooke let out a gentle cough "I mean, I got here on time for Brooke, obviously."

Brooke sat back down. "It is a little odd he's not here yet, but I guess we'll have to start without him."

J.J.'s face lit up. "I thought you would never say those words." He grabbed his chopsticks and was inches away from picking up a piece of sushi when—

"Sorry we're late!" Bradley ran into the room with another man. "Matty's flight got here late and we had to speed to get here," he explained.

J.J. let out of a sigh and dropped the sushi on his plate. "Matty?"

"My boyfriend?" Bradley held on to Matty's hand as they sat down.

"Since when do you have a boyfriend?" Ortus pushed.

Bradley shrugged. "It's not my fault you never listen."

Matty grinned, waving at the group. "Well, I for one have heard so much about all of you."

Emmett offered his hand to Matty across the table. "Welcome to the group, Matty. I'll make sure to arrange an induction packet for you to adjust to the weird friendship of these five."

Everyone burst into laughter and began to dig in. While they ate, they spent time catching up with J.J., who they hadn't seen in a long time. He had left their small town a couple of months ago to be a critic at a film festival.

"I'm sick and tired of seeing films talk about Asian culture, yet no one in those films looks like me," J.J. explained.

"It's so frustrating to see." Ortus grabbed her chopsticks, reaching for her veggie roll. "How many times am I going to see a Black woman portraying someone poor or unsuccessful? Why can't Black women be the successful lead in a film for once?"

Brooke nodded in agreement. "What you're doing is great. I don't think I've seen so much diversity in movies since you started. You must be ruffling some feathers in Hollywood."

J.J. grinned. "I aim to inspire—like Brooke does with her art!"

"Oh, you ..." Brooke's cheeks flushed pink as she poked at her sushi.

"Brooke has accomplished so much with her art gallery." Bradley turned to his sister, nudging her. "I mean, those free art classes for low-income students? You're a hero!"

"You know I don't do it for praise. Everyone should have access to education."

"And that's why you're respected in this town, Brooke." Bradley lifted his glass. "To Brooke and J.J. for making the world a better place."

"To Brooke and J.J.!" everyone said, joining in the toast.

Bradley tapped his glass, and everyone fell into silence once again. "I've seen this in movies. I'm glad it works."

The group laughed.

"Anyway, I guess the brother of the bride should speak," he began. "Brooke,

I'm happy I get to see you get married. I remember your secret binder filled with pictures of what you wanted your dream wedding to look like. You even had pictures of who your perfect husband would be—which is funny, because for the longest time, you told everyone you wouldn't get married."

Brooke shrugged. "I thought this was supposed to be a toast, not a roast."

Bradley grinned. "We've come a long way. I still remember hanging out in our dorm lobby with Ortus, Autumn, and J.J. We would stay up late to go on late food runs. Boy, those were the best!" He looked into the distance.

Ortus coughed, bringing him back to them.

Bradley turned to focus on his sister, unshed tears making his eyes shiny. "Brooke, we're twins. We've shared every moment together since we were in the womb. You are patient and sweet. You are my sister and you're my best friend. I know if our parents were here, they'd be so proud of you too. I wish you nothing but a life full of happiness." He turned to face Neil. "Neil, if you ever hurt her, you'll have to deal with me. Congrats, you two!"

Autumn was leaving the shopping center, arms laden with bags. She stopped before the exit to the parking lot, feeling the humidity pushing toward her from the downpour outside. "I didn't think it was going to rain." She looked down at her stomach. "We're going to have to make a run for it, little one."

She cantered toward her car as fast as her stomach would let her go but came to an abrupt stop as she reached her hand out for the door. Someone was calling to her.

"Autumn!" the voice said.

She scanned the parking lot, but there was no one around. In a moment, the scene changed from day to night. The cars were gone, the streetlights were dim, and she was all alone. The voice had been faint at first, but now she could hear it clearer.

"My love," it said.

No. She dropped her bags, hugging her belly. *No, no, no.*

"My love" it repeated, again and again. She covered her ears, sliding to the ground with her back to her car.

"Autumn," the voice said.

"Autumn," it said, louder now.

"Lil' dove. Wake up, you're having a nightmare," the voice said a third time.

She gasped, eyes flying open, to find a figure hovering over her. Her hand flew up, but he caught it, flicking on a lamp with the other.

"Hey," Emmett whispered, stroking her cheek. "It's okay. You're safe. I'm here."

She was hyperventilating. Her chest ached and her skin was slick with sweat. But Emmett's hand traveled up and down her cheek, grounding her, and her breathing slowed.

"Did you dream about him again?" Emmet asked.

She nodded her head and closed her eyes. She wanted him out of her life, but he had infiltrated her mind like a virus. Was she dreaming of him because of what Ortus had told her a few hours ago at dinner?

"I'll wait for you to fall sleep. I'm here," Emmett whispered, holding her in his arms until she was able to drift back into a slumber.

The morning of Brooke's wedding, dark bags hung under Autumn's eyes. The aqua-toned eyeshadow which was supposed to match her bridesmaid dress made things worse. Her sleep had been sporadic and restless, jolting her awake what felt like every five minutes to scan the shadows for Mason's presence, despite the fact that she was still wrapped in Emmett's arms.

And now, surrounded by her friends at her best friend's wedding, she was terrified, unable to enjoy Brooke's special day. How much more would Mason take from her?

She was standing with J.J., Ortus, and Bradley when a rustle coming from the bushes made her jump, but a cat emerged a moment later, shooting across the twins' backyard and over the opposite fence.

"What's wrong, Autumn?"

Autumn looked at J.J. and sighed. "I couldn't sleep," she said, brushing off the shock of the cat. "My nightmares ..."

Her sister pursed her lips. "Have come back, haven't they? I shouldn't have told you, I'm so sorry. I wanted you to be safe, so I thought if you knew you'd be able to—"

"Move on. I know. I want to. I don't know if I can."

Bradley scowled. "Autumn, you need to try not to stress. It can be dangerous for the baby."

"Maybe we should ask Dad if he knows anything," Ortus suggested.

Autumn had thought about this before. "I don't want Dad to worry about me. Besides, he'd tell Mom, and she would find a way to remind me how it's all my fault." She sighed. "Let's not ruin Brooke's big day, okay?"

She walked away without another word, and her friends followed close behind. The wedding music began to play, and Autumn was the first down the aisle. She tightened her grip on her flowers, her eyes scanning the area and the shadows within the bushes. Ahead, Neil already had tears in his eyes as he waited for his bride to emerge.

Emmett held out his hand. He was already waiting for Autumn at the front row. Her friends had insisted she sat during the ceremony. In fact, they had all decided they would sit with her so she wouldn't feel alone. She somehow felt ... protected.

Bradley began, "Dear friends, we are gathered here today to witness and celebrate the union of Neil and Brooke in marriage. In the years they have been together, their love and understanding of each other has grown and matured, and now they have decided to live their lives together as husband and wife."

"This will be us soon." Emmett whispered.

She smiled. "I can't wait."

"They're so cute together. I can't believe this is happening," Ortus said, dabbing tears from under her eyes.

"Two down, three more to go," Autumn said.

"You and Bradley better hurry up, I'm not going to look this good forever," J.J. whispered.

After the ceremony, everyone headed to the reception at Brooke's art gallery. They arrived to walls filled with art and photographs by the couple, a celebration of their skills separate and together. White round tables and chairs were clustered at the sides of the room, with the center left open as a dance floor, where Bradley and J.J. broke out into some questionable dance moves.

Before long, the twins roped Autumn into dancing. She swayed side to side, feeling silly dancing with her huge pregnant stomach, but couldn't deny her happiness despite being out of breath after a couple of minutes. Ortus, noticing her exhaustion, offered to walk her to a quiet room where she could rest.

In the corner of the room, which was decorated with yet more of the couple's art, a large yellow couch called Autumn's name. She sat, feeling immediate relief for her swollen feet.

She glanced up at her sister, who was making strong eye contact with her.

"Are you okay?" Autumn asked.

"I know you're worried about Mason." Ortus paused. "What he did was unforgivable, and you don't even get to sleep in peace."

Autumn sighed. "It's never going to go away, Ortus. Even if he was in prison, the trauma I endured will always stay with me."

"What do you mean?"

"It's like …" She rubbed her temple. "It's like a box in my brain. A box full of bad memories that I've chosen to lock away. There are moments when the box opens, and the feelings overwhelm me."

"Sis, you have to talk to someone. Process what you experienced. You're about to have a kid and marry a guy that loves the hell out of you."

She stared down at her hands. "I can't even begin to unpack that, knowing he's out there somewhere …"

Her sister leaned against the wall. "Sometimes I wonder if karma crept up on him and took him out in some vicious accident."

"I'd sleep in peace. Not that I ever wished him dead, but it would feel nice to get closure," she whispered.

Ortus shrugged. "He was an abusive asshole. He would've deserved it," she said with no remorse.

They sat together in silence for a few minutes before Autumn held out her hand to Ortus to help her up. "Let's get back. I'm sure Emmett is wondering where I am."

They went back to the reception, where she found most of her friends still on the dance floor. The music had slowed. Emmett came up to Autumn and led her to the center of the room. As she laid her head on his chest, she couldn't help but replay her conversation with Ortus.

She'd meant what she'd said. Even though Mason had caused her pain, she didn't wish him dead. However, she was sure a part of her could try to live free because she knew he wouldn't risk coming back—not when her loved ones were keeping such a close eye out for him. Autumn could enjoy her life with her friends, her fiancé, and soon, her baby.

Hope swung the front door open. There was a subtle light from the living room lamp casting a warm ambiance as her daughter slept on the couch next to Natalie, who was watching the evening news.

"You're back so soon?" Natalie whispered. "What happened to your dress?"

Hope made it back to Natalie's apartment after spending the day spying on Autumn at the wedding. She almost got caught after her dress latched itself to a nearby bush. If there hadn't been a large tree next to it to hide behind, it would've all been over. By the end of the night, she'd grown bored. She hoped Mason would settle with knowing there hadn't been anything interesting going on besides two people choosing to spend the rest of their lives together.

Hope slipped her heels off. "It got caught in a bush. I couldn't stay there any longer. My feet were aching."

Natalie glanced at Hope's daughter. "Well, she just closed her eyes. She might not wake up until tomorrow morning."

Hope walked to the guest bedroom. "Thanks for taking care of her," she whispered as she slipped out of her dress and pulled on her pajamas. "I owe you big time."

Natalie stood in the doorway of Hope's room. "We're best friends, you know you don't. I'm going to go grab us Chinese food for dinner. Call me if you need anything else."

Hope walked back to the living room and covered her daughter with a blanket. She brushed her hand through her hair. She hadn't been able to spend as much time with her because Mason was keeping her busy.

As Hope was about to lie on the couch, there was a knock on her door. She figured Natalie forgot her keys, but when she opened the door, she was disappointed.

"How did you find me?"

Mason barged into the room, closing the door behind him. "I'm a detective, Hope. It is my job to find people," he said as he hung his jacket on the back of the door.

Hope rubbed her shoulder, "It's been a long day, Mason. What do you want?"

He scowled. "I'd be more careful with how you speak to me."

She looked at the floor. "I'm tired, I'm sorry."

"Mama? You're home?"

Hope turned to see her daughter rising from the sofa, rubbing her sleepy eyes. Her heart began to race as a huge smile erupted on Mason's face.

"Luna, look at you. You've gotten so big!"

Hope crossed to the sofa and kneeled to kiss Luna on her forehead. "Hush. Go back to sleep, Luna."

The little girl nodded and closed her eyes.

Hope glared at Mason, "I have no updates. They're all at Brooke's wedding."

"We have to start setting this plan in motion. Have your priorities straight, Hope. I'm not paying you to sit around."

"You're not paying me at all, scumbag!"

A sting on her left cheek. Tears filled her eyes, but she refused to let them out. She wouldn't show him weakness.

"I'm sorry, Autumn." Mason placed a strand of Hope's hair behind her ear. "You get me so mad at times. Remember I'm doing this for us. I want us to be happy again. Now, get better updates!" he said before turning for the door. He stopped before it, met Hope's eyes, looked down past her waist toward the couch. His smile returned, sweet as honey. "I'll see you soon, little one." His gaze met Hope's one more time as his smile turned into a smirk, and he grabbed his jacket and left.

Hope stood there at a loss for words. *Did he call me Autumn?*

"Mama, who's Autumn?" Luna asked.

Hope turned to Luna, who sat up once the door had closed behind Mason. "She's an old friend."

Luna tilted her head. "Mama, why did Cousin Mason hit you?"

A tear trickled down Hope's face as her heart crumbled, she had never wanted her daughter to witness her abuse. "Don't worry about it, honey. Go get ready for bed, and I'll read you a story."

Luna nodded, running to the bathroom.

After Hope showered and read Luna a bedtime story, she sat in front of her mirror, brushing her long, curly hair. Her face was beginning to bruise, and she knew it would take a good amount of makeup to hide the black eye. She could still see the bruise on her right cheek from the last time Mason had hit her.

It had become worse over the past couple of months. Heck, when Autumn told her about the abuse, Hope had thought she was lying. She pushed Autumn away, ended her friendship with her best friend because of *him*. As Hope laid her hairbrush down, she recalled her time in California.

Hope had become successful in real estate and lived in the same complex as Mason and Autumn, so visited often. Autumn's demeanor changed in that time, becoming darker and sadder. At the time, Hope had thought it was homesickness. She had been so naive, but at a young age she had always been told family came first. But one night, Autumn made her question that.

"I think another promotion is on the horizon for me, you know." Hope swirled and gulped her wine, shooting a gleeful smile in Autumn's direction, which dropped when she saw that her friend hadn't touched her drink. She placed hers down. "What's wrong with you, Autumn? You've become such a downer."

Autumn rubbed her arm and turned away, hiding her face, but Hope had already spotted the glassiness in her eyes.

"You're beginning to worry me, Autumn …" Hope said. "Talk to me. Let me help."

Autumn turned back around, tears trailing down her face. Seeing this, Hope sprang from her seat to envelope Autumn in a gentle yet firm hug.

"He hurts me, Hope," Autumn whispered.

Hope pulled her head back to get a better view of Autumn's face. "What?"

"Mason." Autumn's wide eyes found Hope's. "He hurts me."

Hope's arms fell from around Autumn. "How could you say that about my cousin?"

"I'm not lying. He hits me. He controls my every move. I'm a prisoner in my own home. I can't take it anymore—"

Hope stood. "I can't believe you, Autumn. After everything Mason has done for you? I get that you feel alone being so far away from home, but this attention-seeking has gone too far. I can't stand here and listen to you talk about my cousin this way."

Hope stormed from the apartment and never spoke to her best friend again.

As she reminisced back to that moment, she couldn't help but feel like an idiot. Autumn hadn't lied. And now she resented Autumn once more because she'd had had the courage to leave, and Hope didn't.

17

Autumn sat in front of her fireplace reading a book, trying her best to follow her doctor's orders. Emmett had cooked her an appetizing dinner so she could relax, but that night—like every night—the nightmares returned.

She was coming back from the shopping mall, bags of baby clothing dangling from one hand, as she began to feel the gentle patter of rain on her head and face.

"I didn't think it was going to rain," Autumn said, and looked down at where her hand rested on her belly. "I can't wait to splash in puddles with you."

"My love."

Autumn startled, turning around. "You scared me, Mason."

Mason grinned. "What are you doing out in the rain, my love?"

"I forgot my umbrella." She met his brown eyes.

Mason smiled, shaking his head. "Did you at least get the clothes for the baby?"

"I did."

"Let's get you home."

"But I need to get out of here," she whispered, and the rain became her tears stinging her cheeks. She was standing alone at a train station in the middle of the night, a hoodie disguising her pregnant stomach. She had a ticket in her hand that would take her to Seattle.

"Where the hell do you think you're going?"

Autumn, horrified, turned around. "I... wanted to see the cost of tickets. I was planning a little getaway for both of us."

"Don't lie to me, Autumn." He reached for her arm, his grip like a vice. "You're coming home."

A few people at the station looked at them. Autumn looked at each of them, hoping one of them would make eye contact with her, but they all looked away. Mason pulled her closer. She tried to back away from him, but he tightened his grip as he dragged her away from the platforms. Her heart pounded in fear as a weightless sensation enveloped her mind.

"Mason, wait—" Autumn pleaded.

"I knew you'd try to run away," he muttered as she collapsed ...

... into a hospital bed. An unexplainable pain tugged at her insides. She struggled to sit up, but when she did, she looked down in horror at the scar on her stomach. The heart rate monitors beeped faster as panic took hold, she ripped the catheter and monitors from her body as Mason walked in.

"Autumn, what are you—?"

"This is your fault!" she screamed. "You're the reason our little Luna isn't here!" He stepped closer, and she stumbled off the bed. "Leave me alone! I never want to see you again!"

Doubled over from pain and clasping her bleeding forearm, she ran through the hospital halls. Mason called after her, his voice never fading, no matter how far she went. She didn't know where she was heading, but when she turned, he was there.

Someone shook her.

"Autumn. You're having a nightmare," Emmett whispered.

When Autumn woke, she burst into tears. No matter how hard she tried, she couldn't stop. She touched her stomach, taking comfort that it was still there, but it wasn't enough. Her dreams were getting more intense.

Emmett hugged her, letting her rest her head on his chest.

"I know why I'm having these nightmares," she whispered into his T-shirt.

"Do you want to talk about it?"

"In the nightmare, I miscarried when I was with him."

Emmett's lips touched the top of her head. "It's okay, lil' dove. It's a nightmare."

"But it wasn't a nightmare ... it was a memory."

Once again, she broke into sobs, and Emmett held her closer, hushing her, "I've got you, always."

The next morning, Emmett went to grab breakfast while Autumn slept in. He drove through the snowy streets of Maplewood, observing families on their front lawns building snowmen and making snow angels. The day had just begun, everyone was at home, but Emmett felt the need to take some time for himself.

As he drove through town, passing dark windows and closed signs, he noticed a couple of people down the sidewalk, coffees in one hand and *pan dulce* in the other. El Corazon del Pan.

When he walked in, the cozy bakery enveloped him in a warm, cinnamon-scented embrace. Ethan and Marisol were behind the counter, making coffee.

"Whoa, you look horrible. Are you all right?" Ethan asked.

"I didn't get much sleep last night," Emmett admitted, taking a seat.

Marisol placed a cup of coffee in front of him. "Here."

"Thanks."

"Is everything okay? What brings you here at this hour?" Marisol asked.

Emmett sighed. "Autumn had more nightmares last night, and we didn't get enough sleep."

Ethan tilted his head, "Has this been happening often?"

"They've come and gone for the past couple of weeks. She's going to see a therapist today. I figured I'd give her some space."

Marisol tilted her head to the side. "And how are *you* doing?"

"Not well." He placed his hands over his face. "I want to see her smile again. She's been so quiet and sad. I knew she was going to have dark days, but she's never talked about her time in California, and I don't want to push her to process things with me if she doesn't want to."

The torment Mason had put Autumn through lit a fire in Emmett. He promised himself he would protect her, ensure nothing else would cause her pain like this again. It was a promise he intended on keeping, but right now he felt defeated.

"Yeah, you don't want to do that …" Ethan said as he wiped the counter. "But maybe you shouldn't be the one who she processes with. You also need to get some sleep, man."

Marisol nodded. "You can't help her if you don't take care of yourself."

"I know you're both right. That's why I suggested she talk to Dr. Beck. She's seen him a couple of times, but she hasn't stayed consistent with her therapy." He stirred his coffee, "I feel like I need to do more for her, is all."

"Hey." Marisol placed her hands on his. "You're not alone. Talk to her friends. Maybe all of you can think of something together to support her. She's not alone in her struggles, and neither are you."

Emmett adjusted his posture. "That's not a bad idea."

Marisol winked. "I have those sometimes."

Feeling hopeful, he took a sip of his coffee. "Anything special on the menu today?"

"We have some leftover tamales. Want some?" Marisol asked.

"Yes, please, I'm starving. I'll have to take some for Autumn too."

Ethan laughed. "I would think of feeding your pregnant wife first as well."

"I agree she's the one doing all the hard work."

Emmett talked to Marisol and Ethan for another hour. It felt good to befriend people who weren't already Autumn's friends. As the sun rose, casting a golden hue through the bakery's windows, Emmett found himself drawn into their world. Marisol's expressive gestures and Ethan's infectious laughter created an atmosphere of genuine connection. It was as if the three of them had known each other for years, sharing stories and experiences that revealed the depths of their souls.

Emmett couldn't help but marvel at the way life unfolded, bringing these two remarkable individuals into his orbit at the right moment. He realized that their perspectives had always been helpful, and it was now clear to him what he needed to do.

When she found the will to crawl out of bed, Autumn attempted to get ready for her therapy appointment.

After Mason had fled, she'd thought she wouldn't need therapy anymore. She was happy with Emmett, and Mason was gone, so why would she need to talk to a therapist? She had been in a better place, there was no need for month-to-month check-ins.

She now knew that had been a mistake. Dr. Beck had been helpful in the past, but she never thought she'd be in a situation where she would have to see him again.

They had decided to meet in his office. She settled onto the large grey couch, draping a soft yellow blanket over her lap, while Dr. Beck occupied the chair across from her.

"Now, tell me about these nightmares."

Autumn sighed. "I keep dreaming of him. At least, they seem like dreams, but they feel real."

Dr. Beck leaned forward. "In these dreams, what time period does it seem you're in?"

"I have long blonde hair, so I'm assuming it was around the time I was in California." Autumn let out a heavy breath. "Dr. Beck, in the dream, I'm pregnant."

"If you're pregnant in the dream, it might stem from your fear of his return."

"That's what I thought at first too. These dreams are starting to feel like memories. The locations are so vivid, but I don't have any clear recollection of them other than through my dreams."

"Well, when trauma occurs, the mind often does whatever it can to protect you. This sometimes leads to repressed memories that cause pain." After a thoughtful pause, he inquired, "Autumn, is there something you're holding back from me?"

She looked down at her trembling hands. Her mouth opened, but no words emerged. She was terrified. Voicing her thoughts would make them real—the pain, the memories, and the trauma would become undeniable. Which is why she knew she had to say it.

"I was pregnant when I was with Mason," she blurted out, taking a steady breath. "It was already bad between us, but I believed that having a child was what we both needed. I was wrong because I lost our baby two months before she was due."

Dr. Beck raised his glasses to the top of his head. "I'm sorry, Autumn."

"He didn't physically hurt me while I was pregnant … it was as if he was his old self again. He brought me flowers, fulfilled my every need. I felt loved."

"He made you feel safe."

Autumn nodded. "I thought to myself maybe he had changed. Maybe he wanted to be a great father, but …"

"He manipulated you into believing you were the problem?"

"Yeah. Since he couldn't hurt me physically, he hurt me emotionally and mentally." She took a deep breath. "I would cook for him, and when he was unhappy with the food, he'd toss it on the floor, demanding I clean it up. He would say it was my fault because I should've cooked better."

"What impact did that leave on you?"

"A devastating one." Her voice was small, "One evening, while preparing dinner, I placed a skillet with hot oil on the stove. I didn't sense him approach me, and when he did, I bumped into the stove and the hot oil splattered onto his arm."

"He was angry and raised his hand." She continued, "It was the first time while I was pregnant he thought of hurting me. It was enough reason for me to run, because if he was tempted to hurt me in that moment, I wondered what he would do to our child?"

Autumn's voice cracked, "Losing Luna was my breaking point. I wanted nothing to do with him. He destroyed me and I don't know if I'll ever forgive him for that."

"What does forgiveness mean to you?"

Autumn thought about this for a moment. "It means letting go of the past in order to find happiness and healing."

"It can mean that," Dr. Beck said. "I think most people believe they need to forgive those who caused them trauma. The truth, Autumn, is that you don't need to forgive your perpetrator. You need to forgive yourself."

She wiped the unshed tears from her eyes. "I should've known. I saw the warning signs and I ignored them. My mother blamed me my whole life for making foolish choices but marrying him was one decision I was certain about."

Dr. Beck leaned forward, and she turned to face him. "This is not your fault. You did not deserve to be abused. You sought to embark on an adventure and pursue a career you loved, but you did not ask to be abused."

At that, Autumn's emotions overwhelmed her, and she couldn't hold back the tears any longer. She had bottled up her pain since leaving Mason, but now it all came crashing down. Through her tears and anguish, she cried, "My baby, my sweet Luna! It should've been me. Why her?" She screamed, knowing it was what she needed to feel free.

"It's okay, Autumn," Dr. Beck whispered.

"I need some fresh air," she said as she stood up. "Thank you for our session, Dr. Beck."

"Autumn, I don't think it's wise"—" he began, attempting to stop her, but it was too late. She had already grabbed her purse and was out the door.

Autumn had an insatiable urge to wander, no matter where it led her. She couldn't stop thinking about what Dr. Beck had said. She had suppressed her memories of the moments she had shared with Mason in California and locked away the painful memory of her miscarriage. Perhaps the reason she hadn't been able to move on was because she kept preventing the memories from returning; maybe it was time to face her past.

As she walked near the old café, she came to an abrupt stop. Her attention was drawn to a woman with short, shoulder-length black hair. There was a noticeable bruise on her face, and she was engrossed in conversation with another woman. As Autumn approached, she overheard them.

"You've been quiet. Are you all right?" the friend asked the woman.

The woman shrugged. "I'm fine, Natalie. I'm worried about my daughter."

"I told you she'd be fine with Maya."

"I know Maya is great, I'm just paranoid is all." The woman scratched her head. "Does it make me a bad mother to leave my child with someone you've been dating for a few months?"

"It doesn't, I think Maya might be the one." Natalie blushed, brushing away the subject. "Your hair looks good, though. Do you like your haircut, Hope?"

"It's not that, it's—"

"Hope?" Autumn interjected.

Hope's back tensed as she turned to face Autumn. "Oh ... Hi, Autumn."

"What are you doing here?"

"I'm ... here on business."

"Autumn remained silent. The last memory she had of Hope was her not believing her about Mason. She couldn't help but notice there was something off about her now, though.

"How did you get that bruise on your face?"

Hope's eyes widened. "Oh, I ... it was a cat. It wasn't nice. It scratched me, and I fell face first to the ground."

Autumn felt herself grow pale. She was not a stranger to all the possible excuses one could come up with. Hope was lying. She took a step closer to her. "Hope, if you need help—"

"Autumn, this is my friend, Natalie," Hope interrupted. "Natalie, this is Autumn."

"Hi, Natalie." As Autumn looked at the other woman, her vision began to blur. "It's nice to meet you," she said, rubbing her eyes.

"Autumn, you don't look so good. Are you okay?" Natalie asked.

"No. Everything is spinning. I—" she said, trying to hold on to something, but there was nothing. Hope and Natalie caught her fall and supported her to a nearby bench before calling 911. The paramedics were there within minutes.

Autumn lay there, vulnerable and disoriented, as people surrounded her.

They didn't whisk her away in a hurry, as she half-expected, but instead, they maintained a vigilant watch over her. Each measured breath of the oxygen mask felt like a lifeline, a connection to a world that had slipped away.

Autumn's racing heart seemed to echo in the beeping of the nearby medical equipment. The paramedics monitored her vital signs as her blood pressure returned to normal. She sat up, supported by the young paramedic beside her.

Hope appeared, coming to lean against the side of the ambulance parked a foot away. "Hey, how are you feeling?"

"Better now," Autumn said. "I've been under a lot of stress."

"How come?"

"I've had trouble sleeping," she said, touching the side of her head, "the same recurring nightmares, therapy appointments, and an epiphany."

"An epiphany?" Hope's nose wrinkled, with curiosity.

Autumn sighed. "I was making myself my own worst enemy. I started convincing myself that I deserved—" She paused, remembering who she was talking to. "I'm sorry, I—"

Hope shook her head. "Don't be. Please, go on."

"I left for California because I wanted a fresh start. I wanted to follow my dreams. I … I didn't ask to be abused." She said with a firm tone, as if she expected Hope to argue back as she had last time. But instead, she came to sit beside Autumn on the bench.

"No, you didn't. You know, we don't choose our parents, and he detested his."

"I never understood that …"

Hope hesitated for a moment. "Mason hated his father—my uncle—and I think it was because he hurt him too. Did you know Mason's birth name was Diego?"

"What? No. I never knew that."

"That's what his father's name was. And when he was arrested for child abuse, Mason decided to change his name. The name Mason was different, it was unique to him."

"What about his mother?"

Hope sighed. "She left him. She ran from the abuse and left Mason behind. Mason thinks the way to force someone to stay is through threats and violence."

"Thinks?" Autumn rubbed her hands together. "Are you having a hard time with his disappearance?"

"Yeah, I guess …" she said, a slight tremor in her voice. "It's like he's still here sometimes."

They sat in silence for a moment. It was surreal to be sitting next to Hope, as if Autumn was destined to make amends with the people from her past to move on.

"You should get some rest," Hope said. "Do you want a ride home?"

Autumn nodded. "Yeah, I think that would be best."

When Hope hadn't believed her, it had made Autumn question if anyone ever would. There was something different about Hope now, she wasn't as defensive, but instead, she was understanding. Somehow, this was the closure Autumn needed. Perhaps Mason's disappearance was affecting everyone for the better.

Emmett had settled into the cozy living room, basking in the warm glow of the fireplace crackling with merriment. He had returned from an errand, but Autumn was nowhere to be found. It was the perfect opportunity to reach out to their friends and orchestrate a baby shower celebration for her.

As the doorbell rang, his heart raced with anticipation. Before he could reach the door, a whirlwind of faces stormed into the house. Bradley, Brooke, J.J., and Ortus barged in, each bearing bags filled with decorations and groceries.

"When people say you're always welcome, they don't mean barge into their home without their permission," he said, closing the door behind them.

Ortus placed the items she was holding on the dining room table and turned to Emmett. "Are we sure this is a good idea?"

Brooke bit her lip. "No, but—"

"Stop it," Bradley interrupted his sister. "This *is* a good idea. Autumn hasn't been feeling the best. The least we can do is throw her a baby shower."

Emmett massaged the back of his neck, fatigue settling in. "I think Bradley's right. She hasn't been able to sleep, and I think she needs to be around the people she loves."

J.J. approached him, placing a comforting hand on his shoulder. "Speaking of which, Emmett, have you had any sleep?"

"No. I stay up to make sure Autumn is okay." He fell on the couch, displaying the weariness he felt. "I feel so hopeless. I don't know how to help her."

"You have helped her," J.J. assured him. "You convinced her to see Dr. Beck. She needs you to not give up on her."

Ortus sighed, walking back into the living room. "I'm sure my sister appreciates everything you've done for her. Let's get started with these decorations, and maybe you'll be able to take a nap."

They wasted no time in putting up the decorations, a collaborative effort to create a cheerful atmosphere. They had kept the decorations neutral, not knowing the baby's gender, which made the task more manageable. By the time they were finished, their home was adorned with shimmering gold balloons, food arranged on the dining table, and a grand baby shower banner hanging near the stairs in the living room.

Three hours later, Emmett had managed to steal a brief nap, but Autumn had not yet returned. He had attempted to reach her several times but was met by her voicemail. Even if they had not found Mason yet, an undercurrent of paranoia persisted, gnawing at his mind.

"What's wrong?" Ortus interrupted his thoughts.

"I haven't heard from Autumn. I tried calling her and she didn't answer."

"I also texted her to let her know we were here, and no response." Bradley added.

"Did she say where she was going?" Brooke asked.

Emmett shook his head, "No. All Dr. Beck said was she needed some fresh air and left."

"I'm sure she's fine," Ortus reassured him. "She used to do this when we were—"

A sudden commotion interrupted the conversation. J.J.'s urgent voice rang out, "She's here!"

Emmett let out a sigh of relief, making sure there weren't any umbrellas nearby Autumn could use as a weapon. The sound of footsteps on the porch signaled her arrival, and the door creaked open, revealing her silhouette against the dim lit backdrop of their decorated home.

Autumn's hand flew to her chest, her face turning bright red. "What is all this?"

Emmett grinned. "We know you've been having a rough couple of days, lil' dove. We wanted to bring a smile to your face."

"And we know you need your space when you're tired and overwhelmed," Ortus added.

Brooke nodded. "But we also know you'll always find your way back to the people who love you."

"We tried to call you and let you know what we were planning." Bradley lowered his voice, "We know you don't like surprises, but your phone kept going to voicemail."

"Aw, that's so sweet!" For what felt like the hundredth time today, tears welled up in Autumn's eyes. "I'm sorry, my phone died, it's been a long day."

J.J. shook his head and waved his hand at her face. "I'm going to need you to stop doing that. This is supposed to be a party!"

"You're right." Autumn wiped away her tears with a laugh.

Hope entered the room after her. Autumn linked her arm with Hope's. "Emmett, this is Hope."

Emmett smiled. "Nice to see you again, Hope."

Autumn frowned. "Again?"

"Hi, Emmett." Hope rubbed the side of her arm. "Autumn, I think I should go."

"What? No, you can't leave!" Autumn reached for Hope's hand. "You've helped me so much today." she begged.

"I'm sorry, I should get going," she said, already walking out the front door.

Autumn tried to stop her but came to an abrupt halt when Bradley gave chase out the door. She peeked through the living room window, watching Hope standing by her driver's-side door. Bradley stood by the passenger door across from her, his hands on top of the vehicle. Autumn stepped out the front door and walked to the edge of the porch.

"What the hell are you doing here?" Bradley demanded.

Hope stared at her car keys. "I – I wanted her to get home safe."

"Are you serious? Answer me one thing, Hope," Bradley hissed. "Did you know what he was doing to her?"

"Bradley, I ... I didn't know she was telling me the truth."

He shook his head in disbelief. "I asked you to take care of her when you took her with you and Mason."

"I never thought he would be capable of that. He's my cousin—"

Bradley waved her away. "You should go, Hope. Stay away from Autumn. She doesn't need a snake like you here."

"I'm sorry, Bradley, I am," Hope whispered, getting in the car and speeding away.

When Bradley turned around, he saw Autumn waiting for him.

"How much of that did you hear?" he asked.

"Everything." She smiled. "Don't blame her for what happened, though. It wasn't her fault Mason was abusive. She regrets not believing me. I saw it in her eyes today."

"She didn't believe you when you told her. How can you forgive that?"

"I don't have space in my heart for anger and resentment anymore," Autumn whispered. "Mason already takes most of what I have to offer. He's the one I won't ever be able to forgive."

Bradley shook his head. "You shouldn't. You're too nice, Autumn."

"And so are you. It's why we see the best in people, right?"

"You have a point there." He stepped onto the porch and exhaled, watching the street where Hope had disappeared. "Maybe I was too harsh on her."

"It's okay, you were trying to protect me. Let's get back inside. It's cold out here."

Once inside, they were both pulled into dancing with Brooke and Ortus. Autumn was still in shock that her friends had planned a baby shower for her. With everything going on over the past couple of months, she had never thought of having one.

As she danced, she kept an eye on Emmett, who stood by the staircase, smiling at her. Mason had made Autumn keep her friends at a distance. Emmett, on the other hand, had worked with her friends to make her smile. Emmett had changed her life, the amount of support he had given her over the past year had been almost unbelievable. All the pain she had endured was no longer pain. It had become strength.

Emmett walked toward her. "Whoa!" His arms flung to the sides, smacking balloons and streamers aside as he fought to keep his balance. He and Autumn looked down at once, seeing the puddle beneath her spread across the floor.

18

Autumn, her face flushed, and her eyes filled with exhaustion and joy, cradled her baby to sleep on the hospital bed. The soft glow of a lone lamp casting dancing shadows on the walls, lit the room. It was a tranquil moment amid the sterile hospital environment, a moment that seemed to exist in its own timeless bubble.

Emmett sat close beside her. His hand brushed against her arm, a silent expression of support and connection that spoke volumes. They were both filled with awe as they gazed at their newborn girl, a tiny miracle swaddled in a soft, pastel blanket. Autumn marveled at the delicate perfection of her daughter's tiny fingers and the way her chest rose and fell with each peaceful breath.

Giving birth had proven to be an agonizing experience, one that had pushed her to the limits of her endurance. Autumn's memory was etched with the intense pain, the hours of labor that felt like an eternity, and the relentless waves of contractions that had left her gasping for breath. Her gaze fixed on the tiny, slumbering bundle in her arms. Perhaps it was because the experience was impossible to put into words, or perhaps because the reward at the end was so profound that it made the suffering worthwhile.

"Aw, what a cutie!" J.J. exclaimed.

Brooke smacked J.J.'s head. "Could you please keep it down? You might wake the baby."

Ortus looked at Autumn, ignoring the banter between their two friends. "What have you named her?"

After the birth, Emmett and Autumn spent a couple of hours discussing their deep love for their child. Their all-encompassing love for the baby left them with one name in mind. They shared a prolonged, contented smile with each other, letting the significance of the moment sink in.

Autumn turned to her friends and beamed. "I'd like you to meet Dove Joy Evans-Miller."

Ortus grinned. "Such a beautiful name."

"She has your eyes, Autumn, she's gorgeous," Brooke added.

Bradley shrugged. "I still think Bradley Jr. would've worked."

As Autumn looked down at her daughter, she couldn't believe that Dove was the result of their love, their own bundle of joy. Their journey wouldn't be easy, but she knew their love would conquer whatever challenges came their way.

In the months that followed, however, Autumn and Emmett struggled to adapt to their newfound roles as parents. Their whole world had pivoted, now orbiting around their precious daughter, Dove. In the nights that followed her arrival, Dove's ceaseless crying left them sleep-deprived. Keeping track of the last time they had taken a proper shower or hung out with their friends was becoming impossible. Everyone cheered when you had a baby, but nobody stuck around for those moments when you had to rouse yourself in the dead of night, or when sleep deprivation began to play tricks on your mind. Parenthood had also made Autumn put her mental health on the back burner.

One challenging day, after Emmett had somehow managed to catch a few hours of much-needed rest, he approached Autumn with a gentle touch and a concerned look in his eyes. He reminded her that they couldn't continue down this path of exhaustion and self-neglect. So together, they hatched a plan. They reached out to their parents, who agreed to come over and take care of Dove for a few hours, giving Autumn and Emmett a much-needed respite. It was a profound relief to know that they had a support system they could rely on, even in the most challenging of times.

That evening, as the sun dipped below the horizon, Autumn and Emmett set their crafted plan into action. While it wasn't a flawless strategy, it was a lifeline. They took turns resting, catching those precious moments of sleep that had become so elusive. The plan allowed them to rejuvenate, even if it was in small doses, and it made a world of difference. The weariness that had once clung to them like a suffocating shroud began to loosen its grip, and for the first time in what felt like an eternity, they found themselves feeling somewhat refreshed and more in control.

On Wednesday morning, three months after Dove's birth, Autumn decided it was time to see Dr. Beck again. He sat opposite her on his red chair, legs crossed, and notepad propped on his lap.

"It's been a long time since we last spoke, Autumn," Dr. Beck began, his tone warm.

"It's been a hectic three months, Dr. Beck. Dove has kept us up for most of it, and we're beginning to settle into a routine," Autumn explained.

"How is your daughter doing?"

"Dove is great!" She sighed, "I'm exhausted."

"I'm curious, have you experienced any nightmares since giving birth?"

"No, I haven't. Although, when we started asking for help, I began dreaming again. In one of my dreams, I was having a picnic with Emmett, Dove, and—" She paused, her gaze drifting into the past.

Dr. Beck made note, "And who?"

"Luna," she said with a smile, feeling her hands tingle. "She seemed so happy to be an older sister, and it felt so real. We were reunited, and she was happy to see me smiling again."

"Interesting," Dr. Beck scribbled in his notepad, "What did that mean to you?"

"It meant the world to me, it was like I found closure. I never processed the loss of my child or the abuse. I'm on the brink of perhaps finding happiness."

"On the brink?"

She nodded. "I'm still on edge, but I don't think that will ever vanish. I can't shake the feeling that something might happen at any moment to take it all away."

"Do you think you might be self-sabotaging your own happiness?" Dr. Beck asked, his gaze steady.

She tilted her head, giving him a thoughtful look. If Mason was gone, why couldn't she allow herself to be happy? "I suppose that's a possibility. I've been on the run for the past few years, and now I'm home. I don't have to run anymore, so maybe I was looking for a reason to."

He nodded. "That's it, Autumn. You don't have to run anymore, you have people here who care for you. Don't let Mason be the reason you can't live the life you deserve, spend time with your friends."

Autumn shook her head. "I wish I could. It's my turn today to help Emmett get some sleep. We're a team, so I have to be fair to him too."

"Do what works for both of you. I want to recommend not placing your relationships on the back burner for too long. It's important to take care of yourself too."

"Maybe."

"How about this," Dr. Beck said, placing his notepad and pen on the coffee table. "When you decide to go out with your friends, Emmett can care for Dove and, in return, you can do the same for Emmett."

"I do miss my friends. I think it may work if I don't stay out too late."

"All I'm saying is, both of you deserve some rest. You can't take care of Dove if you don't take care of yourself, right? I'll see you at our next session?" Dr. Beck concluded, offering Autumn a reassuring smile.

Autumn nodded, her gratitude evident as she contemplated the prospect of regaining some normalcy in her life.

Once she got home, she headed upstairs to Dove's nursery. She stood by the door for a moment, watching Emmett place their daughter in her crib. She approached him from behind, wrapping her arms around his chest and resting her head on his back.

"Dr. Beck thinks it'd be a good idea if I went out with my friends." Autumn sighed. "Like I could ever leave you two alone."

Emmett turned to face Autumn, tucking a strand of her hair behind her ear as he studied her in silence.

"What's on your mind?" Autumn asked.

He sighed. "Neither of us has had a break from the house, lil' dove. You're right, we're a team, but we've got a system now. I know it's hard to leave our baby alone, but she'll be with me. Besides, I can call Jayden. I think you should go see your friends."

Autumn laid her head on his chest. She knew he was right, and the way they supported each other was something she would never take for granted.

"How did I get so lucky with you?" she mused.

Emmett shrugged. "I could ask you the same question," he replied, leaning in to kiss her.

"Okay, I'll make some plans with them. You'll need to call Jayden, though," she said, heading toward the door.

"What? Don't you trust me?"

She smiled. "I do."

Autumn hadn't left the house since giving birth, and she was beyond excited to spend more quality time with her friends. After making some calls, she sifted through her closet and settled on a pair of olive-colored leggings, a crisp white shirt, and a tan cardigan. She applied red lipstick for the first time in some time too, feeling like a whole new person.

As she drove, the sun hung low in the sky, casting long shadows that stretched like welcoming arms along the winding road. Her friends had insisted on going to the boardwalk where their favorite Italian restaurant was located. As she turned into the parking lot near the Ferris wheel, Autumn couldn't help but feel a rush of excitement. The sight of the iconic attraction towering over the boardwalk filled her with a sense of wonder. It was a symbol of their friendship, a reminder of the countless times they had spun on its wild bright, flashing gondolas, shrieking with delight as they embraced the thrill of the ride.

The car came to a gentle stop, and Autumn lingered for a moment, taking in the joyful cacophony around her. The sound of waves crashing against the boardwalk drew her out of the car. She turned around, watching the waves meet the golden sand. The salty sea breeze was a welcome sensation, and her shoulders relaxed. She could hear the excited screams of children, their voices rising above the chatter of families and the cheerful melodies of street performers.

I've missed this.

As she approached the front of the restaurant, she could see her friends waiting for her through the window. They already had a bottle of wine at the table. After a deep breath, she entered the restaurant, where her friends were already seated, and of course Bradley was desperate to order.

He groaned. "Where have you been? You're the punctual one of the group!"

"I have a baby now, Bradley. Being on time isn't a realistic expectation for me now."

Brooke filled Autumn's glass with water. "All right, but how do you manage to look this good after giving birth?"

Autumn laughed. It felt like it had been months since she had seen her friends. They had visited her during the first couple of days, but both Autumn and Emmett had been too exhausted to participate in their conversations. Parenthood had turned her life upside down.

As their food arrived, Autumn caught up with her friends. Brooke was planning to expand her art gallery, Ortus was being promoted to detective, J.J. continued to work at his production studio, and Bradley was considering adopting.

"I've missed so much already?" Autumn exclaimed, her eyes wide with genuine surprise and affection for her friends.

"You didn't miss out on any major moments. Besides, you have to raise Dove, and that's a lot to handle already. No need to worry about us."

"Thanks, Ortus." Autumn took a bite of her chicken parmigiana, savoring the flavors that had been absent from her life. "Ugh, I needed this," she admitted.

J.J., already a few glasses of wine in, chimed in, "It was my idea! They wanted to take you to the club."

Brooke rolled her eyes. "You couldn't wait to throw us under the bus, huh?"

Bradley shrugged. "It's your fault for thinking Autumn would have the energy to party." He twirled his spaghetti with a fork. "She's also breastfeeding. Do you know how exhausting that can be?"

Autumn couldn't help but giggle. "You've done your homework, Bradley."

"Of course, Autumn! You're my best friend, and I've always got your back. That includes understanding what you're going through. Plus, I need to prepare for my babysitting gig with Dove."

"Speaking of being best friends ..." Ortus began, her expression growing serious, "there's something we need to discuss with you."

"What is it?"

But before Ortus could continue, Autumn's phone rang, breaking the moment. She glanced at the screen, her heart skipping a beat. "It's Emmett. I have to take this," she said, her voice tinged with a mix of anticipation and apprehension, reminding herself that amid the whirlwind of motherhood and friendship, there were other parts of her life that needed her attention.

She stepped out onto the boardwalk to answer the call. Emmett called to confirm he had prepared Dove's milk in the correct manner. As she stood at the edge of the boardwalk, admiring the pier, she pictured herself next to him preparing Dove's dinner.

"Yup! Everything you did was correct." She walked toward the pier and onto the sand as she spoke, since the boardwalk was full of performers, making it difficult for her to hear. The sun, casting long shadows across the wooden planks, painted a picturesque scene. She found solace in the rhythmic crashing of the waves that accompanied her conversation.

"Okay, I don't know why I started doubting myself. It might have to do with the weird looks Jayden was giving me," Emmett said in annoyance.

"It's because you are weird," said Jayden's voice in the background.

She giggled. "I'm glad Jayden is keeping you company. I'll be home soon, okay? Call me if you need anything else. I love you."

"I love you too."

Autumn slipped the phone into her pocket and wandered across the sand, enjoying the fresh sea air and the soothing sound of the waves. She relished the moment, grateful for this small respite. The salty breeze tousled her hair, and the seagulls overhead provided a serene backdrop to her thoughts.

"Ha-ha, I found you, Mama!" a little girl's voice giggled.

As Autumn opened her eyes, she saw a figure standing a short distance away. As she walked closer, she realized it was Hope.

"Luna, you scared me! I thought I'd lost you. Please don't do that again," Hope said, relieved.

"Sorry, Mama."

Autumn was now inches away from them. "Mama?" she whispered.

The little girl turned to face her. "Who are you?"

Autumn's heart dropped to the pit of her stomach. The daughter who existed in her dreams, with her imagined attributes of ebony curls, her skin tone, and her brown eyes, echoed the features of the young girl in front of her.

"Hope, what did you call her?" Autumn whispered, her voice trembling.

"Autumn, I -" Hope tried to explain.

Autumn, feeling panic welling up inside her, kneeled and grabbed the girl's shoulders. "What's your name?"

"Mom, I'm scared."

"Tell me your name, please." Autumn pleaded through her tears.

"I named her Luna, okay! I'm sorry, Autumn."

Autumn glared at Hope, her tears flowing down her cheeks. "You know that losing her tore me apart. Why would you take her name?"

Before Hope could respond, a damp cloth covered Autumn's face. Panic surged through her, and her body fought against the sudden suffocation. Her lungs gasped for air as she clawed at the cloth, but her strength ebbed away.

The overpowering chemical scent filled her senses, seeping into her every pore. It was acrid and nauseating, making her head spin. Autumn's vision blurred, and her surroundings became a nightmarish swirl of colors and shapes. Desperation surged within her, but her limbs grew heavy, her resistance futile.

As Autumn's consciousness waned, she caught a faint glimpse of people arguing.

"What the hell are you doing?" Hope demanded "You could have hurt her!"

"I'm done waiting," a too-familiar voice replied. "Besides, it's chloroform."

The voices seemed distant, like echoes from a far-off tunnel, their words garbled and distorted. Fear clawed at her fading awareness, and she struggled to hold onto reality, clinging to the world slipping away from her. The stranger lifted Autumn in their arms, and in her blurry vision, she recognized the figure carrying her—the ghost she could never escape. Dread clung to her like a shadow as she slipped into the abyss of unconsciousness, the world fading away in a whirlwind of betrayal and fear.

Mason.

As Autumn slipped into unconsciousness, fragments of memories flashed before her eyes. She and Hope were strolling together in the park.

"You walk so slow," Autumn teased Hope.

"And you're so damn sassy when you're pregnant," Hope observed.

She laughed. "Not my fault."

"What are you naming the little squirt, anyway?"

Autumn smiled. "Luna."

"That's cute. I like how it translates to 'moon' in Spanish, a connection to Mason and my Hispanic heritage is important."

Autumn nodded. "I want her to know she has a culture to be proud of, and she's going to be the light to my dark days."

"I might steal that," Hope joked.

"You better not!" Autumn exclaimed. "The name means so much to me. If you stole it, that would be so cruel!"

Luna, Autumn thought.

Luna.

Luna.

Luna!

She repeated her name her name again and again. For a moment, her eyes fluttered open, and a small figure was standing over her, a silhouette lit from behind. They prodded at Autumn's arm, but again that sweet smell came, and her eyes drifted closed.

The next time she woke up, she found Luna sleeping beside her. She rose, not wanting to wake the child, and took in her surroundings. A wooden dresser, a full-length mirror, and a bathroom connecting to their bedroom. Yet, it was the wooden dove figurine on a bookshelf in the corner of the room that made her heart skip a beat. Was this some kind of sick joke?

"No, he couldn't have brought me here. How could he have known?" she whispered.

The bedroom door swung open. She couldn't believe it. She'd thought she would never have to see him again, but her earlier gut feeling was no longer a feeling.

"My love, you're awake!" Mason said, stepping into the room.

She turned to face him. "How are you here?"

He cocked his head to the side. "You honestly believed it'd be so easy to get rid of me?"

"Why did you bring us here? How did you—"

"Know about this place? My love, I never left." He sneered. "You know I was so close to taking you one day. You had reached the point where you understood Emmett wasn't going to treat you any better, and you ran into the woods. I was worried you were going to get too cold and when I saw you collapse, I thought to myself, this is the perfect moment. I can take her and let her see that I'm saving her."

She recalled the footsteps she heard and the fear she felt that day. "Why didn't you take me?"

He scowled. "That idiot showed up."

There was an emptiness in her heart. "Mason, what are you trying to accomplish?"

"Isn't it obvious? I brought you here because this is going to be our fresh start." He smirked. "I even brought back our daughter."

Autumn shook her head. "Mason ... our daughter died a long time ago. You know that."

"No!" He slammed the wall, making Autumn jump. "She's right there, don't you see?" He pointed at the bed where Luna was now sitting, wide awake and looking terrified.

"Okay." Autumn held her hands up. "It's our Luna, you're right. You want to reunite us, right?"

He nodded. "You're getting it."

"But why this place?"

He walked toward the door, looked back at her, and scowled. "Because this is where I lost you forever," he said, slamming the door behind him, leaving behind the faint click of a lock.

She rushed to the door, turning the knob, but it wouldn't budge. Autumn began pacing back and forth. She was trapped in a never-ending nightmare with no escape. He had been stalking her, letting her believe she had rid herself of him. It was all part of his manipulation, making her feel powerless once more.

"Where's my mama?" Luna managed to say.

"She went on a trip to sell a home and asked me to take care of you."

"But I don't know you." Her voice trembled, tears forming in her eyes. "I want my mama."

"My name is Autumn." She walked closer to Luna. "I won't hurt you."

Luna nodded. "I-I remember mama said you were an old friend."

"I am."

Luna rubbed her eyes, tears streaming down her face. "I want to be with Mama."

Autumn opened her arms, allowing Luna to fall into them and cry. It made Autumn's heart ache listening to Luna's cry intensify. Autumn brushed her fingers through Luna's hair, comforting her until she cried herself to sleep.

How long would he keep her? How long would she have to play his sick game? She looked back at the little girl on the bed, who was sound asleep. No matter how long it would take, she had to ensure Luna remained safe. To survive, she had to play along with his twisted game.

19

Emmett sat in the police station waiting for an update from Ortus. It had been more than thirty-six hours since Autumn had disappeared, and no one had been able to give him any updates. He watched as the police officers drank their morning coffee, while the others answered their desk phones, none of them heading out in search of Autumn. He began tapping his foot and covered his ears as he waited, the phone's loud ringing irritating him.

"Can someone answer these damn phones?" he demanded as he stood up from his seat.

"Emmett, you should go home," Ortus said as she approached him. "I promise you we'll call you with any updates, but you should try to get some rest. You haven't slept in over a day."

He frowned. "I don't understand how she's still missing. Dove is crying, she knows something's wrong. You can't expect me to sit around and do nothing."

When Emmett had received the call from Ortus telling him they couldn't find Autumn, he drove over to meet them. They'd searched the boardwalk and found nothing. It wasn't until they walked along the pier and dialed her phone that they discovered her cellphone ringing next to her buried engagement ring in the sand.

Jayden placed a hand on Emmett's shoulder. "C'mon, Emmett, you know they're doing everything they can."

Emmett gripped his head in his hands. "This is the mother of my child we're talking about—my fiancé! I can't ..." He groaned and sank onto a bench, rubbing at his scalp.

Ortus sat next to him. "I know you're scared. She's my sister too," she whispered.

"And my daughter!"

Ortus and Emmett looked up. Marie stomped toward them, followed by Brooke and Bradley.

"Mom." Ortus stood. "What are you doing here?"

Marie placed her hands on her hips. "I'm here to help find your sister."

Bradley stomped his foot. "Are you kidding me?"

Marie's frown landed on him. "Excuse me?"

"You spent her whole childhood telling her she wasn't good enough, and now you have a sudden investment in wanting to be there for her?"

"I pushed her to achieve her potential, so what? If she'd have done as I'd told—"

Now Brooke stepped in. "You chased her away! She clung to the first person who made her feel good about herself, and when that man started abusing her too, she tolerated it because it was all she'd ever known!"

Marie crossed her arms. "I ... I didn't ...Ortus, I didn't ... did I?"

"I'm sorry, Mom, but they're right. We could all see something wasn't right with Mason, though Autumn didn't say it, but you were so blinded by his fancy suits and his job in the city that ..." Ortus trailed off.

For a moment, all was silent as Marie sank into the chair behind her, clutching her chest. "What have I done?"

Emmett sighed, not in the mood to argue. "Ortus, I'm sorry. I get it. I'll try to be more patient."

"You take care of him," he heard Ortus tell Jayden as he walked away.

"I will."

When they returned home, Emmett thanked Marisol for babysitting and took Dove up to the nursery. He rocked his daughter, trying to lull her to sleep, but all he could think of was how much Dove missed Autumn. It took a couple of minutes, but Emmett was able to get Dove to sleep and found himself unable to let her go. He slid onto the rocking chair, feeling the exhaustion catching up to him. His eyelids closed, and he found himself in a small slumber.

In his dream, he pictured Autumn standing on the boardwalk, watching the stars shining above her. Emmett reached for her, but as his hand was about to land on her shoulder, she disappeared in a blink. He scanned the boardwalk and spotted her again walking toward the pier.

"Autumn!" he called out.

No response.

She walked through the sand, and a dark shadow began to follow her. Emmett couldn't distinguish the figure from afar but saw it close behind her. He ran toward Autumn and the shadow. "Autumn! Turn around, he's behind you!"

The shadow figure charged at her and tackled her into the water. Emmett ran toward them, witnessing as the figure forced Autumn's head under the waves. Her arms reached out for help, but as Emmett ran, he realized he wasn't getting any closer. He collapsed into the sand, witnessing Autumn drowning.

"Autumn!" he cried.

"Emmett?" a voice said.

"Autumn, please hold on. Autumn!"

There was a sudden shake on his shoulders. "Emmett, wake up, you're having a nightmare!"

Emmett woke up gasping for air and still holding Dove in his arms, who remained asleep.

"You okay?" Jayden said, stepping away from him.

Emmett kissed Dove's forehead and placed her in the crib. "Of course not. Look how sad Dove looks."

Jayden sighed. "We need to talk, but not here."

"I can't leave her."

"She'll be fine, let her sleep. We'll be downstairs," Jayden said, with the baby monitor in hand as he left.

Emmett gave Dove one last glance before following. He left the door ajar as they descended the staircase into the living room. "It was her first time not being around Dove, and I pushed her to go. Something bad happened and I have no idea what it could be," he said, defeated. Emmett felt like a part of him was missing, an empty piece he didn't know whether he'd ever get back. He studied the photos on the walls of him and Autumn. It didn't matter how hard they tried, somehow life always found a way to separate them from one another.

When they walked into the living room, he was confused to see Brooke waiting for them. "Why do we need to talk downstairs?"

"I'm here to update you." Brooke crossed her arms, looking unsettled. "The police are looking for Hope."

Emmett frowned. "Hope, the real estate agent? Why?"

Brooke nodded; lips pursed. "As you know, Autumn and Hope know each other."

"Okay, but ... but why Hope? Does she have something to do with this?"

"Emmett ..." Brooke started, "Hope is Mason's cousin."

Emmett covered his face with his hands. "Why didn't anyone tell me?"

"Emmett, we didn't know she was even around until she turned up at the baby shower a few months ago, we promise. When Dove was born, Hope slipped out of all our minds. We're so sorry."

He stared at the carpet, unable to meet either of his friends' eyes. "You think she took Autumn?"

"It's the sole lead the police have," Brooke said. "Best case, they find Hope, they find Autumn."

"But why would Hope want to go after Autumn?" Jayden asked when Emmett remained silent.

Brooke shrugged. "She took Mason's side when Autumn came to her for help. And now Mason's life is over. Maybe she blames Autumn for that."

Emmett nodded, lifting his head to look over to Brooke. "You said they're looking for her."

She nodded. "They found out where she's been staying, police are on their way there."

"Why are we standing around here? Let's go!" he demanded.

Jayden stood in front of Emmett, blocking the front door. "And who is going to take care of Dove?"

Emmett turned to glare at Brooke. "She will," he said, already out the door.

Jayden sighed. "I'm sorry, Brooke, he's not himself."

"It's fine, you should go with him," she said as Jayden closed the door behind them.

Jayden chased after Emmett, who was already starting his car. He climbed into the passenger seat and Emmett sped out of his driveway.

"Do you even know where you're going?" Jayden said, holding on to the side of his seat.

"No, you're going to find out for me."

Jayden rubbed his head and sighed, pulling out his phone. "All right …"

As Emmett drove down the road, fingers tapping the steering wheel, Jayden spoke into his phone.

"Ortus? Yeah, it's Jayden … I know you're busy, I'm sorry. Can you let me know the address of—yes, he's with me. Why?"

Emmett's ears pricked up, listening to the mumble of Ortus's voice through the small speaker but unable to understand any of the words. Jayden's eyes flicked sideways to look at Emmett.

"Okay, I'll make sure he knows. Thanks, Ortus. Bye."

As soon as he put the phone down, Emmett asked, "Where?"

"The Maple Apartment Complex, at the end of Oak Street."

Emmett flicked on his blinker to turn right at the intersection, but Jayden wasn't done.

"Emmett, you need to control yourself. We'll be pulling into a crime scene. You can't run in there and—"

"Crime scene? Have they found her?"

"No sign of her yet. But if you find Hope there, what are you going to do?"

Emmett tightened his grip on the steering wheel. "Whatever I need to do to get Autumn back."

When they arrived at the apartment complex, they walked up to Hope's apartment, hopeful they would find something that would lead them to Autumn. They were stopped at the door by a police officer, but as Emmett scanned the room, he noticed it had been trashed. The coffee table was broken, there was a smashed lamp on the floor, and Hope was nowhere to be found.

"The door was left open. She's not here," Ortus said, walking up to them.

"There're are some toddler's clothes in the dressers, but she didn't take any with her. I don't think she's run away," Bradley added.

"Um, why is *he* allowed inside?" Emmett interjected.

Bradley rubbed the back of his neck. "I'm the one that discovered where she was staying. Hope has been staying with her friend Natalie, who I bumped into at the police station. Natalie was horrified when she came back home and found her apartment trashed."

Emmett rubbed the stubble covering his jaw. "What else do you know?"

"We've sent a search team to look for Hope since she's not here." Ortus crossed her arms. "Hope didn't pack her things, but it looks like she packed some of her daughter's clothes ... there's something about this scene that doesn't make sense."

Bradley turned to face Emmett. "Emmett, I know you're upset with us right now, but Autumn wouldn't want you to do this. She'd want you to take care of Dove and not fight us. You know that, right?"

Emmett let out a frustrated breath. "I know. I promised myself I would keep her safe, and so far, I've failed." He looked at the ground, unable to make eye contact with any of them. He needed to remain strong, he needed to for Dove. As he watched the floor, he noticed a faint red trail on the patterned carpet. He narrowed his eyes on it.

"Blood," Emmett whispered, shooting off to follow it.

Ortus gasped. "How did I miss that?"

With everyone behind him, he walked down the hallway until they reached the door of a stairwell. Emmett opened the door slowly, and terror flushed his face. His friends crowded at his back, and Bradley's hand flew to his mouth as they all saw the body lying face down at the bottom of the stairs.

"Guys, over here!" Ortus called to her colleagues as she squeezed past to kneel by Hope's unmoving form. "She's breathing! Call an ambulance!"

Mason made breakfast, lunch, and dinner every day for them. For the past two days, it had been the same grim routine. Each morning, she awoke to a room bathed in cold, dim light. The worn wooden walls seemed to close in around her. Luna, her innocent "daughter" in this sick game, wriggled in her sleep. Autumn's trembling fingers fumbled with Luna's clothes as she dressed the child, the fabric a frail reminder of a life they once knew.

A leak in her breast pulled her away from her thoughts. "Shoot." She scattered to the bathroom to clean herself up. After changing her shirt, Autumn leaned against the bathroom sink, looking at her reflection. In that moment, the tears escaped her eyes falling one after the other.

I miss my baby girl. Autumn yearned to hold her in her arms again and feed her. *What if she cries when I hold her? As if I were a stranger to her…*

She felt like grasping for air, the panic taking over her. *Breathe, Autumn, breathe.*

Luna peaked her head inside the bathroom, "Are you okay friend?"

Autumn inhaled and released a long breath. "Yes. I need to change my shirt and I'll be ready for breakfast."

The scent of Mason's cooking filled the air, but it no longer made her stomach churn with dread. In the past two days, she noticed she didn't feel the fear she once had. As she sat down with Luna, Autumn couldn't help but observe Mason's every move, every nuance in his expression. His face, a mask of fatherly warmth, concealed intentions darker than the depths of the surrounding forest.

Autumn would continue to adapt, driven by an unyielding resolve. Fear had transformed into a determination to protect Luna and to somehow endure this ordeal. Every bite of food, every calculated moment, was a desperate step toward reuniting with Emmett and Dove.

"Did you enjoy your breakfast, Luna?" Mason asked, stirring his coffee.

She licked her lips, "Yes, thank you, Cousin Mason."

Mason slammed his hands on the table, making Luna jump. "Thank you, *what*?"

Luna's hands trembled, "Thank you, Daddy," she whispered.

"There you go. How about you, my love?"

Autumn smiled. "It was exceptional, thank you."

"Good, it's what I like to hear." He grinned. "Now, hurry up and eat. We're going to have an eventful day today."

"What are we doing?" Luna asked, wary in her naivety.

He stroked the little girl's head. "It's a sunny day, so we're going outside."

Luna nodded, her eyes gleaming in optimism. Autumn, on the other hand, wondered whether it was too dangerous to run from him. She couldn't run and risk Luna, he wouldn't be the reason why another child lost their life.

"Where are we going, my love?" she asked as she buttered her toast.

"Fishing! Remember, when we were in California, you said you wanted to rent a cabin and fish? That's why we're here!"

Autumn smiled, fighting the tears in her eyes. "I remember, it was when I was pregnant with Luna."

He grinned. "Yes! Now, we get to do that. Why don't both of you go get ready and I'll meet you outside."

Autumn led Luna back to their bedroom, her heart heavy with dread as they stepped through the door. The room, once a place of cherished memories, now felt like a prison cell. Luna, oblivious to the looming darkness, bounced with excitement, her innocent eyes gleaming with anticipation.

"Do you think my mama is waiting for us?"

"Eh -" Autumn began, "I think your mom might not join us today, but perhaps soon."

Luna's shoulders dropped. "Oh."

"I know you're disappointed hon. I promise we will see your mom soon."

Autumn sifted through the pile of clothing Mason had provided. Each fabric held a disturbing weight, a reminder of her captivity. Her fingers brushed against a silky, crimson dress, and she couldn't help but shudder. Red, the color of blood, the color that Mason favored on her. She didn't know how long she could keep playing this charade.

She watched Luna with a mix of despair and protectiveness as they both changed into more casual attire, donning matching gray shirts and comfortable pants. Luna's innocent excitement for their supposed vacation was like a dagger to Autumn's heart. Every moment spent there was a countdown to an uncertain and ominous fate, and Autumn's determination to protect Luna burned brighter with each passing second.

Stepping outside, Autumn couldn't help but notice Mason had dressed himself in a manner mirroring theirs, his intentions veiled behind normalcy. He loaded fishing gear into the trunk of his new red Toyota Corolla, his preparations executed with an unsettling calmness.

The world around them seemed oblivious. The birds filled the air with their cheerful melodies, contrasting with the looming darkness of their situation. Autumn couldn't shake the feeling that they were trapped in a nightmare, their idyllic surroundings a cruel backdrop.

Mason glanced over at them, his sharp glare causing her to jump. "Luna, come help me finish packing the car."

Luna glanced at Autumn, waiting for her approval. Although Autumn was hesitant, she nodded at her. "Go with him. I'll go back inside and pack our sandwiches."

Autumn walked into the kitchen area and began to prepare some turkey sandwiches. Once done, she peeked out the window above the sink and saw Mason buckling Luna up in the car. Without making a sound, she pulled a steak knife from the drawer and hid it behind a book on the nightstand near the fireplace. She hoped she wouldn't have to use it.

"What are you doing?" Mason asked as he stood on the threshold.

Autumn jumped. "I was looking for Luna's sweater. Have you seen it?"

Mason smiled. "My love, you worry too much. I've already packed it in the car. Let's get going."

The car ride stretched on, filled with an eerie silence that hung heavy in the air. Mason gripped her hand, his fingers a vice that threatened to crush her will. She didn't want him touching her, but she couldn't risk upsetting him. She had to play the part of the perfect wife, all to keep Luna safe.

The car came to a halt beside an abandoned, desolate lake. Mason led them toward a weathered wooden dock that creaked and groaned in protest beneath their weight. As Autumn settled into a folding chair, Luna grabbed a small net and leaned over the edge of the dock to dip it into the calm water.

Mason's hand slithered like a serpent to rest on the back of Autumn's neck. The sensation sent shivers racing down her spine, and her muscles tensed. She fought to maintain her composure, to conceal her panic and dread. Every fiber of her being revolted against his touch, each caress a cruel reminder of the abuse that had scarred her past.

"Are you okay, my love?"

She nodded. "Yeah. I—I forgot our lunch in the car. Do you mind getting it?"

He smiled. "Not at all. I'll be right back," he said.

As Mason walked away, she turned to face Luna. "Are you okay?"

Luna nodded. "This is fun. I'm going to tell my mom to take me fishing more often."

"You should, I'm sure she'll enjoy it."

She continued to watch Luna, making sure she didn't fall into the water as she dragged the net through the shallows.

"Autumn?" She heard someone call from behind her.

She turned and saw Henry, who was wearing a turquoise checkered T-shirt under some brown overalls, walking toward her.

Oh no, scanning to see where Mason was. She spotted him locking the car as he returned to them. He scowled at her, placing his index finger over his lips. He eyed Luna, warning Autumn that if she said anything, Luna would pay the consequences.

"I'm sorry I can't be of more help," she said to Henry.

Henry scratched his head. "What do you—"

"Hi, my love, who's this?" Mason said, placing an arm around her.

"Sweetheart, this is Sam. He's come to visit and was asking for directions. I was telling him that we're visiting too, and I can't help him."

"Mason's lips curled into a chilling smirk, his eyes, cold and calculating, locked onto Henry. "What are you searching for, Sam?"

"Um … a grocery store. Anywhere I can buy a fishing line. I ran out," Henry said, placing his hands in his pockets.

"Oh, is that all?" Mason grabbed a fishing line that was lying on the dock. "We bought extra. Have fun."

"Thanks. Have a good day," Henry said, walking away from them.

Autumn's heart raced, thundering like a distant storm in her chest. Did Mason see through her lies? Did he recognize Henry? She couldn't tell, and the unknown chilled her to her core.

"Here you go, my love," he said, handing her a turkey sandwich.

The hours dragged on as they watched Luna's innocent joy during the fishing trip. Mason kept his arm across Autumn's shoulders, and she closed her eyes for a fleeting moment, trying to conjure the memory of Emmett, his protective embrace replacing the suffocating grip she now endured. She couldn't stop thinking about what would've happened if Henry had said more. Autumn didn't know how far Mason would go, and she didn't know when he would snap. She hoped Henry would look for help and not leave her behind with this monster from her past.

Emmett paced back and forth in the hospital room. His entire body was sore, he had bags under his eyes, and a perpetual headache pulled at his focus. The exhaustion was destroying him. Everyone around them was starting to doubt Autumn was alive. However, his gut told him Autumn was still alive.

"Hope's been unconscious for two days," he whispered. "What if she never wakes up?"

Jayden watched him continue to pace. "Don't lose faith, Emmett. She'll wake up."

Ortus held his hand, forcing him to stop. "We've got eyes on the nearby airports. We know Autumn's still here, somewhere."

"She's got to be okay, nobody would want to hurt her," Jayden said. "I mean this is Autumn we're talking about."

Emmett's patience snapped, his frustration boiling over. He shook off Ortus's grasp. "How can we be so sure? Look at what happened to Hope. She was not recognizable."

Ortus sighed, conceding the point. "You're right, we can't be sure. But Autumn is strong. She has you and Dove to fight for."

Hope's face was beginning to heal, the swelling decreasing. They were convinced it was a hard object that had caused most of the damage. Her eyes remained closed, but for the first time in days, she stirred.

With a faint groan, Hope shook her head, murmuring, "Luna?"

"Get the doctor," Emmett ordered Ortus as Jayden rushed to Hope's side.

Hope's eyelids fluttered open, and she struggled to sit up, wincing in pain. "Where am I?"

"Hi, Hope. My name is Jayden Rose. I was one of the people who found you outside your apartment."

Hope's confusion gave way to horror as she scanned Jayden's face. She attempted to rise but faltered, almost toppling over.

"You shouldn't stand, Hope!" Emmett said, catching her fall.

"Where is she? Where's my daughter?" Hope's voice quivered with panic. She refused to sit back down.

"Your daughter?"

"He took her!" she yelled. "He took Luna!"

"Who took her? Damn it, Hope, Autumn's missing and if anything happens to her because of you"—

"Mason took her! He took both of them."

Emmett's blood ran cold. "I knew it." He massaged his temples, frustration clawing at him. "What was your role in this, Hope? To infiltrate our lives and destroy us from within?"

Hope took a deep breath, sitting back on the bed but not relaxing onto the pillows. "I was supposed to help him carry out his revenge. Emmett, he hit me. I couldn't get out, and I didn't think I deserved any help after pushing Autumn away." She looked at the bruises on her hands. "After she told me what he was doing to her, I freaked out. I never thought he would be capable of doing what he has. He's not well," Hope confessed, tears glistening in her eyes.

Emmett sighed. "Hope, I'm sorry he put you through that. Even if you pushed Autumn away, you didn't deserve it. No one deserves to be abused. But please help us find him. What does he want out of all this?"

"He's trying to rebuild what he lost. Mason told me he wanted Autumn, so he took advantage of the situation and took her at the beach." A tear streaked down her cheek. "He forced me to leave Luna with Autumn in a locked bedroom, he wanted us to go back to my apartment and grab Luna's clothes."

She continued, "I didn't think much of it, I thought he was going to force us to stay with him too. We got back to my apartment, I packed Luna's bag, and that's when he lost it. Mason pushed me against the wall then the coffee table, he grabbed the bag and stormed out of the room. I stumbled but I managed to follow him, I begged him not to take my little Luna, I tried to fight him, I—" Her voice cracked into silence.

"Why take your daughter though?"

Hope trembled as she cried.

"Take your time, Hope," Jayden said.

After a long pause, she took a deep breath and said, "He took my daughter because I named her after the child they lost. They were so heartbroken. I was trying to honor their little girl."

"Autumn and Luna must still be alive," Emmett concluded, hope reigniting within him, but the caution in Hope's tone reined him in.

"Yes, but we have to be careful, Emmett," she warned. "You don't know what he's capable of."

Emmett's phone interrupted, his father's name flashing on the screen.

"I'll be right back," he muttered, stepping into the bathroom. "Henry, I'm sorry I haven't called, I"—

"Emmett, Emmett? Can you hear me?" Henry was frantic.

"Henry, what's going on? Are you all right?"

"Emmett, did you and Autumn break up?"

"No? Henry, she's missing. We've been looking all over for her and—"

"Emmett, listen. I saw her near the large lake where you stayed last time you were here. She was with a man and little girl—"

"Emmett's heart raced as he interrupted, trembling with emotion. "Are they okay?"

"She called me Sam and pretended not to know who I was. I don't think she is. What's going on? Is there anything I can do?"

"I'll explain later, Henry. Don't do anything. I'll be there soon! Thank you so much." He hung up the phone and ran out of the bathroom, finding Jayden holding a bottle of water, his face pale.

"What's wrong?" Emmett asked.

Jayden looked at him wide-eyed. "She asked me if I could grab her a bottle of water. I—"

Emmett turned toward the hospital bed. Hope was gone.

20

When they returned to the cabin, Autumn and Luna remained in their bedroom. After Autumn gave Luna a bath, she grabbed the sweats and shirt she would wear for the night and left Luna alone, reading a copy of *Alice in Wonderland*.

Autumn placed her clothes on the wooden surface next to the shower door, glancing at them for a moment before turning away. The bathroom's warm, dim light did little to alleviate her unease, casting eerie shadows across the old tiles and worn fixtures. She stepped into the shower, the hot droplets against her skin like a gentle embrace, erasing the lingering touch of Mason's cruel hands. Her trembling fingers brushed away rivulets of water, each one carrying away a piece of her fear.

As she lathered her hair, Autumn closed her eyes for a moment, trying to shut out the haunting memories of the past few days. Leaning against the tiles, she let the water beat down on her. She couldn't help but replay her brief encounter with Henry in her mind. Had the desperation in her eyes conveyed the urgency of their situation? Had he seen the silent plea for help hidden beneath her facade of strength?

Autumn felt her fingers prune, aware that she had spent a significant amount of time lost in thought in the shower. She wrapped her hair and body in the light red towels hanging in the bathroom and wiped the steam off the sink mirror.

Glancing at the wooden surface by the shower door, she realized her clothes were no longer there. She let out a heavy sigh.

She opened the bathroom door, hurried to the dresser in her room, and grabbed another pair of sweats and a burnt orange shirt. Luna giggled as she observed her, and when Autumn turned to face her, she realized her hunch was right. Mason had been in the room and left the door open. He watched her from the chair in the living room, a smirk playing on his lips as he admired her almost exposed body.

Autumn ran back to the bathroom, locking the door behind her. She clutched the edges of the sink, wanting to scream. This dangerous game Mason was playing wouldn't last much longer. His temper was growing shorter, and it would be a matter of time before he became more violent. She started to hyperventilate as she stared at her reflection. Was she strong enough to get through this?

"Friend, are you okay?" Luna called from the other side of the door.

Autumn closed her eyes, attempting to steady her breathing. In this moment, there was no time for her to panic. She needed to get through this for Luna. Autumn couldn't risk losing her, not again.

After a few deep breaths, she cracked open the door. "I'm fine, honey," she said, kneeling to give Luna a tight hug. "How are you?"

Luna sighed. "I'm okay, but I'm starting to miss my mom," she said, releasing their embrace.

"What mom?" Mason's voice thundered through the cabin, sending shivers down Autumn's spine. He stomped into the room, his chilling presence enveloped the dim space, "She's right here!"

Autumn stood up and positioned herself in front of Luna. Her heart raced, but she willed her hands to stay steady and raised them in a trembling gesture, a feeble barrier between Luna and the impending danger. "Mason, honey," she said, her voice trembling with a forced calmness, "it's okay, don't worry about it."

Mason looked at Luna. "I knew Hope would cause me more problems, damn it! Let's go, Luna!"

"No!" Autumn argued. "Where are you taking her?"

"It's none of your business. Come here, child!"

"Mason, please don't take her!" she begged, her voice quaking. "It's been a long day. Let me put her to bed, and I can wear that red dress you bought me."

Mason's demeanor shifted, his malevolence transforming into a twisted amusement. A sinister grin crept across his face. "I like that. I'll wait for you in the living room." He darted toward the other bedroom, leaving behind a lingering sense of dread.

She exhaled a shaky breath, her gaze never leaving Luna. "Let's get you tucked into bed, okay?"

Luna's wide eyes met Autumn's, a mixture of fear and trust reflected in their depths. She nodded.

After ensuring Luna's safety, Autumn returned to the bathroom, her trembling hands reaching for the blonde dye box that lay abandoned on the counter. The painful memories of her past flooded back. *I never thought I would have to do this again.*

Hours passed, the scent of hair dye filling the air, as Autumn meticulously transformed her appearance. She exchanged her clothes for the long red dress she had glimpsed earlier, her fingers applying nude lipstick to her lips. In the dim cabin lighting, she studied her reflection in the mirror, her now blonde hair a stark contrast to her previous self; she looked as she did when she was in California. "I need to do this for Luna," she whispered, her voice determined. It was the way to ensure their safety.

She drew in another quivering breath before stepping out of the door, her senses on high alert. In the living room of the secluded cabin, her eyes locked onto Mason, his figure cloaked in an unsettling burgundy suit. With a shiver running down her spine, she couldn't help but recall the first time they had crossed paths in her college dorm room, a time when everything seemed different, simpler.

As the haunting instrumental music swelled in the background, he reached out, his hand extended, waiting for her to grasp it. He gave her an encouraging smile as she walked toward him. Mason pulled her in, holding her close.

They danced to the music, and although the music was loud, she could still hear her heart beating faster by the second.

"You look sexy, my love." His whisper tickled her ear, sending an unwelcome chill down her spine.

"Thank you," she replied.

"Aren't you glad we have our daughter back?"

"Yeah," she mumbled, her voice above a whisper, "I don't know how I'd survive without her."

Their dance ground to a halt, and she found herself ensnared by his gaze, those dark brown eyes drawing her into a terrifying abyss. He inched closer, their lips almost touching. Desperation gnawed at her as she tried to conjure Emmett's image, his soft, curly hair, warm brown eyes, and the love that had filled them.

Mason's lips pressed against hers, and a wave of sickening familiarity washed over her. She clung to the illusion, to the thought that she could continue pretending, until his hands began to roam, caressing her hips and pulling her closer to him. She felt her breasts press against his chest and she could no longer bear it.

"Get away from me!" Autumn's voice cracked as she slapped him across the face and pushed him away.

He glared at her with fury in his eyes. "What else do I need to do for you? I've given you everything!"

She backed away from him. "All you've given me are nightmares, pain, and trauma. I can't continue living like this," she whispered as she walked closer to the nightstand.

"You're so selfish!" Mason's voice thundered through the room. "I made Hope sell her parents' home for you, I let you live with that man for a short time, and I was going to bring Dove to you tomorrow. Why are you not content?"

"Because you're not him!" she yelled. "I don't love you, Mason, I love him!"

With a clenched fist, he advanced, his anger boiling over. His raised fist bore down on her face, but Autumn's desperation drove her to seize the hidden knife beneath the book. With all her might, she thrust it toward his chest. Mason was quick to react and gripped her arm, inflicting a painful twist.

In a desperate move, she stepped forward, catching him off guard, and struck him in the groin. He howled in agony, bending forward. "You bitch!"

Her hand throbbed with pain, but the rush of adrenaline masked it. She clutched the steak knife and slashed at his arm. Mason's agonized screams filled the room as blood flowed from his wounds. "You're going to pay for that!"

Autumn's heart raced, a twisted satisfaction dancing on the edge of her consciousness. It didn't make it right, but it offered her some semblance of control. Her hand was in great pain, but when he looked up at her, she scratched her nails across his face. He cried out as blood trickled into his eyes.

Seizing the opportunity, she sprinted into the bedroom where Luna lay sleeping. Using a soft touch, she shook the girl awake. "Wake up, sweetheart. Let's get going," she urged Luna.

Still groggy-eyed, Luna staggered off the bed, her voice laden with sleep. "Where are we going?"

"No time, let's go," Autumn replied, but as they reached the threshold of their bedroom door, a chilling sight greeted them—Mason stood there, a gun gripped in his hand.

"You think I'm an idiot? I will never let you go, you won't take my daughter with you!"

Autumn shook her head in disbelief. "She's not our daughter, Mason! You killed our daughter when you caught me at the train station and forced me to stay with you. Don't you remember? I miscarried because of you!"

"That's not true!" He shook his head, aiming the gun toward them. "You were trying to leave me Autumn, you left me no choice but to follow you to the train station! It was your fault."

Autumn pushed Luna behind her. "Do what you must, but I won't be with you, and I'll win," she said, turning to hug Luna. She heard Mason cock the gun. "Close your eyes, okay?" Autumn whispered as Luna buried her face in her chest.

A tense silence enveloped them, a pause before the inevitable. They stood, waiting for him to shoot, but instead heard a crash and a loud thud. Autumn turned around, a knot of dread in her stomach as she discovered a shattered window. Glass littered the floor, and Mason lay unconscious with blood streaming down his forehead and someone looming over his body.

Luna's voice pierced through the air, "Mom!"

Autumn's gaze darted to Hope, whose face bore the brutal marks of Mason's cruelty no doubt. She looked pale, fragile, and broken, a mirror of Autumn's own past. "Hope, how did you find us?"

"When he left me for dead, I heard him say to Luna that he would take her back to his mother, where he almost captured you the first time."

"Thank you, Hope." Autumn muttered.

"Let's get out of here," Hope said, taking Luna's hand and limping away out the door.

Together, they fled the cabin, Autumn's footsteps echoing the desperation she felt. Mason had ruined the memory she once had of this place. Now, when she thought of the vacation she had shared with Emmett, she would remember the torment Mason had put her through.

"Luna, sweetie, why don't you wait for me in the car?" Hope said, struggling to get on her knees.

Luna nodded. "Okay, Mom, I love you!" She embraced Hope in a hug before running to the car.

Hope smiled. "I love you too."

"Thank you," Autumn whispered once Luna was out of earshot.

"We don't have much time, the police should be on their way soon. I wanted to let you know how sorry I was," Hope said, fighting back her tears. "I promise you I didn't realize he was going to do all of this. I'm sorry for lying and I'm sorry for not believing you."

"Hope, it's okay. You fell victim like I did, right?" Autumn said, extending her good hand to help Hope maintain her balance. "You didn't deserve any of this, do you understand that?"

Hope smiled. "I do now. You did a number on him. How did you even—?"

"Self-defense. Before he found me, I had to take some lessons in New Mexico. I was terrified." She smiled. "I never thought the lessons would work."

Before Hope could respond, the smile vanished from her face and terror filled her eyes. Autumn had never seen such an expression on her face and spun to find

Mason limping toward them. He spat blood from his mouth.

"Oh, it was most impressive. Besides, Hope deserved what she got," he said, raising the gun once more.

Autumn's muscles tightened, and fear coursed through her body. "What are you doing, Mason?"

Hope walked between them. "Is this how you want to end things, cousin? After all we've been through?"

Mason shook his head. "You betrayed me, and you know if there is one thing I can't tolerate, it's betrayal, Hope."

Autumn's eyes flicked to Luna in the car, the young girl's fear mirroring her own. Terror twisted her insides, but she refused to let it dominate her. When Autumn turned back to look at Mason, he had a smug smile on his face and was looking past her.

"Enough Mason stay away from them!"

"Emmett!" Autumn cried as he came level with her from behind, followed by Jayden.

Mason smirked. "I'm glad you're feeling better after your accident, Emmett. It was a horrifying scene to witness. I'm glad I won our little race."

"You son of a—" Emmett said, taking a step closer, but was stopped by Hope.

"Now, now Emmett. You took her away from me, now I will do the same to you."

In that moment, something fueled Autumn with anger and frustration. For a long time, she had been silenced, for a long time she had been ignored, and for a long time Autumn had been held prisoner by her past. Today, she was going to be set free.

"I'm no one's property, Mason!" she yelled. "I let you torture me for years! I was lost and confused. You took advantage of that. You were supposed to be my safety, someone who cared for me. Instead, you hit me. You would say you loved me, and seconds later you would hit me. The reason why you lost me is because I no longer needed someone to make me miserable. You are nothing to me, Mason, nothing!" Autumn said the words she had dreamed of telling him. She was brave, but she was also afraid, because as she looked at Mason, the smirk he once had was now gone. He looked at the gun, and it seemed clear to him what he needed to do.

"If I can't have you, no one can!" Mason aimed the gun at Emmett as police sirens began to echo through the woods.

"No, don't!" Autumn cried but was pulled back. Emmett and Hope ran toward Mason. The three of them struggled, fighting for the gun, as Jayden hovered over Autumn. In that terrifying moment, the gunshot rang out, its echo reverberating through the forest. Autumn clung to Jayden, her world reduced to darkness and the haunting sound of that fateful shot as she didn't dare look to see who it had struck.

21

Autumn stood resolute before the gravesite, clutching her vibrant yellow umbrella as the rain poured from the heavens above. Her gaze remained fixed on the casket, her heart heavy with the unspoken words that eluded her.

Tears flowed down her cheeks as she murmured, "I can't believe she's gone…"

Luna held her hand tight. "Autumn, I can't stop crying," her voice small and fragile. "I miss her, I want my mama."

Autumn reached for Luna and allowed her to cry into her. Emmett came from behind, wrapping his arms around them. "Remember, Hope saved us so you both could smile. Those were her last words, remember?"

Lifting her head and swallowing her grief, Autumn nodded. They stood together in the cemetery, the raindrops forming a mournful backdrop to the moment. Autumn steeled herself and walked closer to the casket, her trembling fingers brushing its surface.

"Hope, you were my best friend in college," Autumn began, her voice quivering but determined. "You were ambitious, smart, and brave. You never liked to talk about your feelings, but as we got older, I realized all I needed to do to get you to talk was to provide you with ice cream."

Autumn continued, "You will always be remembered as the warrior you were, until the end. Thank you, Hope." Her voice started to crack. "I'll take care of Luna, and I will love her like you did. Thank you for ending our torment."

Their friendship might have deteriorated over the years, but it hadn't been their fault. Both had been ensnared by an abuser. The world was quick to question why they stayed, but seldom pondering why he had inflicted pain upon them.

Back home, Autumn reclined on her bed, her thoughts a turbulent sea. She tried to sleep, but she found herself getting lost as she looked at the fan above her spin in circles.

When Hope had collapsed, the gunshot still echoed through the air, while the police had shot Mason at the same time. His death was immediate, but Hope lay on the ground facing Luna's approaching figure. Autumn had reached Hope first, trying to stem the bleeding from her wound, cradling her head in her lap.

"Stay with us Hope, please," she had said through her tears.

"Mama, what's wrong?" Luna whimpered, drawing near.

A tear ran down Hope's face. "It's okay, honey. Autumn will take care of you."

"Hope, please, we can do this together," Autumn pleaded.

"I owe this to you. I named her Luna to honor your daughter. I promise I wasn't trying to hurt you."

Autumn ran her hand through Hope's hair. "I know."

Hope managed a smile, weak but genuine. "I need you to take care of Luna, and she needs to see that smile of yours. She will remember this for the rest of her life, and she needs more reasons to smile than cry, so be that reason, Autumn. Please."

Autumn had nodded, as tears rolled down her face. It was the last conversation she ever had with Hope, and she'd etched it into her memory. She couldn't help but wonder how Luna would remember this, whether she would warm up to her, whether she'd see Autumn as her mother. Would they be good enough to make her smile again?

"How are you doing, lil' dove?" Emmett asked, as he lay beside her.

"I can't believe Hope saved our lives. I was terrified when Mason pointed the gun at you," Autumn whispered.

He sighed and nodded. "I keep replaying in my head how she pushed me away and ran in front of him. I wanted to stop her, but the gunshots …"

"She got shot, but in the process, so did he. I'm glad the police got there in time, but if they would've gotten there sooner maybe she would still be here." A tear ran down her face. "I know it's over, but now Luna doesn't have her mother."

Emmett turned onto his side to look at Autumn. "But she has us. We promised Hope we'd take care of her. I'm going to love her regardless. She's, our daughter."

"We missed so much already, and she's so confused."

Emmett leaned in to kiss Autumn's forehead. "And now we get to be part of the rest of her life. We will love her so much, and we'll make sure she never forgets Hope."

Emmett cradled Dove in his arms, as he had done on previous nights since the incident. He felt an overwhelming sense of gratitude, and he owed his life to Jayden, who had been persistent in not leaving his side during the search for Autumn. Without Jayden's support and the arrival of the police, perhaps both Autumn and Emmett would have been killed.

A soft knock on the front door pulled him from his thoughts. Emmett positioned Dove in the beige portable crib he had set up earlier. When he reached the door, a composed Henry stood in front of him.

"I'm so glad you're okay," Henry said, embracing him. "I'm sorry for coming on the day you attended a funeral."

"It's okay." Emmett broke their embrace, "Let's get inside."

Emmett gravitated toward to the two chairs by the cozy lit-up fireplace, positioning himself to keep a close eye on Dove. "What brings you here?"

"I needed to see you in person, what you went through was not easy." Henry rubbed his hands. "How are you processing it all?"

Emmett's eyes shifted to Dove, who remained in peaceful slumber. "I was scared," he confessed. "There were times when I wondered, 'What if Autumn doesn't return?'" His voice trembled as he continued, "I would have had to raise Dove by myself, and she would have missed her mother."

"You're what-if questions were valid." Henry locked eyes with Emmett, "And the days that follow will be filled with self-torment and you will replay in your mind what you could have done to stop this from happening. You'll conclude that your actions and decisions gave you the same result —a new family."

Henry continued, "Your fiancé is upstairs, and your baby is behind me. You have now opened your home to a kid who doesn't have either parent here, and I know you will raise her like she is your own. In the end, the person you will need to forgive is yourself."

There was truth to Henry's words. Emmett did blame himself for not doing more to prevent Autumn's kidnapping. But in hindsight, what more could he have done? Should he have kept Autumn from ever stepping outside or confined her to house arrest? That wouldn't be considered living a life, nor would Autumn stand for it."

Emmett veered the conversation, "How are your treatments going?"

Henry released a long breath, "I'm in remission."

"Oh my—that's fantastic Dad!" The words had tumbled from his lips, causing Henry to steal a quick glance at his hands and try to mask the grin that formed when he heard Emmett refer to him as 'dad.'

He didn't regret saying the word, in the past couple of months he had learned so much about his father—both his virtues and flaws. Being seated beside him reaffirmed his dad wanted to be part of his life; he had proven this when he spotted Autumn with Mason at the lake.

"I never got to thank you for your call the day you saw Autumn," Emmett muttered. "If it weren't for that call, finding her might have been impossible."

"The instant she called me Sam and I noticed her discomfort, I couldn't help but wonder, 'What if something's wrong? What if I'm the cause of my son's happiness slipping away once more?' I'm relieved I made the call, but there's no need to thank me for doing right by you."

Emmett shifted his gaze to the crackling fire. "We've come a long way since our first encounter."

"I like to think I'm the living proof that second chances are possible," his dad said, pausing to grasp Emmett's hand, "but we still have a long road. I know that."

Emmett nodded, "We do." Dove's gentle stirring and calm waking sounds brought him comfort. "But for the time being…" he turned to his dad with a grin, "how would you like to meet your granddaughter?"

Henry's eyes brimmed with tears, "It would be an honor, son."

After a much-needed nap, Autumn went downstairs to make grilled cheese. Following Hope's death, her appetite had diminished. The fact she was craving anything at all was surprising. But a knock on her kitchen door startled her, and she clutched her chest. Turning around, she saw her mother standing there, a mixture of surprise and relief washing over her.

Her mother embraced her into a tight hug. It had been a long time since she had been in her mother's arms. Her strong embrace reintroduced her to a warm feeling she had forgotten existed. Still, Autumn couldn't help but wince. "My arm is still sore from when Mason took the knife from me."

"I'm glad you're okay," her mother whispered, releasing her.

They sat in silence for a moment, each lost in their own thoughts, before Autumn took a bite of her grilled cheese. "What brings you here?"

Her mother took a deep breath, her eyes filled with remorse. "Your near-death experience made me realize I need to be a better mother. Did you know that your grandmother wanted me to be a teacher like her? For a long time, I thought I could do it, but I realized it wasn't what I was passionate about."

"Is Grandma the reason why you held me to a higher standard than everyone else?" Autumn asked, her eyes searching her mother's face.

Her mother nodded. "Yes, but it was also your grandfather."

Autumn placed her grilled cheese on her plate and leaned against the kitchen island, studying her mother. "You've never mentioned him before."

"That's because we never had a good relationship," her mother admitted, lowering her gaze. "Your grandfather was emotionally abusive. He told me I was never going to aspire to be better than him. He expected me to cater to my husband and had these ridiculous expectations of me. I never processed it until later, when I realized how it impacted the way I raised you."

Autumn listened, her heart softening as she comprehended her mother's struggles. She had always sensed there was more to her mother's actions, but hearing her mother's vulnerability opened a new avenue of understanding. Her mother had believed hiding her past was a way to protect her children, but opening up would've fostered a better relationship between them.

After a long pause, her mother said, "I'm sorry for pressuring you to do something you weren't passionate about and for saying things to you that have left such an emotional scar on you. I should've done a better job. I'm sorry, Autumn."

Autumn had waited years for this moment, and it washed over her like a soothing balm. "Thank you, Mom."

"I love you, sweetheart. I will work every day to be a better mother to you and an even greater grandmother to both your girls," she replied, wiping away a tear and placing her hand on top of Autumn's. "Now, I believe we have a wedding to plan."

Epilogue

A YEAR HAD PASSED, and Autumn found herself standing before a grand full-length mirror, donned in her wedding gown. The dress she wore had long sleeves adorned with delicate lace, flowing into a billowing ball gown that seemed to expand to no end. She marveled at her reflection, a vision of grace and elegance.

Ortus walked up behind Autumn, looking at her through the mirror. "You better not be thinking about running away," she teased.

Autumn couldn't help but smile. "I think this place is too guarded for me to do that."

"You've got that right!" Brooke chimed in, entering the room with J.J. and Bradley. Her eyes remained fixed on Autumn's wedding dress. "You look gorgeous, Autumn," she whispered, a sense of admiration in her gaze.

Ortus clapped, with a cheerful spirit. "I can't believe this is happening."

And neither could Autumn. As she made her way toward the entrance of the aisle, she reflected on the pain she had endured over the past few years. It had tested her resolve, making her question if happiness would ever be within her reach. Yet now, with people to live for and the love of her life by her side, she felt an indomitable strength within her. Autumn was ready to face whatever challenges lay ahead, determined to protect her newfound family. She knew Emmett felt the same way.

Emmett stood at the far end of the aisle, surrounded by vibrant purple pansies that had bloomed in autumn. He couldn't see her yet, but Autumn's heart raced as she watched him. Nervous knots tangled in her stomach, and her father stood beside her, waiting for her to compose herself.

"I'm so nervous," she whispered.

Her father placed his hands on her shoulders, turning her to face him. "Hey, look at me," he said, his eyes brimming with warmth. "You deserve this, sweetheart. Your mother and I weren't perfect parents, but we both love you. You are worthy of the love you're about to receive."

Autumn couldn't hold back her emotions and gave her dad the tightest hug in the world. "I love you, Dad. Thank you."

Running away from this town had led her to a traumatic experience with Mason. Somehow, she'd gone from a determined woman with big dreams, to someone who was afraid to live. Running away had become her default solution, but all that had changed when she returned to Maplewood.

Autumn was now surrounded by her parents, sister, and friends, and amid it all, she had met the love of her life in Emmett. Being with him had allowed her to shed her masks and be her true self. Even when it seemed like she might lose him, he had come back to her, and not even their troubled past could sever their bond. She was no longer a victim.

She was a survivor.

Her father's grin brought her back to the present. "Are you ready?"

With a nod and a shy smile, Autumn replied, "It's now or never."

She was determined not to be defined by her past, but rather, to let it shape her into the person she aspired to be. As she danced later that night with Luna, seeing the pure joy in her face, Autumn knew her journey included being a loving mother to both her daughters. Her family had filled the void that had long existed in her life, and in the end, she hadn't just rebuilt the relationships she had lost—she had also found herself.

Acknowledgments

When I wrote *Beneath Autumn Leaves*, I was a nineteen-year-old college student who was processing her trauma through therapy. I never dreamt of publishing this story for the world to read until I was older and realized, *why the heck not?*

I have to start by thanking the phenomenal Liz Catwright, the first editor to read *Beneath Autumn Leaves*, who spent time advising me on how to further develop my characters. Thank you for believing in Autumn and her story.

To Cheryl Jaclin Isaac, who proofread my book and caught all my grammatical mistakes. For better or worse, when I lost a version of edits and had to go back to fix the 700+ adverbs I had already fixed, she reminded me to trust the process. I will never use another adverb again …

To the visionary Janna Marie (@mystic.mind), who is the creative mind behind the illustration of the *Beneath Autumn Leaves* book cover. When I shared Autumn's story with you and how I envisioned the cover to fit with both the season and Autumn's name, you surpassed my expectations with the absolutely beautiful illustration.

To Victoria Wolf, who worked on the fonts and layout for the book cover, as well as the interior design. Thank you for capturing my vision!

To my inspiring and encouraging publishing coach, Kirsten Jensen, who at every meeting found ways to motivate me and make this a fun process. Your helpful check-ins and valuable guidance drove me to reach my goal of becoming a published author.

There are many friends who have arrived in my life and who I'm grateful were with me through the journey. Gabby and Tristan, thank you for reading *Beneath Autumn Leaves* when it was still in its early stages and for providing your valuable feedback and support.

Misha, Sergio, Naomi, and Shane, thank you for being my sounding board on the creative decisions I had to make throughout the process.

To my college friends Brandon, Jajaza, Janna, and Justin, thank you for staying by me during the joys and challenges over the past ten years. With you I cry, laugh, and am reminded that I don't need to go through my darkest moments alone.

Of course, I couldn't have stayed motivated without my family. My brother and sister, thank you for encouraging me. I love you both, especially on days when we're not annoying one another.

A dedication to my mom:

A mi querida madre, a pesar del sinuoso camino que nos trajo hasta aquí, eres la prueba viviente de lo que puede pasar si le das a alguien una segunda oportunidad. A lo largo de los años, has abrazado tu vulnerabilidad, has reconocido tus errores y te has convertido en la admirable mujer que siempre quise conocer. Gracias por ser mi madre y por creer siempre en mí.

For those curious, the translation is below:

To my dear mom, despite the winding journey that brought us here, you're living proof of what can happen if you give someone a second chance. Over the years, you've embraced your vulnerability, you've owned up to your mistakes, and you've become the admirable woman I always wanted to meet. Thank you for being my mom and always believing in me.

Finally, to my dad, who passed away a little more than a year ago. I miss you. When you arrived in this country, you did so dreaming of finding a way to better provide for my grandparents in Mexico. You faced every obstacle imaginable—poverty, racism, discrimination, and more. Yet, you held your head high and ensured my siblings and I had everything you didn't. The most profound wisdom you gave me was to keep my heart open and have empathy for others because we never know what obstacles they may be facing.

One of your last texts to me was, "*Yo siempre quise darles alegria y felicidad,*" and it's because of those profound words that I was inspired to create Alegria Ink Publishing. Without you, I wouldn't have been brave enough to publish my book. I'm grateful for the love, the valuable life lessons, and the inspiration you gave me to follow my dreams.

About the Author

LIZBETH J was born in Los Angeles, California, with a rich Mexican heritage she's proud of. She currently resides in Denver, Colorado, with two cherished companions—her cats Leia and Luna. When she's not writing, Lizbeth enjoys participating in thrilling Dungeons & Dragons sessions with her friends, getting lost in the pages of her beloved romance novels, capturing the beauty of nature through her photography, or relishing the genuine Mexican dishes served at small establishments.

Invite Lizbeth J to Your Book Club!

Starting a book club or already have one? Invite me to one of your meetings by visiting www.lizbethj.com and submitting the Contact Form!

Made in the USA
Middletown, DE
01 April 2024